The Diary of a Trophy Wife

By K. Phoxx

The Diary Of A Trophy Wife
Copyright © 2021 K. Phoxx
All rights reserved. No part of this publication may be reproduced or transmitted in
any form or by any means without the written permission of the publisher.
All rights reserved.

ISBN: 1956884005
ISBN-13: 978-1-956884-00-5

Contributing Editor: or all services completed
by Imprint Productions, Inc.
Cover Design: or all services completed
by Imprint Productions, Inc.

Printed in the United States of America
Published by Imprint Productions, Inc.
First Edition 2021
10 9 8 7 6 5 4 3 2 1

CONTENTS

ACKNOWLEDGMENTS

All things are possible through my heavenly father. As long as he is with us, nothing or no one can stand against us.

This book is for: Nuas, Cavalrice, Missy, CaBreall, Queenie, and Prissie. I also dedicate this book to my mother, Valerie Benson.

With love always,

-K. Phoxx

Foreword

From Your Daughter,

D. L. Phoxx

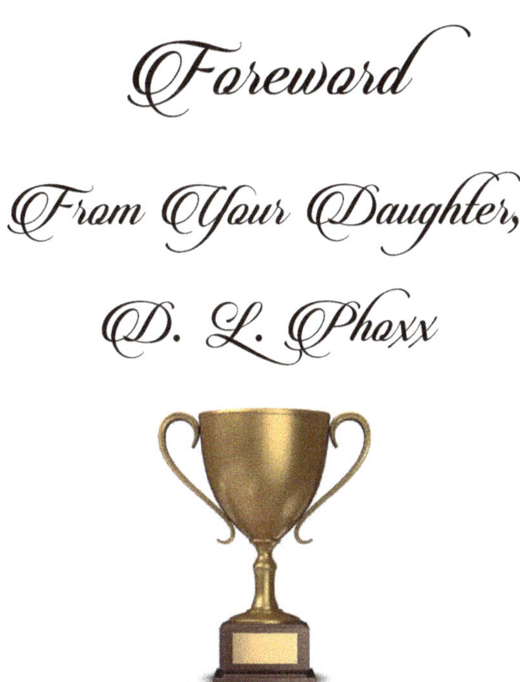

As a growing young woman, I often wondered what made my mom so strong. Was she born that way? How could I receive just a piece of her strength? If it were ever possible, I thought, I would salvage a piece of her and instill it into the core of my soul.

I was told the stories of her childhood throughout my adolescent years. I saw all of what she had gone through that made her so strong and confident. I realized that we are all carved by the path that God has blessed us to have.

And I could not be more grateful to have such a mother who is so God-loving and unselfish to ensure that her daughters have a fire for God, love, passion, and desire for the best in life. But, unfortunately, I've often seen some mothers have had the desire to outshine their own children. They dared do this to the most precious of souls: flesh and blood that was created in their very own wombs.

My mother, God bless her forever, is like a Sequoia. She is tall, strong, and big on everything around her, not too big to block the sun with her leaves from reaching the ground where her seeds were planted.

She then becomes a palm tree, taking on the toughest of storms to bend back enough so the water can reach her seeds in the ground. She wants me and my siblings to become just as tall and strong as she is. Of all the popular and inspirational African American women of success to look up to, I have always looked up to my mother, even as a child.

Whatever path God has for me, I am sure that the foundation of love, respect, and pride I have in God and myself that my mother has built will help me endure the worst of storms. Within the storm is an eye of peace, and growth follows.

My mother is my blessing. Yet, I often wonder how I would be had she not been my mother. Would I be lost? Would I have fallen victim to the cursed mental yokes that my grandmothers before me were enslaved with? God only knows that I am blessed not to know.

And for other women out there my age, I don't mind sharing my mother and honoring them as my soul sisters. But, I know that they may not have had the best relationship with their mother.

We all might be at one point in our lives where the roads are perilous, and the storms over the seas are tumultuous. I have often heard it said, "This too, shall pass." I have witnessed this very phrase happen with my parents. So, I know with all my heart that when the storm comes and challenges us, we will indeed find our way, so long as someone somewhere helps us to our feet and teaches us to walk. We are sure to find a smoother past and peace within the eye of every storm. We are all capable of that with prayer, faith, and patience. Of course, this is all easier said than done, but very well possible through God almighty. Not everyone knows this, though. And if my mother is one of those appointed by God, then, with a generous heart, I will gladly point them in her direction so that she can point them in God's.

As for my father, I have always admired his strong will and individual personality. I thank God that he blessed me with such a father to give the example of what a man should be like and how important a father's role is to his family.

Despite having such a rough childhood, he has never relived his childhood with my siblings and me. Instead, he has proved to be a better man than his father. He never saw taking the easy way out as an option. I watch him as he works, and I say to my Heavenly Father often, "Lord, you have truly blessed my father."

I owe God all my thanks. I was blessed with parents who defied the logic of the hand that they were dealt in life. Witnessing these things lets me know that anything is possible with God on our side. We will see this as long as we take the initiative and are receptive to His teachings and love.

I am truly blessed to say that as my own person, I am complete.

Prologue

The beauty of an award reflects on the accomplishments of another. That tall, gold, silver, or red, shiny object is the envy of those who want one. A trophy is to be admired. It showcases how hard someone has worked to obtain it. However, the trophy does not reveal the pain, the work, the sacrifice, and the difficulty of the endeavor. Upon receipt of the award, the hard work exhibited to accomplish the feat is unforgettable. I compare this experience with the birthing of my children. I remember when I was in labor and all of the hard work it took to push my baby out into the world. But if you asked me specifically about the pain, I could not tell you. Listen, no matter how intense the contractions were, no matter how much anguish and how the pain escalated, once I held my beautiful babies in my arms, the memory of the pain was gone! The extreme pain of birthing vanishes when I see the result; the eyes of my beautiful babies. Let me encourage you. When you fix your eyes on the prize, the sacrifices will not take priority over the process. That prize, goal, or trophy will be what you will ultimately remember!

Let me caution you to buckle up. We are going down some streets that can get provocative, erotic, and even sexy. When a man embarks on a pursuit to attain a new toy, house, car, or even that trophy (a woman.) He will not stop until he wins. He is on his best behavior. He makes himself available. He opens his wallet. He does things that he usually will not do. When he reaches that goal, when he wins that trophy, the accomplishment is gratifying! The prize, goal, or trophy may be available to all; yet, all men do not reach the target. Some of them miss opportunities for whatever reason to win that prize, goal, or for example, the trophy. These men missed securing their trophy wives. It's interesting when men say that some women are high maintenance, too expensive, or bougie. I will share in-depth **"The Diary Of A Well Kept Trophy Wife."** Some men think of their wives as a "trophy." When he sees that woman as a "trophy," it takes on an entirely new meaning. Some men look, stare, and take the risk to win with failure as no option. But when the achiever receives it, it is his. His claims his stake. He sanctions bragging rights and confirms his honor.

When he wins, everybody admires him, envies him, but he knows he has got it. He has earned every bit of it. But what if that trophy could talk? What would it say? Will she explain the rigor of being carved into a trophy? How much it hurts to hold the gold medal? What will it say?

Chapter One

The Eight Ball

Damn it! I whispered to myself, "It's hot as hell in here!" I removed the covers from my already soaked and sweaty body. It was storming like crazy, making my Fibromyalgia hurt even worse. My body was feverish due to the flair-up, but I still wanted to ensure our children were alright.

The loud thunder outside didn't wake my hubby at all. But, unfortunately, when the lights went off, so did the air-conditioning, which made it even worse for all of us. Not only was the house pitch black, but so was the entire neighborhood because the streetlights were out as well. "Where the hell is my phone?" I asked myself! As I felt around on my nightstand. Then with the tip of my long stiletto, designed fingernails, I suddenly rubbed my nails against the face of the phone.

I immediately turned on the phone's flashlight, went into the bathroom, drank some cold water, and took medication to calm the pain. Afterward, I checked on the babies and got back in bed.

"Mmmmmm," I moaned in pain while getting under the covers. The rain, the thunder, the lightning; still, none of that woke up hubby. But the moaning made him toss and turn until he turned towards me. It's normal because, for whatever reason, he thinks my moaning is a mating call. "Baby," he whispers," I want you."

I responded with I'm tired baby, and the rain is making my body hurt. I was explaining all of this as he turned me over in bed. When I felt him, he had already risen to the occasion. He rubs my body all over with his big, strong, rough, albeit soft hands. He began to massage the feverish places on my body, "Damn, baby you're so fuckin' fine," he'd whisper.

Ok, so at this point, he's not going to go back to sleep until I put him there. Up and up my shirt he goes, over the breasts and into his mouth. And that point, it doesn't matter if I'm hurting or not, because now I want him to. I couldn't help myself. I was so intoxicated from his foreplay I had no choice but to give in. I truly believe that his tongue and hands hold some type of magic. He honestly touches, licks, and kisses me in all the right places, just at the right time. And at that point, it's game over. He wins as usual. After two and a half hours of intense lovemaking, it was time for a shower. The last thing I wanted to do was to wash his scent off of me. So, I laid in bed a while longer as he got up to head to the bathroom.

"Hey," he says on his way to the shower after he had finished making sweet, passionate love to me, "Pretty girl, I didn't pay for all of that for you to tease me with."

I looked up at him as he was passing by the side of my bed and said, "You think you own me, don't you?"

"Baby, I bought you from your Mama, LSB."

"LSB?"

"Lock, Stock, and barrel. I own every part of you. And I plan on getting my money's worth," he laughed as he walked into the bathroom. And as soon as he walked into the bathroom, BLING! The lights popped on. "Come take a shower with me. I wanna see what you taste like when you're wet, anyway."

I needed a shower too, so I got up and hopped in the shower with him. He lathered up the sponge with my favorite soap. He washed my body all over slowly, caringly, lovingly, and protectively. The soft soap and warm water accompanied by his hands felt so good on me.

His dark-skinned arms and hands melting into my caramel complex body made the scene of a decadent caramel-filled chocolate dessert from an upper-echelon restaurant. He picked up a heap of my hair in his hands, "You smell so good, baby. I can smell you all over my hands." He separated my thighs to wash between my legs. He got down on his knees to wash my vaginal area. And then suddenly, I felt his tongue doing more of the washing than the sponge.

"Ahh!" I yelled quietly, "Honey! Please, Baby, please!" Before I knew it, he had lifted one of my legs over his shoulder. His head was between my legs, one of my hands rested on the back of his head. "Oh my gosh," I said to myself. It was feeling so damn good I put my other hand on the back of his head. The deeper his tongue penetrated, the harder I pressed his head. The harder I pressed his head, the more the orgasms came back-to-back, and the more they came, the more I lost my balance.

"Baby, please!" I yelled softly over and over again.

"Please, what?" he whispered. I felt like I was losing my balance. I thought I was gonna fall. "I got you. You ain't going nowhere." He was right. He had me. He really did have the very part of my soul that God said belonged to my spouse. He had me. That very part of my soul, he has consumed it all; it was his LSB.

My hubby was confident, and he made damn well sure that he was gonna claim every single inch of what God gave to him, leaving nothing behind.

After a very long and hot, smoking, intense shower, we laid down again, and out of habit, I laid on his chest. The next day was Saturday. Judging by the storm the night before, I didn't think the following day would be so beautiful. However, hubby had already awakened and got dressed.

"Good morning, pretty girl. Come on and get dressed so we can go get breakfast," he said as he passed back and forth in a great mood. He put on his black and white Nike outfit with his black and white Nike shoes.

"Damn, he's fine," I thought to myself. "Mmm! How the hell can one woman handle all of that chocolate?"

As blissful as I was, I knew I had to break out of that daydream and get on with the business of the day. So I went to the closet to pick out a lovely skirt and a white top. After I got dressed, I looked on the floor of the closet for flat shoes. Hubby saw me trying on different kinds of flats.

"No, no, no, no, no, no," he shook his head while waving his index finger, "You know better than that. You know how I like you in those," he said while pointing at my white, six-inch Stilettos.

I was tired and didn't feel like wearing heels. But I knew what he liked, so I put them on. Besides, what's wrong with a man enjoying his wife? He worked so very hard so I wouldn't have to. I wanted him to be proud of who he made his wife.

After I finished getting dressed, I met with hubby downstairs, "Which car are we driving?" I asked.

"The BMW," he replied, "But first. Let me examine you." He'd look at me up and down and have me turn around in a full circle, "You look amazing! Well-groomed, well-moisturized, just like I like you to be."

We'd walk out the house together, and he'd open the car door for me. After he gets in, he pops in Keith Sweat, and the melody plays, "Your body all over my body. My body all over your body. It's your body, baby."

We drove while listening to the CD until we arrived at Starbucks about ten minutes away from the house. From the time we left home until we arrived, he held my hand tightly in his. He didn't let go until we had parked. When we got out of the car, he made sure my skirt was lifted up enough, and my top was low enough. "Go ahead," he told me.

"Are you coming in with me?"

"I'm right behind you."

He waited outside for a minute and watched me walk into the restaurant. While I was waiting in line to order, a very handsome well-to-do-looking gentleman began suggesting that I order the Caramel Mocha that matched my skin. He was so funny. As soon as the cashier started taking my order, hubby walked in. The evidence of a funny joke was left on my face because the smile was still there.

"Yes, let me have two Venti Green Tea Lattes made with Almond Milk, two Splenda's in each, and whipped cream for the froth."

"Wow," said the gentleman, "You ordered as if you were reading poetry."

Hubby saw the guy flirting with me, but said nothing. Instead, he sat in the chair and watched. He always waited until the guy was comfortable no matter how long. He knew exactly what he was doing.

"Shawny?" the waiter called. "Shawny? Is that your name?"

I looked at him and nodded, 'Yes.'

"Shawny for two Venti Green Lattes," he called again.

Hubby got up and walked over to help me get the lattes. He had that "Yeah nigga she's mine" type smirk on his face, then he tilted his head, motioning for me to come.

"Is he referring to you?" the guy asked. I didn't say anything. I walked up to hubby, he gave me my latte, then put his arm around my neck then let his hand fall to my butt. It was like he was letting the guy know, 'Yeah, nigga, I won.'

"So?" hubby stated.

"So, what?" I asked.

"What did he say?"

"What do you mean?"

"I saw him talking to you," He kept looking at me, waiting for me to say something.

"Baby, it's the same thing they always say or ask," I replied, "Honey, you should be used to that by now."

The look on his face was as if he could never get used to it. It's like a game that he plays. In public, at the grocery store, just period. He and I can go almost anywhere, and he allows me to walk in front of him to the point where I'm walking away from him; not too far, but just far enough for him to have a bird's eye view of me. He waits and watches as other men throw themselves at me. Then he slowly walks up; they look at him as if he had lost his mind or as if he was just plain lost. Then he starts to say something to them to let them know that he's not my brother or my friend. Then, deliberately, he will hold my hand and walk away with me. And that look! That look that he has! That sideways grin creeps upon his lips! That, 'Yeah, I won dip shit! I didn't know whether or not to be proud or pissed, but that's him. He stopped questioning me about the guy, and I was not about to stroke his ego.

So, we headed off to Buckhead on our Saturday afternoon date. We ended up going to the mall where I purchased some make-up and some other things I needed. While I was doing my thing, hubby went to Brooks Brothers, his favorite store.

Another store in the mall had a badass lace dress that came down over the knees that would suit me just fine. I wanted to try it on, but the dressing rooms were packed. The cashier told me to pay for it and try it on in the bathroom to see if it fit. If not, I could exchange it for another size, or they would refund me. The dress was one hundred eighty dollars. I wanted hubby to see me in the dress to know what he thought about it.

We both went to the restroom labeled "Family" where I knew I would have more wiggle room to change. I quickly got out of my clothes and left my heels on. I wanted to get a good assessment of the dress by seeing how it would come together with my heels. So I tried the dress on, and damn! It fit perfectly. I stepped over to the other side of the bathroom area to show Hubby.

"So, what do you think?"

He looked pensively with a frown while tilting his head from side to side. His slow response pissed me off, and unenthusiasm ruined my excitement. My smile disappeared quickly wiped off my face.

I took a deep breath in and out and thought to myself, "What now?"

"Something is missing," he finally said with a sincere look.

He took me over to the mirror that started from the ceiling and ended at the floor. He turned me around and said, "Look!"

"I'm looking!" I yelled, "I like it!" then I walked away over to the sink.

"No, baby. Look in the mirror. Something is missing." He was standing behind me. He put his hand gently around my neck. Then he whispered, "This is missing."

It was a gold box with a beautiful pearl necklace inside. I was speechless. "How did you get this?! We've been together the whole time."

"Well, while you were shopping, I slipped into the jewelry store. And I know how much you like pearls. Besides, you needed a new pair anyway." He placed the necklace around my neck and fastened it, "Now that's what's up," he said with a huge smile on his face, "Now, be good to Daddy and give me some sugar."

"Baby, not in the bathroom in the mall…right?" I asked.

"You know how we do it."

I got on my knees for a long ten or fifteen minutes, soaking wet BJ with his eyes half-closed and weakened knees; he lifted me from the floor, turned me around facing the mirror, and lifted the newly bought dress.

"Now look in the mirror and see how beautiful you are when I'm fucking you."

My body was getting hit so hard from behind that I could barely look in the mirror. "Say it! Say it! Say it!" He said forcefully.

"Fuck me! Fuck me! Fuck me!" I yelled.

"Yeah, you know what to say."

My six-inch heels were holding me up like a champ. My five-foot stature would not have been tall or strong enough to handle him on my own. I don't know how long we stayed in that bathroom, but we had to walk out like nothing happened. I, on the other hand, was weak.

It was a good thing the Pizza Kitchen was right next to the restrooms. Aside from being weak, I was thirsty and hungry. This intense, passionate love-making lasted for at least an hour. After which, I could barely walk. My va-jay-jay was sore and swollen. It felt like I just came out of a fight with Mayweather.

He considered this spontaneous fling as another one of his star moments. He's rough, and he knows he is rough. I often wonder if he's trying to prove a point. While I'm several years younger than him, I often wonder if he's trying to show me that he's still got it. Well, I'm not complaining. Hell, I have to keep Tylenol 3 on hand just in case. I have both the Tylenol 3 and at least two 800mg tablets of Ibuprofen on my nightstand on most days. My sister Jay knows this, and she says, "He should be ashamed of himself. This man fucks like it's going out of style or some shit! Like he has to go all-in, or somebody is gonna take the pussy away from him!"

Honey, I tell you. I can feel the evidence. My clitoris swells like a fuckin' balloon. I need my medication. Good thing the wait was short, and we sat down immediately.

"Is there anything I can get for you all this evening?" asked the host.

"Sure," I started quickly, "May I have a tall glass of ice water with lemon, please?"

"Okay, ma'am. Your waitress will be right over."

"I know the waitress is coming ma'am, but if it's no trouble, may I please have some water to take my meds? It's an emergency," I explained calmly.

"Sure! Sure thing," she responded quickly.

"Babe, are you okay?" Hubby asked, "Is it me being too rough on you? I'm sorry. But baby…you got some good pussy, though," he spoke every word with a look of concern.

"No, baby. It's not you," I trembled as I drank the water the waitress had just brought and placed on a napkin. I didn't want to tell him that it was his fault, but he knew the truth. "I can slow down," he said.

"No, honey. I'm okay. Honestly," I said. Then a flashback played in my head. When I was a little girl, I overheard my Godmother telling my mother that men from Alabama had big dicks. So, although hubby was from California and raised in Alabama, it had to be something in that Alabama water.

When the flashback ended, I downplayed it as the medication sat in and then changed the subject. I asked my hubby what kind of pizza he was going to get. I didn't want to complain or make him feel like I was too sickly to handle him. On the contrary, I yearned to satisfy him and make him happy. He does it for me all the time. For years he sacrificed himself to give our children and me this amazing life. God Almighty blessed our family and us repeatedly.

Taking care of me is something he'd always done. For years he sacrificed himself to give our children and me this amazing life. So, for him, I will be what he wants me to be. I will do whatever he asks me to do. I will submit it to him. You see, I've never had to work hard for anything because he's done everything I have asked him to do for me. So, for this man... this amazing man... who will give his very life for me and damn near did on more than one occasion, I will submit to him.

I am the mother of his children, his wife, his sex toy, his girlfriend, his friend, his lover, his side chick, his mistress. Never shall he ever have to step out for any unfulfilled desires, for I am his eight ball in his side pocket. I am his high. His addiction to me turns me on, and all he has to do is take a hit of me to get his fix. I truly thank God Almighty for blessing our family. But things weren't always this way….

Chapter Two

The Process

We talked and discussed the pizza flavors and agreed on the Hawaiian chicken pizza with BBQ sauce. We enjoyed a glass of wine and conversed over our lunch. I thanked him again for the pearls. And then we left.

I fell asleep in the car on the way home. I was exhausted. I woke up as we pulled into the driveway and was surprised to see my mother's car. I hadn't seen her for a couple of weeks so I couldn't wait to go inside to see her.

I walked in the house, went up the stairs and saw my mother sitting on the couch in my bedroom, surrounded by several packages that had just arrived in the mail. My name was on every package. "Yeah girl, come on in here," she called to me, "I couldn't wait until you came home and opened these bags and boxes. I stayed over here longer than I wanted to just so I can see what all that man bought for you now," she said with a detailed look on her face.

"Hello, Mommy," I said with the biggest smile, "I missed you." I gave her the biggest squeeze.

"Okay! Enough with the pleasantries. Let's get on with it!"

"Okay," I had an embarrassed, bashful look on my face. I started with the boxes first. In the first was my Dooney & Bourke bag. In another box was another Dooney & Bourke bag. Another box had my brown, knee-high UGG boots; the other had shoes from a luxury retailer.

Next were the bags. Most of them were outfits from Fashion Nova, Versace, and Vera Wang.

Mom looked at me and shook her head from side-to-side and then said, "You know, your husband owns you."

"WHAT?!" I yelled.

"Yeah. Your husband bought you."

I started laughing like, 'Yeah right, Mom, but don't play me like that.'

She had the most serious look on her face and said, "He bought you. He did."

Welp! That killed my vibe. I just sat all of my new things on the bed, spent the day with my mother until the visit was over, then sat down in disbelief until hubby got home.

He walked up the stairs to see me sitting on the couch pissed off.

"What's wrong, baby? Everything okay? How was the visit with your mom?"

"Honey? Do you know what my mother said to me?" He didn't say 'What' orally - but his face did when I asked the question. "She said that you own me and that you bought me! That is the most hurtful and the meanest thing anybody could say to a person!"

While repeating what she said, I walked to the bathroom and started prepping some bathwater for hubby and me to bathe together. He came into the bathroom as well. He began to take his clothes off and put them on a hanger to have them ready to be taken to the cleaners. While he was doing that, he asked, "Okay. Well, what's wrong with what she said?"

I was shocked! "What do you mean what was wrong about what she said?! All of it was wrong!" I yelled.

"I don't understand," he spoke earnestly and quickly.

"What's there not to understand?! Honey, she said that you bought me and that you own me," I answered.

"Well baby, she's right. I do own you. And I bought you," he agreed with my mother wholeheartedly.

"Baby? Now is not the time for joking. I'm being serious right now," I said sadly.

"Baby, I'm not joking. Technically I do own you. And I did buy you. Not like how you purchase something from the store. When I met you, you were a minor. Therefore, I assumed the responsibility and the cost of raising you from childhood to an adult. I relieved your mother of that obligation by taking you off your mother's hands, he explained.

"Baby," I replied, "I could have worked, but you didn't want me to. Rather, you told me to take care of the home and the babies. I could have taken care of myself."

"Well, you can say that now, because that the kids are grown. You did a great job on raising our kids. That phase is complete. Besides, you have a preexisting condition. How were you going to work and do anything?

"If I knew this was how you felt these past twenty-plus years….,"

"If you knew about what?" he cut me off, which is something he always did because - to him - his way of seeing things is always correct. He has to be right about every damn thing! "You were fourteen or fifteen years old when we got together. I practically raised you!" he yelled.

"And now you own me. You have given me a great lifestyle, you have built me, polished me, placed me on a pedestal, and you show me off. So much that all of your friends have traded in their wives to compete with you. You'll keep me in the highest of heels and badass expensive clothes. You don't want me to buy a cheap synthetic wig. You buy me the best lace with real human hair down to my ass, and you make sure I'm shining. You say it all the time. 'I love how your beautiful skin glows.' Why? Why?! Why?!" I yelled.

"Everything that you have, I bought. From your hair, to your teeth to your body. I bought it!" hubby yelled again. "I get my ass up every day and work to pay for your life! Your family ain't never did shit for you! You didn't have shit when I got with you! I brought you up!" he argued.

"Yes, honey, you did bring me up. And then you conveniently tear me down!" I yelled as tears fell from my eyes. But this wasn't the first time he brought up everything that he has done for me. I guess it's to remind himself of what I owe him. I don't know why, but he's gotten better.

I took off my clothes and got in the tub after the water ran. Hubby got in right behind me. "Baby, I don't want the peace in our home disturbed," he continued calmly, "I love you. And you're a great wife, a great mom, and an amazing woman. You made me a better man."

"Baby, I thank God for you, but please, do not treat me like an object. I'm a real person with real feelings. And I feel guilty because I didn't help financially with us."

"Well, first of all, I thank God for blessing both of us with each other. And don't ever feel like you've never contributed to our family. You've done an awesome job with the kids and with me. I'm sorry for yelling at you," he said as he bathed my back. He started to kiss my back all over.

I took a deep breath, in and out. My mind felt burdened with the whole 'I own you' stuff. He, on the other hand, was thinking about fucking. As I tried to get out of the tub, he held me down and stuck his thumb up my ass and his finger in my swollen, sore va-jay-jay. "Didn't he get enough at the mall?" I asked myself.

I didn't say anything. I just took the pain. If he had known how painful it was, he would have stopped immediately. But, again, I didn't want to complain. There was blood in the water.

"Are you on your period?" he asked.

"No. I just went off. I'm just sore," I humbly said.

He got out of the tub first and then helped me out. Afterwards, we stepped into the shower to wash off. Once we were done, we dried off and went back to our room, "Lay down," he said.

I wanted to say, 'Baby, not tonight.' My body soon became feverish from the pain settling into my muscles. "Lay down," he begged again.

I laid on the bed. He opened up my legs and saw how badly swollen my vagina was. He went into our medical box, where I kept all of the first aid material. He got my vaginal cream, Q-tips, and some cotton balls.

He squeezed some cream on the tip of the Q-tip and gently swabbed around the swollen areas. Then he dressed me in one of the long t-shirts that I use as a nightgown. Afterward, he put me into bed and tucked me under the covers.

"Baby, you can't suffer in silence. You're not supposed to take the pain. It's not normal. And somehow, you have learned to accept pain. But taking it is a whole different thing. You learned to stay out of the way and not complain, but sometimes you gotta say something. You can't accept or take pain like that."

What he said registered just in my ears and not in my soul. I was an inconvenience. I was always somebody's inconvenience. Pain had become my best friend; hurt became my comfort; the tears were my normal. Hubby didn't know how often I cried behind his back. He only knew some things. I didn't tell him everything. I didn't tell him everything because, in an argument, what I say is often used as a weapon against me. So I kept a lot to myself, and it burns on the inside.

I had forgiven a lot on the surface. Initially, I forgave so that I could move forward mentally and get on with life. Then, emotionally, I forgave to cope with life. Then, I forgave so that I could spiritually have peace with God and pray. Finally, I have forgave primarily to have a relationship with my family.

But for some reason, I have not forgiven my soul. My soul still hurts, and it hurts badly. As a little girl, I felt my soul. Yes… my soul. What does a little girl know about a soul? As far back as I remember myself, this was the first memory starting to know who I am.

Chapter Three
Who The Hell Am I?

The first memory of learning and knowing that I existed was when Granddaddy woke us up early on summer mornings. He would often yell at his kids because he wanted them to clean the yard.

He told them that they had no idea who would be coming to visit that day. Grandma looked pissed at him. Later on, she said his yelling was a stunt that he pulled whenever she got ready to go somewhere.

Grandma said that Granddaddy would raise hell when she left the house. Well, this was a Sunday when my Grandma was getting ready to go to church. While Grandma prepared my clothes, because I was going with her, my Granddaddy went outside. He was out for a second, then, suddenly, he ran into the house yelling, "DAMN IT! Them damn bees stung me!"

Grandma knew her husband well. He would do anything to keep her home. So when Grandaddy went to the refrigerator, grabbed the red and white pack of tobacco cigarettes, and started to wet them, my grandmother began taking off her clothes back off. By then, she knew he did not want her to leave.

Granddaddy laid down on the bed. I laid beside him. I can't remember what I was thinking about at the time. I just remembered him shaking and then falling on the floor. "MAMA!" I yelled.

Grandma ran into the room and started shouting, "Bayboy! Bayboy!" She quickly sent for our next-door neighbor because she was a nurse. Soon, the ambulance and everything was at our house. Grandma was crying. Everybody looked sad. Over the next few days, I was wondering where Granddaddy was. I hadn't seen him at all. Then, one day, a lot of people came to our house. They were our guests. And one of the guests was one I knew I would never forget. It was a lady. She was light-skinned and angry-looking but still sad.

Days had gone by, and Grandma dressed me up in a pretty dress with tights. My baby brother, Zay, looked nice too. Then this long car pulled up in front of Grandma's house. That car was awesome! We got in, and the car brought us to… this place… where a lot of people were. Everyone was dressed nicely; however, they were all lined up one after the other, crying. I remembered somebody telling me, "You're about to see your Granddaddy."

"Oh, goodie!" I thought. I hadn't seen him in days. I couldn't wait to tell him about all the sad, crying, unhappy people. I couldn't wait to tell him how much I missed him and that Grandma had been crying a lot. I guessed that a lot of people wanted to see Granddaddy, too.

Then, someone else lifted me up and said, "There's your Granddaddy."

I didn't understand. To me, he was asleep. Then I thought, "Granddaddy is gonna raise hell with all these people looking at him like this." I couldn't wait until he woke up and started shouting. But he didn't get up.

After a while, some people there closed the bed that he was lying in. "Grandma!" I shouted, "He can't breathe! He can't breathe!"

"He's dead, baby. He is never coming back anymore," Grandma told me.

What did dead mean? I had no idea. But I did know one thing for sure: Grandma was right because Granddaddy was gone. I never saw him again.

Grandma began to take on what Granddaddy had done, which was fussing all the time. Mainly at Lilly, Shane, and Joey, and sometimes Derek. Lilly and Shane were the youngest boy and girl. Derek started to drink alcohol a lot while Joey put on Grandma's wigs and hung out with other boys in the neighborhood. They called themselves "The Ladies of the Night."

I didn't know why Joey wanted to be a lady so badly. He had too much hair on his face and the odor of a sweaty man. Being a lady was something he should not have opted into. But in the mind of a child, nothing made sense, but everything made sense.

Joey did a lot of sneaky things when Grandma's back was turned. He had a pack of cigarettes hidden in her vase. Joey put on women's clothes and walked like a woman. He loved Barbara Streisand and Diana Ross. He would sling his hair back with his eyes closed as he sang their songs using the broom as a makeshift microphone. When the songs ended and he opened his eyes, he realized that he was a hairy-faced man with a kinky afro. I watched him and took notes because, for some odd reason, I wanted to be just like him. Free and unapologetic. But that was until his big ass, muscle-bound brothers came around. They tried to beat the shit out of him when they saw him acting like that.

He was scared of them, and I could tell. The moment Grandma came home, everybody stopped their sneaky shit and got quiet. But I saw everything. I gave Grandma complete reports about everybody except Joey because we were friends.

I liked it when Lily and Shane were home. They were like my older sister and brother. Zay, being younger than me, was not impressive at all. He just ate a lot, and his breath smelled like bologna.

Again, that same mean-looking light-skinned lady brought her angry ass to visit. She was frowned up as always. She was looking like somebody had stolen something or slapped the piss out of her. She looked like she had a chip on her shoulder or a bone to pick with somebody.

All I knew was to avoid her. Lily and Shane were telling her about something awful I had done. That angry ass woman then found me and pinched the damn shit out of me! She took my damn skin off! It seemed as if she had nothing better to do than to fuck with me! I wanted to haul off and hit her ass, but I was too scared of her. So instead, I hid from her.

Every time her mad ass came around, I hid. Under my Grandma's skirt, under the bed, and even in the damn closet until she left. I hated that lady and hated when she came to the house. I wanted Grandma to tell her to just stay away, but Grandma didn't.

She was nice to Zay. But, when it came to me, she would look at me as if she hated me just as much as I hated her. Her gaze at me was with disgust and an emptiness. Anyway, however she felt about me, the feelings were mutual. Everybody else liked her, and I didn't see how. She was nice to everybody except me, and I was okay with that because I was happy and free when she left. So much so that I went to the vase where Joey hid his cigarettes.

After I snuck one out of the packs, I went and got Zay and sat him down on the side of Grandma's bed with me. Nobody was paying us any attention. They were all getting ready to have a party. Grandma had the house decorated so nicely. She had gone downtown to pick up her cake from the bakery and was gonna stop by the record store to pick up Marvin Gaye's song "Got to Give It Up." She said before that she was gonna listen to that song and party all night long.

Well, Zay and I were going to party, too. The side of the bed where we were sitting had exposed plastic that was covering the bottom mattress. I struck a match to light the cigarette. Before I knew it, the plastic from the bed had caught fire. The fire spread so fast that I pulled Zay by the shirt and ran out of the room.

Joey was outside talking to the ladies of the night when we ran to him. He turned to see smoke everywhere. He started grabbing his afro – which, I guess, he thought himself to have long beautiful flowing hair - and he screamed to the top of his voice.

I don't know who called the fire department but there were big red trucks and lights everywhere. The loud noises and sirens were so terrifying. I really didn't understand what was going on. The last time I saw these many trucks and lights was when Grandaddy had died.

The next thing I knew, the neighbors had come outside to see what was going on and what they could do to help. Then, the Marta bus came by Grandma's house, where she got off the bus to see her house in flames.

She stood there with a big white box in her hands, the cake she picked up for the party. And oh my God, the look on her face. It was the saddest thing. I have seen her miserable and unhappy before, but not like this. So many people came to her and gave her hugs as she broke down and cried.

I remember feeling awful on the inside. Like I was in trouble. I knew I had done something wrong. I knew that I had made Grandma sad. The hurt in her eyes and the pain on her face; I did that. Me. The little girl that she called Shawnie. I did all of it, and there was no place for me to hide.

So many cars started to pull up to the yard. So many people were crowded around looking at the burning house. The moment someone asked what had happened, Shawnie did it!

After the fire department put out the fire, everybody started to go inside and assess the damage. The house was mainly filled with black soot. All of Grandma's beautiful white walls and her beautiful furnishings were all black. Everyone walked around, looking at their belongings - or what was left of it.

All of my dolls and toys that Zay and I played with had melted onto each other. This burned, charred rubble could have had us lying there with it. But, of course, the blessing was that we got out of there in time. But nobody even cared to notice that.

All of Grandma's kids had come over. Then, out of nowhere, that mean-ass lady came again. I finally found out her name when somebody said, "There goes Pat!"

"What happened?!" she shouted.

Grandma started to talk, and I knew my name would eventually come up. Grandma was wearing a coat. She would usually have a huge skirt big enough for me to hide under. Underneath the bed was no longer an option. The closet had no place for me to hide either. I grabbed onto the belt of Grandma's beige coat.

I had the urgent sensation to pee badly or run out of my skin whenever that lady looked at me. All she needed was a reason. She hated me just that much. I could tell she hated me. Every time she looked at me, she had a frown on her face. No matter how much I wished she would leave, she never left. Then the moment I so dreaded came. I braced myself,

"So, what started the fire anyway?" she asked.

"Well, Joey said that Shawnie and Zay were playing with matches and Shawnie set the house on fire," Grandma explained.

Oh my god, my heart started beating fast as hell. Before I knew it, "I'm gone' beat yo ass!" Pat yelled.

There. Pat had her reason. Then WHAP! There it was - a slap on the side of the head and that infamous pinch that took my skin off. I remembered looking at her as if I could kill her.

Then her brother, George, walked up and said, "Pat! Don't hit that child. We just lost our father a couple of months ago, and y'all up here talking about a party! This is God's doing! What y'all gon' be mad at a child for? Daddy is gone, and y'all wanna party!"

Everybody got quiet. Then Pat, who kept her eyes set on me as her brother spoke, looked at me as if she was casting a spell. And then she rolled her eyes and turned her head slowly as if she was saying to herself, "I want to kill her, but it's not worth it," or, "I changed my mind."

Grandma started to gather what little things she could salvage. Lilly and Shane helped her out. Joey just disappeared. Maybe he hid= his cigarettes that I was attempting to light so Grandma wouldn't find out that he smoked.

After a long day of packing what could be salvaged, Grandma said, "I'm going to be staying at Esther's house until I can get us an apartment."

Zay and I followed behind Grandma and Uncle George where his little blue car was waiting for us to get inside. Grandma then turned around and looked at Zay and me and said, "No, babies. Y'all are going in the other car."

As far as I knew, we've never separated from Grandma before. We were always with her. But nothing in the world could prepare me for what she was about to say next. The words that came out of her mouth shattered my tiny little world. She finished, "Y'all aren't going with Grandma. Y'all gotta go stay with y'all's Mama."

"Who?" I asked myself, "But... you... you're our Mama." As a child, I didn't know the difference between different relatives.

"See over there," she pointed, "y'all gotta go with your mom," she repeated.

I looked to see where she was pointing at the very same lady of whom I shared mutual hate for. Pat!

Although many years have passed, I can still feel that hurt - that let down - like it was yesterday. I actually had to pause just now while writing this to let out a few tears. Just like back then, I shook my head as I thought to myself, "No, no, no! This can't be true! Maybe Grandma got it wrong, or perhaps she was angry at me for setting her house on fire. Possibly, this was her way of punishing me. If it was, then it was one of the worst punishments in the world. Yet, this was real. I was not dreaming. And this situation was no joke. What had I done that was this bad for her to be my mother?

I wanted to magically give Grandma her house back and promise never to burn her house up again. But, as much as I wish I could have, I could not unring that bell.

"Go and get in the car with your Mama," she had to say several times before we really got it.

I was so scared of her and so nervous. Zay and I got in the car. I don't recall the ride or how I was feeling at the moment. However, I do remember that when we got to her apartment and went inside, the smell of cinnamon and apples filled my nose.

Otherwise, she had a massive picture of an owl on her wall in the well-decorated living room with a couch.

Then, there was a man in her apartment whom I had never seen before. Later on that night, I laid down on the sofa and kept my eyes on that owl. I was hoping that bird wouldn't jump out of the picture and get me. I watched all night until I fell asleep.

Chapter Four
In The Mind Of A Child

The following day, I remember her making us cookie crisp cereal. Seeing the cereal made me remember when I saw a commercial about them on TV at Grandma's house. It made me wanna go back home. But I knew that wasn't an option anymore.

Then I wondered about Grandma and what she was doing. Then I heard, "Shawnie and Zay?" said the guy whose name I later found out to be Tony. The way he called our names was as if he had known us our whole lives. He was nice to us, though, nevertheless.

Soon, Shane had come over to visit. We were so happy to see him. Shane stayed at Pat's house with us until Grandma got us an apartment.

Even though I was terrified to speak to Pat, Zay wasn't afraid to talk to her at all, although he could barely speak. As time went on, and the longer we stayed, I started to warm up to her. I remember looking in her purse one day and smelling the scent of lipstick and Doublemint chewing gum.

When I looked up at her, I saw her smiling about something. I looked at her with that huge smile on her face and thought, "Wow! She's pretty." Her skin looked as if she bathed in milk. She kind of looked like the lady I saw in Grandma's magazines. Back then, I didn't know the woman's name. I now know her name to be Marilynn Monroe. That was exactly how my mother looked. Big, red lips and a snow-colored face.

She was indeed entirely African American, but her skin was like buttermilk. My skin was like hers, but I was more of a Cherokee Indian complexion like my Grandma.

Zay and I bravely called my mother by her name. We acknowledged mother by her first name as if we had known and communicated with her all along. 'Pat this' and 'Pat that,' we said. Then she sat Zay and I on her dresser and asked us, "Listen. Do y'all know who the devil is?"

"No," we both said.

"Well, the devil is mean and evil, and he lives in the ground. He has a tail with a pointy arrow, and he carries a pitchfork. He lives in the flames of fire, and he sticks that fork in people's backs and takes them down to the ground where he lives. That place is called Hell. So do not call me by my first name. If y'all call me Pat or Patricia there will be consequences. That devil is gonna stick y'all with the pitchfork and drive y'all to hell!" she shouted, So y'all better start calling me Momma!"

All those times she pinched me before felt like hell, so anything worse than that I didn't want any part of it. So after what she told Zay and me about the devil, I've been calling her Mom, Ma, Mother, Mommy, and Ma'am ever since from that day to this one.

Later in life, I thought about that day and asked myself, "Why would a parent have to threaten or scare the living shit out of their child into calling them Mom or Dad?" At that point, one would have to wonder, "Are they even worthy of being called Mom or Dad?" All one would have to do is be a mom or dad. Fuck the theatrics! Earn the name, and the child will learn the name!

Grandma never had to threaten us to call her Grandma. Me calling my Momma, 'Mom' was wrong on so many levels. Because I called her Momma out of fear and not love, admiration, respect, and certainly not out of the happiness of having her as a mother. In my little mind, I already had one.

More days had gone by, and I wanted to go home even more. I was missing Grandma like crazy. I didn't want Momma to see me sad because her pinches were a calamity that I didn't look forward to.

I might have warmed up to her, but it didn't mean that I took to her. The funny thing was, Zay took to her. He really liked her. I guess if I did something terrible and she hurt another person instead, maybe I would like her too. I say this because whenever Zay did something awful, I got the punishment. So the best thing for me to have done was just stay the hell out of her way.

Over the next few days, I watched the rain come down. The rain filled into a long ditch that looked more like a trench in the back of

Mama's house. It was like a fast-flowing creek. I stared at it for a while, wishing I could dive in that water and let it carry me far, far away.

Mama showed up a few minutes later and told us to get in the car. Zay and I did what we were told and got in. We rode for a long time. After a long ride, we finally stopped in front of a house. We got out and walked towards it. Soon, I heard her voice. It was my Grandma! I walked quickly inside and looked for her. And there she was. I ran to her and gave her the biggest hug.

I was so happy to see her. It felt like an eternity. Zay, on the other hand, was more concerned about the smell of the food. He walked up to my Aunt Esther and asked, "May I have a coffee sandwich?"

Everyone burst into laughter. Once I got old enough to understand what coffee was, I understood why it was so funny coming from a small child.

Grandma was packing up her things, "Maybe we're going home now," I thought. Everything that belonged to her, she took to Aunt Esther's house in a box along with some other items her sister had given her.

The rest of the day, Zay and I played with each other. Finally, when nightfall came, Momma returned back to the house. I was so ready to go home until Aunt Esther's daughter, Nell, walked into the room where we were playing.

"You see that man over there?" she said, "That's your daddy." She pointed through the door that connected the bedroom to the front, screened porch.

I looked at the man, and he was very, very tall. Then I thought to myself, "He looks just like that man from Staying Alive." The movie that I now know is named Saturday Night Fever. The man that I thought he looked like was John Travolta.

The man sat down on the couch. He wasn't so tall when he was sitting down. I looked at him with my finger in my mouth. I was scared to get close to him. I guess he might have heard me breathing because he looked directly at me.

Slowly, his jaw began to move back, and his eyebrows started to raise. Then a great big, beautiful smile appeared on his face. "Hey Shawnie!" he said through his smile, "Come here!"

I walked up to him, and he picked me up and sat me on his lap. I still had my finger in my mouth the whole time. Then, out of nowhere, Zay showed up in the dark, screened room. "Hey, Zay!" I guessed he knew both of us. He sat Zay on his knee, then he introduced himself, "My name is Neno."

"Neno?" I thought. I was so happy that he didn't have a whack or a pinch or a slap, along with a gruesome threat to force us to call him Daddy. He talked to Zay and I for a long time. He even played with us. "Look, Shawnie," he pulled out a device, "This here is a phone. Do you know how it works?" I shook my head no. "Well, come look-a here. You see? This is how you call me." He started pressing some numbers on the face of the phone.

Even after all of these years, I still remember the number that he taught me. Frankly, I can't recall the numbers that I've ever had growing up. But for some reason, I still remember the number he gave me as plain as day.

It's strange to say that even though I couldn't wait to go home with Grandma, I wasn't ready to go when she was. I wanted to stay with Neno. Patricia was my mother, and Neno was my daddy, and boy, did I have the best daddy in the whole world.

As I came to know myself and how things pretty much worked, I started to realize things pretty fast. But as a child, I couldn't change anything because I was a child. Nonetheless, the following day, we got all of our things and headed back home. We went with Grandma to stay with Aunt Esther, which was now home, but this house didn't look like home.

It was a brick building that had stairs on the outside. Grandma called this dwelling an apartment and we would be living here until the house was repaired. Me, Grandma, and Zay were not the only ones to have packed up. Lilly, Shane, Joey, and Derek moved back in also.

Momma stayed with us for a few days. After several days of getting settled in, I fell fast asleep. When I woke up, I remember it still being dark outside and hearing a lot of whispering. But it wasn't calm and soft. It was more like jarring, quiet talk. All I could make out through all of that was, "I'm gonna kill the nigga!"

I walked into the hallway where Shane stood outside Grandma's bedroom door holding a stick wrapped with black tape. Then Shane went to the bathroom to demonstrate just how hard he would hit the 'nigga' he was talking about.

He aimed at the back of the toilet. He swung that stick so hard that it broke the glass toilet tank cover. "Wow!" I said as I was now able to see inside the tank of the toilet. The pump and all the other parts fascinated me for some odd reason. But it wasn't gonna fascinate Grandma. Nah. She was gonna raise holy hell when she woke up!

The morning had come fast, and the beatdown for this person was short-lived as Shane realized Grandma was gonna do what she called 'slap the shit out of you!' I guess the thought of her long fingers going across what he called a 'handsome face' was not worth the risk.

So later on, Grandma emerged out of her room along with a man. This was not normal. "Who the hell is this?!" I thought. Whoever it was, it was her new boyfriend. Oh my gosh! This short, little man with no teeth in his mouth, with buck bloodshot eyes looking at everybody and addressing us all by our first names as if we had known each other our whole lives! He was a grubby little thing. And how did he weasel his way into this family? What the hell was Grandma thinking?!

Is this who was supposed to replace Grandpa? Where were his dirty clothes and boots with the smell of cement? Where was his hard hat like the one Granddaddy used to wear? Where were his overalls like the ones Grandaddy put on before he went to work? Who the hell are you, sir? This was the question we all had and wanted answered.

Where did Grandma find this? Take it back and get your money back! Sue, protest, complain! Call corporate and the local dealers! Call the fucking cops and get him out of here! But Grandma kept him in the house with us, unapologetically.

She went to the kitchen and made breakfast. "Here's your plate, Crawly," she said as she handed him a plate.

"Crawly?" I thought to myself, "This nigga's name is Crawly?" It was nothing dignified. Then I thought, "Really, Grandma? Really? He's the replacement of shit! He looks like a bug! You mean to tell me you couldn't meet a roach? Hell, even an ant would do. At least they worked all the time and built their own shit!"

An ant could move the whole family in his shit because it was big enough. But that motherfucker there was brave! He not only squeezed his ass in that tiny ass apartment but also squeezed himself in with Grandma's seven big ass sons. Conversely, this excludes Joey because he was not a son or a daughter. He was a queen, and nobody was gonna tell him anything different. But he had no problem with dragging Crawly's ass out of there whenever it came to it.

I never thought that I would see a man that Joey dislikes. But Crawly had me doing the hail Mary every time I mentioned his name. It was something about the way he was. In my eyes, he was a sloppy or maybe even a lazy opportunist. Nevertheless, there is nothing wrong with being an opportunist -just be smart about it.

Later, I learned that he was the type to get to know you really quickly; learn names fast to create an angle to get to know people or run games on them. He was slick and sneaky, just like a crawly little creature.

I did not like Crawly, and neither did Grandma's other sons, George, Teddy, Ronald, and Richard. Each of them was about the same age as Crawly.

They were grown, married men. But my poor Uncle George loved grandpa so much that all he could do was swing on the limb of a tree in the backyard after Grandpa passed away.

George had hurt and anger brewing in his soul, making him hate

Crawly with all of his heart.

Sometime later, Uncle Rich came by the apartment to look for Grandma. But she had already left with that, that creature. Mama, Shane, Lilly, and Joey were all talking to Uncle Rich in the kitchen. When he asked for Grandma, Lilly and Shane told him, "She left."

"With who?" he was eager to know.

Mama hesitated before she told him, "She left with Crawly."

Uncle Rich jumped high into the air and smacked the cabinet out of pure anger. To me, it looked as if they wanted him dead. If ever there was a giant shoe, they for sure would have used it to crush him like the bug he was.

Somehow, they managed to stay quiet and out of the way. Crawly knew he wasn't liked. So, he played nice. Besides, when Christmas came, he lifted Zay and me and told us to look in the sky at Santa coming. "See? Look right there. Do you see his reindeer?" I don't remember my reply, but I knew he was just trying to be kind.

After months of living in the apartment, we were finally able to move back into our house. I was so happy to be back at the home that I knew. I was even more delighted when Mama brought Neno to live there with us.

But Mama looked different; her stomach was big. Then I found out why her stomach had become so big. There were babies in there! I was going to be a big sister again! But, while I was excited about my own life, a little boy named Noah was somewhere else in the world.

Chapter Five

The Wrath Of A Father

Noah had a rather unconventional start in the world. Instead of being born in the hospital, Noah was birthed at home by his father, Edward, who worked in the Army's medical field. All of Noah's siblings were born at home, save for his three oldest siblings: Angeline, Jamal, and Samuel.

Normally when a child is birthed at a hospital, they are given a birth certificate and a social security card. This wasn't the case with Noah and the other few children. They had no legitimate birth certificate nor social security cards. Thus, they had no records anywhere to prove that they even existed.

Noah's family was "religious." His knowledge of himself was completely different from mine. He loved peace, animals, and the big, green pastures of the farm where he and his family lived. The farm belonged to someone who shared the same religion.

Noah loved it. He could run for miles. He could escape to his own world like hiding under the belly of a cow and smelling that fresh country air. Noah feared nothing in the world. Except for nightfall. Not because he was afraid of the dark, but for an entirely different reason. When the sun started sinking into the land, Noah knew it was time to go home.

His father, Edward, was the head of Noah's household. He was also well-known throughout their religion. He would wear the brightest of smiles as he worshiped and cooperated with other men who all stood firm in their belief of being a good husband and father.

Whenever Edward returned home to his family, religion was no longer God's religion. It was his religion. Beat the wife and the child. Harm the girls and hurt the boys. Sadly for Noah, his days of him escaping on the farm had come to an end.

That beautiful farm, the wonderful piece of God's serenity, was burned down. The cows, the house, the land…everything. So the family had no choice but to move. However, Edward packed them up and moved them to a remote location in Alabama.

Now living in their lonesome, Edward had taken control even more than before. He had become twice as abusive. Noah's mother, Martha, was a very soft-hearted woman. On the day she married her husband, Edward showed her just who he was and his intentions. He hit her as hard as he could and told her that he was in control.

This was the madness that Noah had to live in. He loved his mother, but he was too young to do anything about the circumstances.

There were times when Edward would leave home for days, sometimes months at a time. When he came back, he brought food with him. I'm not sure how much, but it wasn't enough for several people; therefore, it never lasted long.

Noah and his siblings stayed hungry. Due to their religion, there was food that they were forbidden to eat. Noah's older brother, Jamal, couldn't take living like that anymore, so he left home and turned to the streets to survive.

His eldest brother, Samuel, who was the most responsible, couldn't take watching their father beat up on their mother, so he left as well and moved to the Carolinas. Thus, Noah, his two sisters, and two brothers were left behind.

Martha had been beaten so much that it caused her to become both mentally and physically ill. One day, Noah wanted to go into her room just to see her. Deep down, all he wanted was to seek the connection to the woman that shared a nine-month bond with him.

"Mama?" he called softly.

"Go back in there little one," she responded softly, albeit so sad and lonely.

Noah did as his mother said and went back out of the room, closing the door behind himself. Noah and his baby brother, Messiah, were the babies of the family. As children, they needed that maternal connection. As the next best thing - and closer to a mother figure - they depended on their oldest sister, Angeline, to provide that maternal, tender, love, and care.

Although that was the case, Angeline herself was also in survival mode. She was dealing with the daunting task of keeping herself out of the path of their father. Then there was Mavis, the second-born daughter. Their father's abuse was so bad that she began having spells out of sheer fear of him.

Martha, as I said before, has a very soft heart. Every day, not only did she endure her own experience of Edward's wrath, but she also endured watching her children suffer at his hands. She knew the kind of man she had married. All she wanted to do was to gather the strength she needed to leave.

Even through all of the sufferings behind the walls of that structure of misery, she never lost her faith in God. She learned from that situation that there were wolves in sheep's clothing. After being called bitches, whores, sluts, and getting hit, how could a woman with a wounded soul and spirit and a hurting body possibly soldier on for her kids?

The physical, mental, and verbal abuse wasn't the only challenge. Hunger was another issue. However, God was so good that he blessed them to have a pear tree in their yard. Martha would pick many pears from the tree and make as many dishes out of them that she could. They ate this for days.

One morning, Angeline picked some pears for the children to eat for breakfast. Noah refused to eat. "Boy, you better eat this pear!" she demanded.

"No! I refuse to keep eating pears! And if I were seventeen, I'd buy my own food!"

This worried Angeline. "Man, this little baby gon' starve himself to death. Come on, Noah. You gotta put something on your stomach."

"No! I refuse to eat that!" he said again while shaking his head with his eyes closed. That day, it was a blessing that their father had come home. He had been gone for weeks and had come back with food. Noah was so happy to see the food. Seeing Edward was a different story.

Noah, even as happy as he was to see the food, steered away from his father. He paced the house, stomach growling, and everything. Eventually, he walked toward where Edward was. He heard Edward telling the family how bad his day was.

"Come here," he told Noah when he saw him. Noah came closer into the room where his father was, "Yeah, that's right! I had a bad day! You see, your brainpower made me have a bad day! It's all your fault!" he yelled as he threw an unripe pear toward Noah. The pear missed Noah's head and hit the wall, making a hole in it.

If that pear had hit Noah like it was intended, Noah probably would have lost his life that day.

The same way I found ways to avoid my Mama was how Noah found ways to avoid his father. Even though I couldn't understand why my momma beat me so much, Noah's understanding was far clearer than mine. He was beaten because he was dark-skinned.

Martha, Jamal, and Angeline were all the same complexion as Noah. The other kids weren't as dark, but according to Angeline, the darker-toned kids were treated the worst. Because Martha was a God-loving and God-fearing woman, one lesson that she did teach as a mother was for them:

"Listen children. I don't care how badly someone treats you because of your skin. Never forget to love yourselves and never be ashamed of who you are. God created the world out of the darkness. Everything that is great comes out of the darkness. Even a seed is planted in the dark. In the dark is where we get our strength, how we learn to grow, and how we learn to stretch."

Noah hung on to his mother's words. Her words gave him the strength to carry on. As her body weakened, her health started to unravel. She knew that in order to live longer and see her children reach adulthood, she was going to have to leave Edward.

Elsewhere in the Carolinas, where their older brother Samuel lived, he made money after finding a job doing construction work. Every month, he sent money to help his family. Martha depended on that money.

Then Edward left home again. The moment he left, Martha rented out a house down the block from where they lived and filed for a divorce. She left the children at their current house because she couldn't afford to take them with her. That's why she rented a place close enough so that she could keep her eye on them.

Over the years, I often wondered why she didn't take them with her. I later found out from Angeline that if she had taken them with her, Edward would have just moved in also. As a mother now, I often find myself debating that decision because the kids were still in harm's way. I guess she did what she thought was best for them.

After Edward returned once again, he came home to find that his wife had moved out. Angeline and the others knew where she was but refused to tell him how to find her. Edward was then left to take care of the family on his own.

After a few months, Edward came to the decision to pack them all up and take them with him. Instead of leaving for great deals of time on his own, he just took them all. Edward was not only abusive. He was also a schemer.

He knew that the children would want to say goodbye to their mother. So, he was nice this once to go and take them to see her. On doing so, he managed to find out where she had been all that time. The house where Martha was staying wasn't the best-looking place. To her, she would rather live in a house with rats than stay with Edward.

At that point though, it didn't matter if he knew where she was or not because they were moving. Noah was worried about her. Martha was fine because she knew she had God on her side. Even with all of the struggles she had - no money, no family, beaten until she was ill, and with the loss of the family that she had with her children - she still prayed to God and kept her faith in him.

They all gave their farewell and piled into a small brown 1970 Ford Maverick. Noah sat in Angeline's lap. He reflected on all the car rides they shared with their mother. The last time she was in the car with them, Edward landed into her something serious.

As a child, Noah heard his father call his mother bitch after bitch, whore after whore. This Godly woman that tried to be the best wife and mother that she could be. He heard her try to fight Edward back with words, but they weren't as rough, loud, brutal, or as cruel as his.

Angeline, however, just wanted her mother to stop arguing altogether because Edward dominated the shouting match. He was drowning Martha out to the point where she couldn't get a word in.

They all witnessed how dominant their father was. And they could see that he knew it also.

The fatigue that she had to have felt, the exhaustion, and the fear she had of him pulling the car over to beat the living shit out of her. How helpless she was. She didn't know that she was teaching her daughters how to be treated and accept pain. She was setting the example of how to become less than, and accept, next to nothing. That mindset of living a pitiful, poor, broken down way of life; taught them how to become defeated and dominated. Most importantly, she taught them how not to fight back.

When it came to Martha's sons, she taught them that a woman wasn't supposed to fight back. They were used to seeing their mother sit back and take it because daddy paid the bills and bought food. They were used to seeing their mother being dominated and abused with hands and words. Therefore, a woman defending herself was not an option, especially for a helpless woman.

Angeline described her mother as a beautiful, dark-skinned woman in the beginning. After five years of living with Edward, she looked like she could be her own grandmother. Angeline and her younger siblings inhaled all of this as children would.

As a little boy, this was the blueprint that was set up for Noah. But Noah was Noah. He never knew his father as father and son, but he knew him. Whenever his father was gone from home, he was at peace.

Chapter Six
The Struggle

Although Noah's father was chaotic enough, things were about to get even more difficult. The place where Edward chose to relocate them was a life they were not used to. They were country people moving to the big city of Atlanta.

They moved into a duplex located in the heart of one of the toughest neighborhoods known as "The Bluff." Even the mailman was afraid to deliver mail there. The people there were rough and just as cruel. Noah and his family weren't like that. They had come from a completely different world.

They had never gone to a physical school before because their father "home-schooled" them. So, it was difficult for the family to mingle and understand the intentions of those around them.

Noah and his siblings, having the friendliest spirits, wanted to get to know their new neighbors and make friends. Because they were from the country, they were used to walking and running barefoot. The folks from the bluff would always watch them. On occasions, they would even ask Noah and the others to run barefoot.

To Noah and his siblings, they thought that their barefoot attraction was impressing people. Little did they know, they were being ridiculed about it. They would get called 'Africans' and 'apes' and 'monkeys' all behind their backs.

Not long after they moved to the bluff, Noah turned nine years old in March. Although the ridicule, in the beginning, was hard to see through, the jokes had become more apparent. And some even more blatant than others.

Of course, little boys are going to talk to little girls that they like. Whenever Noah attempted to talk to a girl, he would always be told, "Ew! You are so black and ugly!" And because they came from little to next to nothing, they were also ridiculed for being broke and not being able to afford anything.

But they were people on the outside looking in. They didn't know that their father, Edward, made so much money that he could get expensive suits tailor-made exclusively for himself. He was even able to make large donations to their place of worship and donate to other people. But he never spent a dime on his children. He never bought them clothes, shoes, nor enough food. Even when his children were down to their last watermelon, Edward had to satisfy his thirst of being a people pleaser that he gave it away - taking food from the mouths of his children. While he was worried about people liking him, he should have been more concerned about the way his kids felt about him.

Noah might have been young, but even his little 9-year-old self didn't bother asking his father for anything because he knew he wasn't going to get it. He never approached his father with his wisdom because he refused to get into any pointless arguments or trouble.

Noah and his siblings never attended school; however, they were provided social activities revolving around learning administered by their ministry of faith. Although their "homeschooling" by their father wasn't fruitful, they could still get somewhat of an education through their activity programs.

This, however, wasn't enough, but Noah didn't know. He and his brothers and sisters were always seen walking around during the time their peers were at school. Eventually, this was seen by one of the neighbors, and it was reported to the authorities that there were children that were idly walking about and not attending school.

When someone did come to visit their residence, Edward assured the people that his children were being homeschooled and getting the education they needed. Even after they had left the house, they continued to press on the issue of the children going to a structured learning environment until they were all placed in a school.

Although they had some learning in their religious programs, the learning was inconsistent. They knew some things on their level, below, or above. So, when Noah was accepted into school, he was placed in the fourth grade.

Now finally able to get the education they needed, Noah and his siblings continued to endure their father. But Noah didn't have to worry about feeling alone whenever he avoided his father.

He befriended a little boy - his neighbor - named Calvin. Calvin and his mother didn't have the best of a relationship, so he understood Noah. The only difference between their parents was that Calvin's mother never let him starve, and he always had a fresh, clean school uniform.

There were times when Calvin would invite Noah to his place to have a meal. But Noah had so much pride that he kindly refused the offer because he didn't want to show just how poor and hungry, he and his family were. The saddest part of it all, when I think about it now, is that they didn't have to be.

Edward made almost one-thousand dollars per week in the '80s! That was a lump sum in those earlier times. Even though I think about it that way now, Noah got the idea when he was a child. He knew he didn't have to be hungry.

He had to wake up - hungry, go to school - hungry, hang out with his friend - hungry, and then return home - hungry.

One day, Calvin's mother ordered a family-size order of fried chicken from Church's Chicken. She sent Calvin to pick it up. But the order was so large that he needed some help carrying everything.

Of course, Noah agreed to help his friend. They both went to the fast-food restaurant and waited on the order. When it was done, Calvin grabbed two boxes - one in each hand, and Noah did the same with the other two.

As they walked back towards Calvin's house, the aroma from the chicken filled Noah's nose. The salivation that the smell triggered filled up in his mouth. His stomach was crying out to be fed. Noah wanted so badly to stop and ask Calvin for just one piece to quell the anger in his belly.

Again, his pride wouldn't let him do it. God, somehow, he found the strength to keep from asking for what was so easily accessible.

Again and again, he knew that he did not have to go hungry. Every day that passed, Noah would always see some boys working at their local grocery store putting people's groceries in their cars for a few bucks.

That summer, when school ended, Noah put it in his mind that he wouldn't be hungry anymore, nor was he going back to school with the same shabby clothes. He walked down Bankhead Highway to the local Food Giant.

From there, he began to ask people if they would allow him to put their groceries in the car. Next, he pumped gas at gas stations. Before long, he knew how to hustle. After a long summer of hard work, he was able to buy himself some decent school clothes, shoes, get a haircut, and at last…he was able to buy himself some food.

Noah wasn't the only one of his family who had made friends in the big city. His sister, Angeline, also made friends who taught her how to sign off for food stamps for herself and her siblings.

Somehow, Jamal found the family after they had moved from Alabama. Soon enough, Samuel regrouped with everyone as well. Edward felt that the family was coming back together. The only person who was missing was his now ex-wife, Martha. He knew that she wouldn't willingly come where he was. But he had a fix for that.

He explained to his returning boys that their mother was living in a run-down shed that was infested with rats and snakes. He also told them that she refused to leave the hellhole where she was residing and needed their help in getting her out of that place.

Tugging at their heartstrings for their mother, he convinced them to lie to Martha about their baby brother, Messiah, being so sick that he was hospitalized and was about to die. And so, it was done. The two boys lied to their mother, thinking it was for the better good.

In reality, Martha was just getting better. Her mental stability and her overall health was slowly being restored thanks to help from her neighbors. As good as things were beginning to go for her, she received word from her sons about little Messiah. As a loving, caring person and mother, there was no way she was going to allow her child to suffer. She immediately went to see her son.

Jamal and Samuel helped her move to Atlanta so that she could be close to her "dying" son. Since the family lived in a duplex, the men stayed on one side while the women on the other. The moment she was back good enough, the cycle that started in Alabama repeated itself.

Although they were now divorced, Edward started back beating the woman.

In due time, Samuel managed to find a woman that he loved, and the two married. He moved out of the duplex to start his own family. Jamal, however, found comfort with friends in the streets and moved out as well.

It was like before, with Angeline, Mavis, Noah, and Messiah enduring the madness in their residence after their brothers moved out. The children saw Edward beat her so severely that a Varicose vein burst in her leg. As if this evil wasn't enough, he shaved off all of her hair and forced her to take all of her clothes off. He then ran her outside of the house in the nude in front of everyone!

This happened in front of Noah's friends, the neighbors, everyone. Angeline couldn't take it anymore. She went elsewhere in the city and rented an apartment. She gathered up her mother and her things and moved her mother in with her.

Martha was doing very well in Alabama without Edward. Why the hell did he have to disturb her? He was just pure-fucking-evil!

Chapter Seven

Samuel's Rage

Once Martha, Mavis, and Angeline had gone, Noah and Messiah continued to live with Edward. Like before, Noah avoided Edward by staying gone all the time, mainly because he was working at the Giant Food store.

As it so happened, that same Giant Food store where Noah worked was the very same Giant Food store my Grandma, and I always went to all the time.

As far back as I can remember, I recalled seeing this little boy standing and waiting for finished shoppers to exit the building to ask to pack their groceries. I could tell that he was a little older than me.

Out of curiosity, I went up to the boy and asked, "Where's your Mama and daddy? Why are you at the store by yourself?"

He looked at me as if he didn't feel like answering my questions. I was climbing all over the rail that framed the ramp for grocery carts, "Why are you just standing there?" I asked again.

He was looking like he was thinking to himself, 'Lil girl stop asking me so many questions' or 'why are you so nosy?'

I was honestly concerned about him. When Grandma called to me and said it was time to go, I got off the rails and ran to her. Before there was Uber, older men would wait outside the store to give shoppers a ride back home.

They were not certified taxi cab drivers, but they were still making some extra cash under the table. Mr. Bennet was one of the older men who was participating in this side hustle. He was the one my grandmother got to drive us back home.

After we got in the car and drove off, I looked out of the window at the boy and wondered if anybody cared about him. He had the look of nobody wanting him. As I looked out the window, his eyes met mine through the glass.

After that day, I've always told myself that I would have taken care of him. And that I would have brought him home with us.

Back at Noah's place, he and Messiah received a call from Angeline. She instructed the two of them to come to her place. Though Noah found it strange for Angeline to demand for them, he took up Mavis' hand without question or hesitation, and both started their journey to their sister's apartment.

As they were walking, Edward drove up on the side of them and stuck his head out of the window, "Where are y'all going?"

"To Angeline's house," Noah answered.

"Get in the car. I'll take ya there," he told them. They did as their father said. The moment they parked in the lot of Angeline's apartment, they saw Samuel and his wife standing on the sidewalk boarding the black asphalt.

Samuel swiftly jotted to the car and opened the passenger's door, "Y'all come on and get out!" he said in a demanding tone. The two boys got out of the car and ran onto the sidewalk where their sister-in-law was.

"What's going on?" Edward asked.

Enraged, Samuel explained, "Angeline said that you sexually assaulted her and Mavis! What kind of man are you! You'd better get as far away from here as fast as possible! And don't you ever come back here again!"

As he was explaining, the rest of the family came outside, including Martha. The children all stood in front of their mother and at each other's side, ready to give Edward the ass-whooping that was a long time coming.

Edward, heeding their warning left, went back to the duplex, packed up his things, and moved to Texas.

After he left, things started to get better for Martha again. Angeline helped her to get herself together. After then, Martha was able to apply for assistance and rent her own apartment. She moved out of Angeline's place and took Noah and Massiah with her.

For many years, that poor woman was finally able to get peace of mind after much suffering. She started teaching the words of worship, and many came to respect her. As happy as she was becoming, she wanted nothing more than to move back to Alabama--the only home she'd ever known.

I'm not exactly sure how things happened between Martha and her children, but I do know that most of them had become lost to the world. They had to figure it out for themselves. Jamal, by far, was the only one of them that had quickly adapted to the streets. He lived his life the way he wanted to.

After I was told this story at first, I couldn't understand why Edward would marry a dark-skinned woman if he hated the complexion so much. Why torture the hell out of a person for being born of God's choice? In my own opinion, it's a beautiful choice.

Look at me. Look at me! Now stand with pride

Somebody said blackness was ugly

Well, that somebody lied

Your melanin is a threat,

Proof that God is real

You're matched with the universe

And all that is his

Love yourself. Love yourself! Your skin is not a sin!

To divide you from yourself,

Is how the enemy can win

Your hands, your hair, the depth of your shade

Clay carved out of darkness,

Beautifully hand-made

Every race comes from you; you're the parents to the earth

But to keep you uninformed was to decrease yourself worth

Now raise your head. Raise your head!

My melanin people

The true and living God made us as his equal

Let that sit in. your skin is not a sin

Somebody lied so that they could win

God loves us all

Poem: Melonin To My Mother Mary By: K. Phoxx

As things changed in Noah's life, they also changed in mine. Momma ended up giving birth to twin boys whom she named Rashad and Brashad. They were the cutest little babies in the whole wide world.

During this time in my life, Mama and Neno were staying in Grandma's basement. Whenever I woke up in the morning, I couldn't wait to run downstairs and play with them. But momma would tell me that I had to go to school.

At that time, I had no idea what school was. All I knew was that I wanted to play with my baby brothers.

Not long after, she ended up putting me in school. On the first day, I knew that I hated it! One morning, I was adamant about not going back. I hid under my bed and waited for the school bus to come. I came out from hiding after I knew it was gone.

Mama found out that I didn't go to school, "Girl, I'ma beat you good!" she yelled. Well, by me staying home and not going to school, I'd say the beating was worth it.

She and Neno were going to take me to school themselves, but she mentioned that she had to go to someplace called "the welfare office." Her appointment with them was that morning, so she didn't have time to take me to school.

I was with them the entire day. The appointment took hours. When they were done, momma and Neno went straight to their side hustle. Neno sold scrap metal and all kinds of other stuff to provide for the family.

One of his miscellaneous scrap parts was an old, large bucket of glass. They sat the bucket on the car's floor, and I crawled up onto the dashboard underneath the rear window. Neither my mom nor Neno knew how I was sitting in the back. They weren't paying attention. Now the day before, it had stormed something serious. The storm was so bad that a tree was subsequently toppled over and landed halfway in the road.

Since we were driving down a hill, Neno was blindsided by the slope of the road. He ended up crashing into the tree, thrusting me from atop of the seat and into that bucket of glass.

After the shock of the crash, momma and Neno asked if we were alright. I tried to lift up, but I couldn't, "Mama!" I yelled.

Neno swerved around to see me in that bucket, "Don't move Shawnie!" he exclaimed. Other people who were nearby started running to the car and asking if everyone was alright.

"My lil girl is hurt!" he told them in a panic.

Soon, I heard everyone debating if they should move me or not. Somehow, I don't recall clearly, someone picked me up and laid me down on my stomach. I could still feel the pieces of glass that penetrated my back.

I still remember the look on my mother's face. It was one of disgust. Now, I can't remember if she said this aloud or if I imagined her saying anything because the way her expression was as if she was saying, "You make me sick! You should have went to school."

She always told me that I made her sick. Although my memory of some of the events that day was fuzzy, I clearly remember being loaded into an ambulance truck, taken to the hospital, and getting stitches in my back.

Due to the incident, I was out of school for real. Since I was unable to attend school for days, my teacher, Ms. Lennon, came to visit my grandmother. I couldn't stand that woman. She always picked at me. She always said things like, 'y'all welfare Mama is no good, and y'all are gonna be just like them.'

After her visit, momma told me that I had to go back to school. Of course, I had to wait a few more days to get my stitches taken out. When the time came for me to get them removed, I believe my mother was too lazy to take me to the doctor, so she decided to remove them herself.

When she did, it was too painful for me. I cried and screamed so loudly. She had no other choice but to take me to the doctor. After I had them removed, I was able to return to school. By this time, Ms. Lennon was orchestrating a charity session with the classroom, "We need for everybody to bring at least one can good so that we can help the poor and the needy. The poor and the needy have no money to buy Thanksgiving dinner. So we're going to decorate a box, put in the food, and give it to the poor people."

When I went home, I told my Grandma about it. She gave me a can of something that nobody ate, and I took it. I helped in making and decorating a box. I put the can that my Grandma gave me into the box.

Days later, when I got home from school, I saw where Ms. Lennon's car was parked outside our house. She was just leaving as I was walking down the driveway. When our eyes met, she smiled and kept walking until she got in her car and drove away.

I walked into the house and went to the kitchen. That same box that we had decorated in class was the same one sitting on the counter. I didn't really understand what all of that meant.

The next day, Ms. Lennon gathered everyone's attention, "Hello boys and girls," she began, "I want to thank you all for bringing your canned goods. We were able to feed the poor and needy families. We even took a box to someone in our class yesterday who is sitting with us right now."

Bitch looked right at me, and so did the rest of the class. She knew what the hell she was doing. I often wonder if she is alive somewhere because I just want to tell her, "Look at me now." But I know that vengeance is the Lord's.

The following year, I moved on to the first grade. But I wasn't the only one going to school anymore. Zay started attending school as well. He was in my old class with Ms. Lennon. I was so happy that I would finally have someone to talk to.

One day, we were in the cafeteria. I saw him standing up in line with his classmates. But his face wasn't the only familiar one that I saw. Ms. Lennon had an empty tray in her hand going from child to child to see who didn't want their cornbread or milk so she could put the cornbread inside of the milk.

She did the same thing the year before when I was still in her class.

After a while, she began to look like someone who took people's food. On this same day, Zay was in line with a tray. I sat down with my own class. When I looked back at Zay, I noticed that his tray was gone, and his head was held down. I quickly got up and jotted over to him. "Where's your food?"

"The lady took it. She said Mama didn't fill out the paperwork."

Then Ms. Lennon walked over to me, "Go back to your seat."

"My brother doesn't have any food," I explained.

"That's because y'all welfare Mama didn't fill out the forms," she spoke disgustingly nasty to me.

"How much does his food cost?" I asked.

"Twenty cents."

'Twenty cents!' I thought to myself, 'Two dimes is all it costs to feed a hungry child?! You lowdown motherfucker you! You roll your big ass around with an empty plate to the top for yourself every fucking day, and you mean to tell me that you can't even do that for a child?! A wicked creature you are!'

I hated that woman, even until this very day. As much as I know, hating is wrong, but that's one woman who needed to feel the wrath of God.

I wanted to make sure my brother ate, so I said, "Well, he can eat with me."

"No, he can't eat with you."

I sadly went back to my seat. What I did was get a few napkins and wrapped up some of the food that was on my tray, and crept it into my pocket. After school was out and we were on our way home, I took the napkin from my pocket and gave it to Zay. I made sure he ate something.

That's why it was important to make sure that Zay because it might have been all we had to eat for that day. When I went home, I begged my momma to fill out the form for my brother. When she finally filled them out, I watched carefully and taught myself through her how to fill them out. I knew at that point that I would have to be responsible.

As it happens, my mother was expecting again. When she gave birth, she named him Lashaud. All three of my youngest brothers look like triplets. After a few years, they were old enough to attend school. Now, we were all going to school together.

We mainly lived with Grandma during the school days and went with Mama in the summer. And every summer that came, I dreaded it so. I hated going to her house! The only reason why I liked going there was because of my daddy. He was such a good dad.

He taught me how to ride a bike, do my homework, color, and many other things. But Mama, on the other hand, was sneaky! Whenever my father went to work, another man was always coming into the house.

I wanted to tell Neno so badly, but Mama made sure that I didn't. She gave me a taste of what I would get if I ever told. The pain that I felt from her beatings made me just want to die. But the pain for her beatings wasn't the only thing hurting me. It was also my back where the stitches had come out. And then, so did the rest of my whole body.

I tried to tell my Mama, but she didn't listen or care. The blessing was that I had brothers. Since they were still small, they used their feet to massage my legs and wherever else I felt pain. Their massaging helped me to feel a little bit better.

Chapter Eight
Backdoor Jodie

At this same time in my life, Mama and Neno would argue all the time. It was chaotic in our home. So hectic that some days, Neno would have to take us to school and was late every day for work. Then one day, he told me that he got fired. I learned what that meant very quickly.

But still, he got up every day and tried to do something. He was stressed out. Soon, he started drinking. Every day he went out. And the moment he left was when Black Jesus would show up. Yeah, that was his name. Real talk. Black Jesus did ungodly things like laying up in another man's bed while that man was at work; however, a weak woman had to allow it.

I could tell when Mama wanted to be with Black Jesus. She would start fights with my daddy. One night she wanted to be with Black Jesus and go to The Silver Fox, a nightclub on Bankhead. But the car would not start.

Neno went outside to check on the battery. The battery ended up exploding in his face. During all of this, I was asleep. I didn't even know that anything had happened. All I knew was that when I woke up the following day and saw my dad, he had gauze wrapped around his eyes.

I sat down on the steps. I was afraid to go near Neno. He rocked back and forth on the couch for hours. Mama later tiptoed down the steps and went to the front door. She started signaling for Black Jesus to get his attention.

He knew my dad was home. He looked at my mom with the look of, "Are you crazy?!" But she kept signaling to him. Then he tiptoed toward the door with an evil smile on his face. Finally, she motioned for him to come to her, and he went like the damn fool he was.

Poor daddy had no clue! After he had come up, she led them both upstairs and looked at me like, "You know you better not say a word!" When they were out of sight, I went nearer to my daddy and sat beside him. I didn't leave him. I would never leave him.

Who does this to a person? Mama dogged my daddy. She ran over him, steamrolled him, and he took it because he loved her. She talked to him like he was useless. Like a nobody. How could a person be so cruel? How could a person kick somebody while they were down?

After Daddy got better, things went back to normal for a while. Dad always played Elton John's whole record. His favorite song in the album was "Rocket Man." To this very day, I still cry whenever I hear the song. It makes me think of the days of just sitting with him for hours as he drank beer after beer and played his record.

When Mama got tired of Black Jesus, she brought in another one. His name was Hurbert. But everybody called him "Walking Tall." A big lazy ass Nigga! Daddy had gone to the club with Mama one night.

Hurbert saw my dad with my Mama, walked up to him, and slapped the hell out of my daddy. My dad didn't even know this man or seen that slap coming. Hurbert pulled a fuck nigga move by catching him off guard. My dad was going to retaliate, but people around held him from hitting this nigga back!

He did not know Mama was fucking this nigga. My father is a man who had a reputation for bursting holes in concrete walls. Strong enough to open jars and eat hot peppers from Church's Chicken like they were chips.

My dad is a strong man. I thought him to be Superman. Because of this, I felt that women were the only ones that could cry; big, bulky, strong men did not show emotion. Truthfully, I believed that, however, I thought that, But that changed the day I walked downstairs to see my daddy rocking. He used to chew gum on his tongue out of habit.

"Shawnie," he called to me. So, I walked over to him. He said, "Sit down." Notably, I sat on the floor close to his legs obediently. "Shawnie, you're growing up to be a big girl. And I know you know what your Mama is doing to me is wrong. But let me tell you something. I want you to make me proud. You're my only daughter, and I want you to know that your Mama hurt me pretty bad."

Then, tears started to roll down from his eyes and down his face, "I know that's your Mama. But I don't want you to be like her. I want you to do better than her! Don't ever walk in your Mama's footsteps, ya hear? When you find a good man, be good to him. Don't ever hurt anybody the way your Mama hurt me. You hear me?!"

"Yes," I answered, "I will never hurt a man this way. I promise." I didn't think he could cry. 'This isn't right,' I thought to myself, 'This is wrong. Very wrong!'

After my dad finally got enough, he packed up and moved out of the house and back with his parents. When Daddy left, Hurbert moved right on in. This nigga beat the hell out of Mama and ate all the food.

There was no food in the fridge. But I was able to go in the freezer and dig out some old hotdogs and cook some flour and water mixture that I came up with so that my brothers and I could eat. My brothers were outside her door earlier that day, knocking and asking her to cook them something.

Then I saw them push the sock covering a hole in the door where a knob should have been. After that, the boys started peeking in there to see what she was doing.

That was the day I learned how to cook. I had to take matters into my own hands. At this instant, I realized my Mama was ill-equipped for motherhood. I started cooking, and bathing, and taking care of my brothers on my own. Mama just provided a place to stay. I wanted to dial Daddy's number so desperately. I even imagined myself building a wagon and attaching it to my bike, pulling everyone with me to my daddy's house.

I cooked the hotdogs and flour and water stuff. It came out looking like pancakes. The boys ate. Then this big, lazy nigga gets up and asks for a hotdog. I said, "No!" Shit! Didn't he already eat?! I wish I were old enough back then to tell his little pussy ass, 'you are what you eat!' Then this stupid ass dude threw beer bottles, busted Mama's windows, hit her in the head with a bottle, and went to jail! Then she went and got him out! Meanwhile, daddy started doing good. He got another job and a new car while this 'walking tall' Motherfucker walked everywhere he went. Mama was sick in the head. She had to have been.

But things changed when one of the twins fell down the stairs, and one of his teeth went up in his gums. He went immediately, rushed to the hospital, and daddy was back! I hated that my brother hurt himself. But daddy coming back around kept Hurbert's pussy ass away! He wasn't gonna fight a real man straight up! He knew what was good and got the hell on.

Then he started dating a lady two doors down from my mother's apartment. That lady had kids his age. And whipping her ass was not an option because her kids would have killed him. He was just like a lot of these lizard-ass negroes that live from project to project with different females. Then have the females out there fighting each other like some damn fools!

His name isn't on any lease, but he knows the game. He goes from one hole to the next, telling one girl one thing and telling another girl something else. Neither not realizing that he owns nothing. Her residence is his home. God forbid that he drops babies and diseases in the wake of this madness, but he does.

There are a lot of Hurbert's and Black Jesuses all over this country, half-baked. Nobody cooked him well-done, so he beats the shit out of women to make himself feel like the man he has never become. His mother could be young herself. Misused and unraised, so the trait is passed on to her children--to her boys.

His lack of compassion and maturity says that he's a man at 3 years old. So when he falls and hurts himself, they say, 'shake it off. You're a man.' News flash! He's a baby! Children need love and affection. But nobody showed them that love. Love is a luxury that some can't afford.

So they look for women like my mother, weak and clueless. And now who's affected? Me. Her child. And the cycle can continue to go on and on unless somebody is brave enough to stop it.

Finally! Mama was approved for her section 8 and was able to move us into a house. We left the Hollywood Court apartments forever. The new neighborhood we moved to was called The Dixie Hills Community. We lived on Wadly street.

A white lady, named Mrs. Hill owned the house. She allowed Mama to rent out the four-bedroom home. Although it was four bedrooms, the house was so big that it had at least seven rooms. The Dixie Hills Community in the early '80s was good. But the apartments behind them started to become unsafe.

We pretty much avoided going near the apartments at the time. But, sometimes, we had no choice but to go there because Uncle Teddy and his wife, Sandy, lived there with their three kids, Lizzy, Lawanda, and Lashawn. Lawanda and Lashawn were twins.

At this time, mommy and daddy had started to fix televisions and sold them for a living. Dad worked at a furniture company, and Mom went to the Salvation Army and bid on buggies of TV's. Sometimes, she even bid against her own brother, Uncle Ronald. They were all in a Flea Market-type business.

Mama was good at hustling and making money. But then, she and Daddy started to do well, and the jealousy from others began to grow. Usually, Mama would get out and cheat on my dad. But this time, she stayed focused.

Uncle Shane lived with us, and Aunt Lilly and Uncle Joey came around from time to time. Uncle Shane was like my big brother. I loved when he was around. Uncle Shane went in on Mama whenever she tried to do something to hurt my daddy. He even told my dad what she was doing behind his back.

Nonetheless, Mama and Shane were very close. And to us, he was a big kid. So whenever Mama had adult cookouts and things like that, Shane disappeared and hung out with the kids more. So, for example, the Fourth of July parties were filled with adults, but the kids were hanging out with Shane somewhere.

After Mama's last Fourth of July party, certain family members noticed that my dad had a new Cadillac, Mama had a new Cadillac, and both had an extra Sedan Coupe Deville in the yard for no reason.

Then before I knew it, different family members started moving in. Daddy better not had said anything because Mama would always defend her family. After they moved in, their friends would be at the house often. It went from quiet to crowded.

Even Crawley's no good ass moved in. So let me get this straight! Not only did he move in. He brought his stankin' ass feet with him! The same stankin' ass that moved into my dead grandfather's house.

My grandfather bought and died in that house. His death paid off the house, which he willed to his wife and children.

Crawley laid up in my grandfather's room with my grandfather's wife, got to make friends with my grandfather's neighbors, then broke in their houses when they were gone. The motherfucker had no shame!

So Grandma met a decent man named Raymond. Raymond was very well-to-do; he had class and was very dignified. Raymond had enough respect to take Grandma out on dates and to his apartment. He respected her children and grandchildren. There wasn't a holiday that went by that he didn't send Grandma a gift. Raymond loved her. He would not disrespect the memory of my grandfather under any circumstances.

Even my grandfather would have given Raymond his blessings by being the man his wife and children needed.

I think Grandma was lonely when she met Crawley. One Sunday morning, while Crawley was still with Grandma, she got up and got dressed. Crawley had spent the night. Grand said to him that Raymond was on the way to pick her up.

I'm not sure if she was looking for a reaction from Crawley to see if he would get jealous. But in true Crawley's fashion, he also jumped up and got dressed and the sand, "Arita! Ask Raymond to give me a ride to Bankhead!"

Dude! Have you no shame! This man was so lazy and prideless that he asked his girlfriend to ask her new boyfriend to give him a damn ride! Most men refuse to allow themselves to look like a loser in the eyes of another man. But Crawley's Spam-eating ass was a different breed. He drank and smiled and ate cheap ass mediocre minced meat called Spam. From that day on, I had to come to learn that sorry ass men ate that shit!

I'm sorry, but every man I've ever met who ate spam is coincidentally wretched as fuck! Spam--Sorry, Pathetic Ability to be a Man. I believed that was the purpose of the acronym. And if he didn't have Spam, he would get a piece of bread and place a tough piece of pork skin, add some hot sauce, and then gnaw on it with his eyes closed while having no teeth!

I guess his eyes were closed to brace himself for the pain that was about to fuck up his gums. It should have served him right! Seeing him gnaw reminded me of Dusty, Uncle Ronald's old dog that didn't feel like barking. A damn dog that didn't have the strength to bark. Her barking went something like 'rrrrrrr.'

I'm shaking my damn head as she laid her big, dusty, long-ass in the middle of the dirt. She was gnawing on a ham bone. At least Dusty had a reason--she was a dog. Crawley on-the-other-hand had none. But he dragged his ass to our house and moved in. The next thing I knew, his cousin, Leroy--a married man with kids--started showing up also while Daddy was at work.

We thought that he was coming over to see Crawley. But, naw, Patricia was who he had his intention set on. Daddy got up to go to work, then came home to fix all the TVs he had piled up in the living room. After he got done with that, he polished them up, loaded them into the truck, and went out and sold them. His appreciation? Patricia is cheating on him repeatedly. Daddy always came through for the family.

Sometimes when we didn't have anything to eat, he would leave early in the morning and walk. By the time it was dark, we would see him walking through the apartments in front of the building that Mama had lived in with bags of groceries in his hands. Now, as a grown woman, I can see the actual distance from Bankhead to Hollywood court. And I'm not talking about the Bankhead where Kmart was. Or even closer to what was West Fulton High School.

He carried big bags of leg quarters and several other things in those bags in each of his hands. I could tell the bags were heavy because when he stretched out his arms, the strain from the weight of the bags made his veins visible. His tall, slender physique thrust him forward as fast and as hard as he could just to make it home.

The caring spirit that God gave me allowed me to take notes, see the hurt, and try to understand it all. As a child, there was no understanding - just a lot of worry. I saw my father find money without a job; make a Christmas every year even though the year was challenging. I saw him numb the pain that came from his health and heart--all he wanted was love. Still, love is a luxury that some cannot afford.

Chapter Nine

Sick And Tired Of Being Sick And Tired

After moving into our house to get a fresh start, I thought that Mama could put the temptation to cheat behind them by moving away from the apartments. But for a foolish woman with a weak mind, it found her anyway.

Shane was upset, and so was I. I confessed to Grandma that I wanted to tell my daddy. She later told my Mama what I said, and I got beat so badly. Laying there getting whipped with guilt hurt me more than the three sticks that were supposed to be switches going across my body.

The pain from the beating was extreme. She beat me on my legs and back. Additionally, the muscle soreness in my arms was an excessive reminder that I got whipped! "Why did God let me live?" I thought to myself. As a ten-year-old, I grew so tired of living.

I wanted to be free of Patricia's beatings. I wanted out so much that I would sit down and write poems and songs and call radio stations and music stores, wondering how I could become a singer. The same year, I got a Hello Kitty diary. In it, I wrote everything that had happened.

Usually, I would keep it with me. But one weekend, I forgot it and made the mistake of leaving it at home. It was under my bed where I last put it. Later that day, Grandma's phone rang with Mama on the other end crying. She was telling Grandma that Daddy had found my book and read it.

She said that I had written a book of lies about her. But everything that was in it was true! What hurt Mama the most was that Daddy found it and saw where I said, *'Mama didn't love us. She had different men in the house while Daddy was gone. She beat me a lot because she said I talked too much. Everything I saw her do, she told me not to tell my daddy if I knew what was good for me'.*

I had to talk to somebody. I had to get it out of my soul! I didn't tell my daddy. I told my diary, and I did not give him my permission to read it. But God works in mysterious ways. Because of how I hid that book, only God himself could have led him to it.

Mama then started playing her invisible violin, wanting someone to feel sorry for her. She told me that she was going to die to play on my guilty conscience. I thought to myself, 'Naw. You're gonna live, but you're gonna get punished like hell for cheating with a married man that clearly used her for sex.

As I think about this now, it's like this; imagine you and your kids are walking home. All of you have on your coats. You stop and take a shortcut through the woods because it's getting cold and dark. The babies get scared, and so do you. But you can't let them know you're afraid, nor can you start to panic because they believe mommy can do anything.

You have the baby bag with about three diapers, baby wipes, two full bottles, one-half bottle, two bottles of water, a candy bar, chips, and maybe a sandwich bag filled with dried cereal for a snack. Then, as you're walking, BOOM!

You fall into a hole. You're now stuck down there, yelling for someone to help you. Then this handsome, fine-ass dude says to you, "Baby, you look so beautiful down there. You're fine and sexy. I can help you and help you with your kids."

So, he throws down a rope. As soon as you grab a hold to the rope and begin to climb, he says,

"No, baby. I'm about to get down there with you." so he climbs down into the hole.

The only little bit of food you have to survive on is such a small amount. There's barely enough food for you and your kids. So, not only did he climb in the hole with you. This motherfucker didn't bring any food or a coat! So the little that you have for you and your kids, he wants some of it also.

So now, he's taken your food and warmth. You, your babies, and he are gonna need more because he's a big ass man in this tiny ass hole! So, instead of helping you up, he climbs in there with you. When a man walks by that can help you, he refuses because there's a grown-ass man in there with you WITH A ROPE!

The Motherfucker is too sorry to pull himself up and bring you and the kids with him, and it is more comfortable for him to survive off of you! And who is paying for it all? The babies! Because they are too young to help themselves. But the hungrier they become, the more they resent you as a mother because as their protector, you should have told him not to get his ass down there with you.

You should have said, 'Keep it moving! We will stay in this hole until somebody is responsible enough to pull us out.

Well, that was the situation with my mother. She didn't want a man that could pull her out of the hole. She couldn't see, respect, or appreciate when there was a man who could. So she gave every man the green light to get into that hole with her. But they could leave and come back whenever they wanted - even Hurbert, A.K.A. "Walking Tall."

When she ran out of food, he would say, "I'm going to my sister's house to eat," or "I'm going to my mother's house to eat." So instead of saving the girl with five hungry children that you just finished fucking, you save yourself?! But how much could I blame him when she allowed it?

But the man that's trying to save everybody gets dogged the fuck out! So now, it's Leroy's turn to do the dogging. He was a big dude! Good-looking nigga with his own business. But what did that matter? We never benefited from it.

This nigga came over, dapped my father up, and had broken his home down by fucking his woman. Even as a child, I knew the shit was wrong. But then, the fussing started again. And the disrespect from my mother's siblings playing loud music and drinking, "Whatcha doin' this weekend, Pat?" they'd ask.

And she'd answer, "Oh, we can play cards and get some beer and shit." 'Beer and shit' was a known phrase. Beer and motherfuckin' shit! If it's 'shit,' who needs it? But what the heck, that was Pat's house. Daddy's name wasn't on the lease; therefore, they could do whatever, and Mama said nothing.

Her family walking all over her, using her, and making her feel guilty was a sport they all played well. But Daddy better not have opened his mouth or else. I lost respect for Mama at a very early age because she did not fight. To me, she was weak. She had no backbone nor moral fiber in her anywhere. For these reasons, I wondered why Daddy stayed, why he put up with it. I didn't know or understand.

I wanted Daddy to cheat on Mama so desperately so that she could see how it felt. So she would get her act together and hold on to this man. One time, I lied to her and told her that he was talking to a lady named Betty. But that shit didn't work. She continued her behavior. She continued to allow her family to take over our house.

Daddy's only escape every day was going to work at Comfort Furniture Company Downtown Atlanta. It was like every other month; Daddy was bringing in a new sofa. All so her siblings could sit on it with their nasty ass feet and have their kids piss on the couch. The last beautiful sofa I remember Daddy buying was a peach and green-colored set.

As expected, everybody with their nasty feet climbed onto this light-colored furniture, and not even a month later, pee rings were everywhere. Daddy was getting fed up day by day. It was frustrating to him that he couldn't voice his own opinion. A house filled with overgrown negroes where nobody worked. All the bills he paid and all the food that he bought, he had to keep quiet.

One Friday night, he had come home to everybody outside on the porch drinking beer and playing music. By this time, he already knew about Leroy, and the pressure had built up. Consequently, he pulled into the driveway and got out of the car, already exhausted from a long week. I don't remember who said what, but I remember Daddy throwing a Budweiser up against the house, and the beer splashed on everybody.

Then Lily and Joey both ran up to him and started fighting him. Then Mama jumped in. Uncle Richard had just pulled up to our house, and I begged him to help my daddy. But his fat ass took the opportunity to jump on my daddy too. When Shane saw what was going on, he started beating the shit out of his siblings. He told my mom how fucked up it was to let her other siblings beat Daddy like that.

I hated them after that. My mother's siblings had it out for my daddy, and I think it was because he cared about her. As long as he was around, they couldn't use her the way they wanted to. They wanted our family torn apart. Once when my dad came to pick us up, we all shouted, 'Daddy's here! Daddy's here!' Lilly told us, "That's not your real daddy. He's the twins and the last boy's daddy. Not yours and

Zay."

That was the most challenging truth I had to swallow as a child because it was true. Mama didn't know who my father was. She said that when I was born, I was so ugly that she hid me. Mama told me that all the other girls had pretty babies. She even told her friends that she sent me out of town because she was so embarrassed by how ugly I was. Whoever my father was, mama didn't like him. So apparently, whenever she looked at me, I reminded her of a failure that had occurred at one point in her life when she decided to get pregnant by someone with whom she regretted having sex.

But that fell on her. She was always quick to remind me how she wanted to roll over me and smother me and pretend like it was an accident. I didn't care to know this. I was already getting bullied and called names at school. All of this information wasn't necessary, but to confirm that Neno, the only father I had ever known, was not my father, was hurtful. But he never said anything to me about it.

He always told people he had five children. Never once did he say that I was not his daughter. To me, his blood, sweat, tears, pain, grief, hurt, sacrifice, and love was all the DNA I'd ever needed. I am my father's daughter, and I still hated them for jumping on my dad, and I am angry at my mom for allowing it.

After the incident, Daddy's back was bruised and scarred. As time passed on, the outside wounds healed but not the scar on the inside. Daddy eventually started speaking back to mom's siblings. But he and Shane had a very tight bond. He was closer to my daddy than his own brothers.

Chapter Ten
A Childs Broken Heart

Mama was close to her brothers for other reasons. For instance, Richard disrespected Big Ma, Grandma's mother, even though she raised Richard, he did not respect her. He often used profanity in front of her. Grandma didn't talk to her kids like they were kids. She spoke to her eldest children as if they were making a business deal by answering 'Yes' or 'No.'

With the youngest ones, she'd haul off and slap the shit out of them. I often wondered if Grandma feared her oldest children like Richard's disrespectful ass. Ronald and George were respectful to her. Teddy, on the other hand, stayed in jail. Always in trouble. Mom's closeness to him was off and on.

Teddy stole one of momma's TVs during one Christmas, and they got into a horrible fight. They ended up not speaking to each other. That Christmas, it felt bizarre because normally, he and Sandy would walk down to the house and bring their kids with them. But, they didn't come that year.

Christmas was gone, and January passed by. Teddy came by the house to see Grandma since she was living with momma because she didn't have gas at her home. Since it was too cold for her to stay at home, she stayed with us.

Later that night, Auntie Esther and Uncle Hale's grand Uncle, their grandmother's baby brother, came by for a visit. They were playing music and enjoying themselves. Mom and Dad were getting along. Then, suddenly, Crawley came running through the door yelling as loud as he could, "Teddy just got shot!"

Grandma had hurt her ankle weeks back, and she started trying to walk back to Dixie Hills. I don't remember who picked her up, but Uncle Hale said, "He might already be dead."

"Don't say that!" I yelled.

Mama managed to get to the ambulance to see Teddy. He was trying to cover himself up because they had taken his clothes off while attempting to perform procedures to save his life. Teddy placed his hand over his private area. Shortly after that, Mama saw Teddy take his last breath. They had not spoken to each other up until that night. That hurt her so much; it crushed her. Even I felt sorry for her. Nobody deserved to live with that. All of the money she saved up, she used to help bury Teddy.

After that happened, the guilt of not speaking to her brother weighed heavy on her heart. After that incident, she began to allow her family to steamroll all over her even more just as long as they weren't angry with her about anything.

Sandy was pregnant when Teddy died. We thought that the baby was his, but come to find out, she had been sleeping around on him. He was shot because a fight had broken out in the liquor house he was in, and he went to see what was going on. One guy pulled out a gun intended to shoot the guy he was fighting with. But Teddy took the bullet. He was an innocent bystander.

When Lilly told Sandy that Teddy was dead, she was apparently sitting in her apartment with the man she was messing around with. As fucked up as it was, that guy had nothing to do with Teddy's death. He was a married man. He wasn't looking to be serious with Sandy. About a year after Uncle Teddy died, Sandy sent the baby to live in Fitzgerald, Georgia. We didn't even get the chance to see the baby, to see if she looked like us to know for sure if she was really ours.

Sandy soon started dating this guy named Bobo. This big, heavy, dark-skinned dude that beat the hell out of her and Teddy's kids. One day, we went by her house to visit and saw that her kids were at home by themselves. Uncle Ronald and Lilly knocked on the door. Lizzy opened the door and let them in. They had been home alone for a while. Sandy had a reputation for being unfit. She beat her kids for crying when they were only a few months old. The kids had been eating cake icing. Sandy and Bobo came home, and Bobo took off his belt and beat Lizzy in front of us for opening the door. Ronald walked out of the door because he wanted to kill him for putting his hands on his brother's children. He had no business putting his hands on another man's children. Mama left in tears. The guilt of Teddy dying like that almost ate her alive. But what could anybody do? Sandy was another woman who decided to put a man above her own children and even herself.

As time moved on, so did the way to hustle. The TV--selling became too slow, so Shane, a young man now, was tired of struggling, tired of trying to get by, opted into the dope game and introduced Mom, Dad, and Aunt Lilly to it also. The days of not being able to pay bills were gone. Days of not having food and money came to an end.

We had money. Lots of it! Shane once bought us one-hundred tacos from taco bell and two hundred wings from J.R Crickets. He drove a 1985 Mercedes Benz and wore Kangol and Borsellino hats. Most of the kids in my class had family members that either sold drugs or used them.

It was a jackpot! The sellers in our community, people who worked a 9 to 5, were making more money than they had ever seen! And there was no age limit on who sold it. It was a hustle that brought about a sound called rap music, which I loved. I could write it, perform it, and be it. All I needed was a chance. Shane told me that he knew this well-known rapper named M.C Shy D, and he was going to introduce me to him. Almost every night that Shane came home, I waited to see if Shy D would walk into our living room. The only person to walk into our home was Tammy, Shane's new mystery girl.

Shane's main girlfriend was named Breanna, and they were together for years with two children. He also had two other children by Sandy's twin sister, Cindy, and a son with Aunt Lily's friend, Leslie.

Later, he and his childhood girlfriend, Mary, got together. Mary had class. I didn't know what he saw in Tammy. Joey said that she was a stripper. She looked like she could be a stripper. Tammy was tall, dark, very well-shaped, and had long hair. She was very beautiful. Shane told us that she lived in her brother's car and asked if she could live with us. Her brother had a nice, fixed-up car with rims and everything on it. But he was in prison on drug charges. They had come from Buffalo, New York because their father was a detective for the Fulton County Police department.

We figured out who their father was when we learned that her brother's name was Darnell Jr. Their father was Darnell Rice Senior. We wondered why he distanced himself from his children. Darnell was well-known. He was one of the officers over the Wayne Williams story about the missing and murdered children. That was big in the headlines.

But his son was doing time while his daughter was living in our home with Shane. Shane was a big-time drug dealer. I didn't understand what the hell was really going on. Even though Darnell Jr. was doing what we thought was a long sentence, Tammy knew he would get right out. And got right out, he did.

Jr. hardly served any prison time and was able to get off on all the crimes he committed. Not too long after this, Tammy found out that Shane was a whore, for lack of a better word. We loved him, but so did the ladies. He had babies being born, child support, and other women bringing his clothes to the house and throwing them in the yard. Shan was a mess! He didn't drink, smoke, or do drugs even though he sold them. He still acted like a big kid, and hanging out with us kids was the highlight of his day.

As beautiful as Tammy was, none of it was enough to keep Shane from whoring around with other women. The only woman I could see Shane settling down with was Mary. She loved Shane for most of her life. They had gone to high school together and grew up in the same neighborhood. Tammy knew about Mary and found her to be a threat. Tammy and Shane fought almost every night. One night, he told her that he wanted her to leave my mother's house. And knowing what I knew, Mary was a few months pregnant. Shane saved enough money to get out of the game. He sold his Mercedes and was about to buy a Jaguar, so he was driving the extra car Mom and Dad had. He was going to settle down and work on building a family and business. Tammy and Shane were barely talking. He asked her to leave weeks before, but she didn't. Then Shane stopped coming home altogether. When he did come back after a while, she was still there. All of his clothes were still at home. He hadn't fully moved out yet. He just didn't want to be there because of Tammy. Finally, she told him that she had no place to go and didn't want to be without him.

Shane's bedroom was right next to mine. Whenever he wanted to go to the club or the skating rink, he knocked on my door, which was also his door on the other side, and paid me twenty dollars to iron his clothes. Or he paid me to lie about him not being home when different girls would call. Because I missed all of those things, I wanted Tammy to leave also. Then the night when she decided to leave, she took her time packing her stuff. Shane went in the Freezer to get out a Coke he put in before. But he mistakenly left it in there too long, so the Coke froze. Then he sat down at the table and started counting money. "Shane! Why don't you take that girl to her aunt's house in the morning!" Grandma yelled to Shane as he was trying to drink his frozen Coke. Tammy butted in and said, "He's just gon' drop me off, Mama!" "Can't he wait until it gets daylight? It's only a few hours away." she looked at Shane next, "Shane, don't you leave this house," warned Grandma. "I'll be back, big woman." His nickname for Grandma was 'Big Woman.' "He so damn hard-headed," Grandma said to herself out loud.

Shane and Tammy were on their way out the door when Shane stopped by Mama's room, "Pat! I put the money up in my room! Pat come ride with me!" he said. But Mama and daddy were knocked out. So Shane went ahead and left. After about fifteen or twenty minutes after Shane left, the phone rang. Grandma picked up the phone, and a woman was on the phone. It was Tammy's aunt, "Ms. Benson? Your son Shane was shot, and they shot my son too!" Grandma yelled, "Pat! Neno! Wake up! They shot Shane!" Mama and Daddy jumped up. After that, everybody went to the hospital except for us kids. A while later, Joey called home. "Hello?" I answered. "Shawnie? Your Mama wants to know if anybody called." "No," I answered, "Where's Shane?" "He's dead." I dropped the phone and started screaming. Uncle Derrick was a stone-cold alcoholic, but even alcohol couldn't numb the pain of him losing his baby brother. The whole family was devastated. People from Bankhead, Techwood, Bowen Homes to Hollywood Court, Perry Homes to Joyland, and everybody who knew him was hurt.

The old football coaches that called him "Bubblegum" were hurt. Even though this happened years ago, I'm still in mourning to this very day over him. He was my big brother. He showed me how to dance and rap while staying on beat. He could dance his ass off in shoes or skates. He told me that I was smart and that I was going to be somebody one day. He was proud to let people know that I was his little niece. He was fair and my protector, and I lost him.

When the following day came, police officers in plainclothes came into our house. Only one of the policemen had on a uniform, and he went by the name of Dexter. The plain-clothes policemen made everyone sit in the living room. Mom, Shane, and Lily knew Dexter from high school. "What's going on?" they asked. "I don't know. I received a call request for a uniformed police escort," Dexter said. "You know Shane got killed last morning," they both told Dexter.

"What?!" he responded in shock. Mom went into Shane's room earlier to see if she could find the money that Shane told her that he had hidden. Hence, Mama tore that room apart, looking for that money. But the undercover plain-clothes police officers went straight into Shane's room. Mama quietly followed them.

She saw the white cop lift the ceiling in Shane's room and get the money he hid. The only two people who knew where the money was were Shane and Tammy. The undercover cop searched everybody. Sandy was there at the time, and she had weed on her. They should have locked her up if they were looking for drugs, but they didn't bother her. The information that came in was that Shane dropped

Tammy off. He was about to pull off when Tammy told him that her brother, Junior, wanted to see him in the back. So he got out of the car and left it running. Then these three guys came up and yelled, "RED DOG! Get on the ground!" The Red Dog was a drug task force put in place to bust drug dealers. Guess who was over the Red Dogs? Darnell Rice. Tammy and Junior's father. They walked over to Shane and shot him in the head. And Tammy's aunt, who said her son was shot, was walking around Grady Hospital unharmed.

Right after the shooting, Junior asked to speak to Shane. I told him, "He's dead." Now, as an adult, I know that it was a confirmation call to make sure my uncle was dead and gone. The police got on TV the next day and said their Red Dog squad was nowhere in the area. That was a lie, and they knew it. Ironically, the same day they killed Shane was when Tammy's mother came and got her on the first thing smoking back to Buffalo, New York. I don't know where the bitch is today, but hell is a decent place for her. As a woman of God, I'm sure it's okay to hate the Devil. The Devil is no creature in the ground. The actions of that beat lived in the souls of the ones who worshipped him. And they worshipped him whether they knew it or not. Consequently, life for my family was never the same. A hole was now in the center of our world.

Chapter Eleven
A Whole New World

Mom and Dad moved out of the house. Drugs and alcohol had taken the essence of my father. He tried to soldier on with what was left of his spirit because part of it died when Shane died. He loved Shane like his own flesh and blood. Living in that house had Shane's spirit everywhere.

We moved into Lily's apartment that she had abandoned. After that, Mama and Daddy broke up for good. Not long after that, Mama moved into another house. It was the first place we had ever lived without Daddy. He left, never knowing many things, including the first time I was molested sexually by one of Lily's homeboys. When Lily found out about it, she wanted to kill the guy! But Mama rolled her eyes at me and was pissed because we had to go to court to press charges.

Because we got to court late, the man was set free. Mama told me never to tell Daddy what happened. The most hurtful part was that I couldn't even tell Shane either. Even when I was punched in the eye by a boy at school, Lily laughed at me, and Mama didn't blink! I felt numb, but not for long because Mama was getting high, and someone had to care for my brothers. So I did.

Mama blamed Daddy for introducing her to drugs. But how do you ask a sick man to heal you? He was on it heavily. When she tried it, she said she felt nothing. But she said it was his fault.

That year was my last year in elementary. All I know is that I barely went to school. Daddy tried his best to send us as much as possible, but we were kept back anyway due to lack of attendance. For this reason, when Daddy left, we fell off. Whenever we could go to school, the teachers would ask us why we hadn't been attending. Mama would tell us to tell them that she was in the hospital or that she was sick. But it was always a lie. She always made up sympathetic excuses to get her way out of stuff. I've never even seen her try. I used to tell people that my mother worked for the government. Every time she tried to do something, and it was wrong, she never wanted Dad's help. I found out later in life what the reason could have been. When Mom met Dad, he was on a break from college. His family was middle-class--or at least they aspired to be. They were such beautiful people. Their fair complexion would allow them to almost pass for white or at least biracial. Yet, they were Black and Indian with thick, black curly hair. My dad's parents had two girls, and I think four or five boys. They all looked like Italians from Saturday Night Fever.

Daddy's parents wanted him and his siblings to stay in school. My dad was a college basketball player, and he had played with some of the most well-known legends back in the day. So his parents thought that he would make it to the majors.

Dad had been to three different colleges because his parents wanted the best for him. So when Mom got pregnant, they wanted her to have an abortion. But our family didn't believe in abortions. His parents had no desire for my father to be with a woman who already had two kids by two different men. At that time, Mom told Dad that Zay and I had the same father. Dad dropped out of school to be with Mama because she was pregnant and to help raise two kids that were not biologically his. Nevertheless, he made us his own. He didn't have to give up his dreams, but he did. And I think that was why Mama never asked for his help.

I remember I took to him like a duck to water. Mama always got angry with me whenever I took his side. But she was wrong 99.99% of the time. Daddy had his faults too, but his faults paled in comparison with Mama's actions. Her lack of responsibility carried on while his responsibility as a father was crippled by drug abuse. Mama knows she didn't try to help me with schoolwork or homework. She never talked to any of my teachers nor checked up on me at school to see how I was doing. But Daddy did. When we were all still together, he came to my school one time to pay for my school pictures. When he was about to leave, one of the teachers stopped him and told him that I was very smart, but I needed to come to school more. All the other kids in school used to brag about how their parents knew each other from meeting each other at PTA meetings. I felt bad because my mom never came. But one day, that all changed when I heard a teacher tell another teacher, "These parents don't care about their kids. They never came to find out how their kids are doing. But I spoke to Shawnie's father, and he was very cooperative, and now Shawnie's doing better." I held my head up a little bit higher that day because my father came and talked to the teacher. I was no longer grouped with the children that 'no one cared for.' Daddy really did try. I remember our clothes getting washed. And if they didn't get dry in time, he would iron them dry. He would weave the iron back and forth while chewing his tongue and falling into a trance-like state as he ironed.

Then my seventh-grade prom was announced as the school year was coming to its close. For the first time, and unexpectedly, my mother helped prep me for my prom. She bought me a pretty dress. She did my hair and everything! That was a moment I would cherish forever. She smiled, and so did I. At that moment, I felt that I really did have a mother. My date to the prom that night was with a boy named Calvin Corey. My cousin and Teddy's daughter, Tanya, picked us up and took us to the prom. Afterward, Mama came by and said, "I just wanted to see you." Then I told Mama, "We're going out to eat. Do you have any money?" She went into her pocket and gave me her last seven dollars. I was so happy. Corey and I left the school and went to a restaurant. When we got there, he bought another girl some food. I was thankful to God that Mama gave me some money because I wouldn't have been able to eat. I will always cherish that night.

The next day was graduation. Mama was back to being Mama again. She didn't want me to go to the graduation ceremony, but I did. And I was blessed to make it there in time.

During the graduation, so many other kids were getting called for awards. I wasn't getting called for anything. After the graduation was over, Mama looked at me with that familiar face of disgust. Then she told me that I basically embarrassed her for not getting any awards, "Don't invite me to no more shit like this anymore," she said.

But that was her fault. It was her failure as a mother that she was at war with. Not me. She put nothing into me, and she got nothing in return. But from that day forward, I decided that anything I had done would be for me and from me.

So that following summer, I learned how to take care of myself. I learned how to do my own hair, my own makeup, and how to dress. Grandma was a fashionista. She was always in style in her clothing, her hair, and housekeeping and cooking. I learned a lot by watching her.

When I was still in elementary school, Ms. Lennon told so many lies on me to every teacher I had throughout my school years. One of the lies was that I was boy-crazy. That bitch didn't know that I was sexually molested; that made me scared of boys. But something changed that summer.

So many boys started liking me. I had never received that kind of attention before. But one boy really caught my eye. He went by the name Ron, but his real name was Tarell Jenkins. He was tall, light-skinned, and a very handsome young man. He attended Columbia High School. I wasn't to start high school until the fall.

I would sneak behind auntie Lily's apartment just to see him. I told him that I was living with my aunt and Grandma, but sometimes I would spend the night at my Mama's house in Adamsville. I was head-over-hills for Ron. I knew almost everything about him. He lived with his mom and two older sisters. He was about 5" 9,' and I was about 4" 10. He was way taller than me, around the same height as my father.

Looking at him, you would think that he was all the world of 21 years old, not sixteen or seventeen at all like he was. I didn't want Mom to know that we were talking. I didn't want to get into trouble. But she ended up finding out anyway.

One day we were playing in the parking lot, and Mama saw us, "You might as well bring him down here," she yelled, "I done seen him now."

I took Ron by the hand, "Well, come on and meet my Mama."

Mom and Lily were well-known queen pins on M.L King and Delmar Lane. After Shane taught them the dope game, they were like celebrities because they played it well. Ron was honored to meet my Mama, and she was honored to meet him.

The following days after their meet and greet, he would come over to see me without fear. He and Mom got along well. A little too goddamn well. Every day, I dressed up to look cute just for him. But his attention was no longer on me. Instead, it was on Mama. They played with each other more. At the time, I thought maybe she was accepting him. But one day, they were both outside. I forgot what he had done, but she looked at him with those sneaky flirtatious eyes and said, "Stoooooop!" I caught that! I tried to let it go, but I couldn't.

Mama and Lily Rented hotel rooms on Fulton Industrial. Their main one was Motel 6. That's where they made more money. One night, I watched Mama, and Lily get in the car to go there. Then Ron got in the back seat.

"What the hell does he think he's doing?" I said to myself out loud, "His Mama is gonna beat his ass!" Then I saw Danny get in the car also. He was the boyfriend of my best friend, Shay. I called her and told her. Danny was about two or three years older than Ron.

She and I both started crying because we felt betrayed and hurt that they wouldn't at least tell us they were involved with Mama and Lily.

The next day, all of my homegirls came over, and we were all on the porch. Mama was out there also. 'Shawnie!" yelled Tish, "Where's your boyfriend?"

I humped my shoulders because I was pissed.

"How long you and Ron been talking anyway?" she asked again.

"Who y'all talking about?" Mama butted in.

"Shawnie and Ron. They love each other," Tish answered with this weird-ass look on her face. She looked at my mom like she had a problem with her.

"Shawnie is too young to have a boyfriend," Mama said.

"Hold on, Pat! You were okay with it at first! But now you're not? They are both in high school, and they are both teenagers! I don't understand what the issue is!" Tish said to Mama as if she was standing up for me.

Mama knew I was afraid of her. She knew I wasn't going to stand up for myself.

Days after that, Shay and I went to Adamsville to spend the night with Mama. To our surprise, Ron was there. I made many efforts to try to get back to him, and I tried putting on a bathing suit and walking around the house. I even tried talking to him over the phone and promising my virginity to him. I did everything, but nothing worked.

Shay and I started drinking behind closed doors because come to find out, Danny was messing around with Lily. My aunt took my best friend's boyfriend, and we were both hurt.

When Shay confronted Danny, he hit her in the face, blackening her eye. Shay and I leaned on each other for comfort.

Mama had always had this cold way of treating me. But the way she was treating me was colder than ever. I knew that lady hated me, but I never knew why. That fall, I started eighth grade. In order for me to get to school, I had to stay at Mama's house.

Chapter Twelve

When Little Girls Cry

Shay and her family moved to Pool Creek. From there, she introduced me to a boy named Steve. My feelings for Ron were fading. I didn't even try to fight for him anymore. But I did leave a letter for him before I caught the bus for school one morning.

The letter explained how much he hurt me. All the things that I had ever shared with him about the very person he was now teamed up with had hurt me. While at school, my pager beeped with a 911 message which means to call home because it was urgent. So, I did. I called home, "Hello?" I answered.

"Yeah! I got ya little note," Mama said.

"Well, it wasn't for you," I told her.

They both read the letter, and she called me, confronting me like 'Yeah, I took yo man. And? Then I said, "You know what, y'all can have each other." I wanted a mother. Not a goddamn adversary. I needed love, not a competition!

She was supposed to have been the person that I ran to when getting hurt by a boy. She was supposed to mend my broken heart when a boy cheated on me. So, who could I turn to when the one who should have been there to help me caused the broken heart over a boy I had my heart set on? Her excuse was I was too young to have a boyfriend. But she allowed me to talk to other boys. What she should have said about Ron was, "I don't want you talking to that boy because I want him for myself." In time, I got over it. And Ron saw how I paid him no attention.

I started making new friends because my old ones felt sorry for me. They heard the laughter and chatter behind my back. They heard people saying things like, "Damn! Ron had the Mama and the daughter!" That shit pissed me the fuck off! This news spread like wildfire. I was haunted by it day in and day out and then having to see it.

Them being together no longer bothered me. But the embarrassment almost killed me. Steve knew what was going on because I told him everything. My mind, my heart, and everything else was totally about Steve.

Soon, Mama and Ron started to have issues. I knew it was bound to happen. He didn't know her like I did. Mama was a broken person. If anything was fixed, she'd break it. Psychologically, she was not normal. She thrived on both pity and sadness. She was attention-hungry but for empathy and sympathy.

She, again, is that woman in the hole with her kids. In order to get out, she would have to be 'fixed,' 'saved,' and 'heroic.' But no, she'd rather destroy things. Nothing was good enough. Anything good was never acknowledged or appreciated, like fixed things were not a part of her DNA. And Ron was about to see it.

Faithfulness and loyalty were not who she was. I, on the other hand, was glad that I wasn't on the receiving end. Before long, Mama asked me to fix her hair up one day because she was about to go out with a new guy named Nod. She picked me up from Lilly's house and told me she would bring me back after I was done.

Well, I gathered my things, and I went with her. I was doing her hair when all of a sudden, we heard a loud knock on the front door, "Who is it?" Mama called, "That might be Nod. Go open the door."

I ran downstairs to open the door to Ron. "Uh oh," I thought to myself. He walked up the stairs and went to the bathroom, where Mama was getting dolled up for another man. And boy, she was sharp as hell! I said nothing.

He looked at her up and down and then asked her, "Where you finna go?"

"None of your business. I'm grown!" Mama yelled.

I was laughing my ass off! The same thing she did to my daddy to leave the house on some sneaky shit was the same thing she was doing to Ron. She would start an argument. But with Dad, she made up shit to argue about. Ron was about to get the Patricia special.

"Whatcha mean you grown?! You must finna go with another nigga!"

"And if I do, So what?! I do whatever the hell I wanna do when I wanna do it!"

BOOM! And that she did. Nod blew the horn outside for Mama to come out. "Wait ma," I called for her before she went down the stairs, "Let me get my stuff. Y'all gon' drop me back off, right?" I asked.

"Just go in your room and close the door. I don't want Ron to come out here and see Nod," she said as she ran out the door and jumped in the car with Nod. I was pissed. I didn't want to stay at the house with Ron. So I went to my bedroom, shut the door, and called Steve.

Steve and I had a habit of falling asleep on the phone together. And that's precisely what happened. Deep into my sleep, I thought I was dreaming when I felt something heavy on my body. I felt like I was suffocating. When I woke up, it was Ron on top of me! "Move! MOVE! Get off of me! Get off!" I yelled. He didn't move.

He was heavy and outweighed me. His heavy body made me hurt. And the pain quickly set in. I couldn't fight anymore. Then, I felt his long fingernails go into my vaginal area to stretch me open! They felt like blades cutting me on the inside. Finally, he was able to penetrate me. It felt like I was getting gutted. When he was done, I started shaking really badly. My throat was sore. When he left, I stayed in the same position he left me in. He said to me before going out of the room, "That stuff on the bed. Be glad it's on the bed and not in you!"

The next morning Mama came home, and she had my brothers with her. She must have stopped by Lily's house and picked them up before coming home. She and Zay came into the house. Ron was sitting in the living room on the couch. I stood at the top of the steps when she came inside, "Mama," I said, "Ron had sex with me last night. I tried to stop him, but he wouldn't stop."

"What you mean he had sex with you?!"

"He raped me, Mama," I cried.

"How the hell can he rape you? Y'all are about the same age," she said.

"I didn't want him to. Forget it!" I knew she didn't care, "I'll just call the police," I said as I picked up the phone.

Mama smacked her lips, "Zay, y'all go ahead and get y'all stuff. All y'all need to go. Ron, you too," she said in a fit. It already looked like she had an attitude when she got home. Then she looked at me, "You trying your best to break up my family! When I get home, I want you gone!" she yelled.

I was sore, bleeding, and hurting from the inside out. So I called Shay and her mother. They told me that I could come and stay with them. I didn't bother asking Mama for a ride. The bus fare was one dollar then. I also had some food stamps on me that I either got from Mama or Aunt Lily before.

But I couldn't pay the one-dollar fare with that. So I searched all over the house that day until I gathered up one hundred pennies. After that, I looked around for some paper to write a note on. But all I found was a piece of white cardboard that was packaged with some Nylon stockings.

I didn't have a pen, so I used some black eyeliner. I can recall some of the words that I wrote:

Dear Mom,

I am so sorry for being born. You asked me to leave, and this is where I will be. I will come back when Ron leaves. I can't take him putting his hands on me.

By the time I got to Pool Creek, the cuts on me had turned into blisters. Shay and her mom, Cheryl, ran me some bathwater with vinegar and salt so that I could soak. But, my God, it burned badly.

That night, I sat outside in the cool summer breeze, wondering what would become of me. Ms. Cheryl begged me to go to the hospital. I didn't go because I didn't want Mama to get in trouble. She had already accused me of trying to break up her family and turn my brothers against her. She had manipulated them into thinking that I was the enemy, so they were angry with me too. Therefore, I didn't go because I didn't want to make things worse for myself.

All of a sudden, the police came to Shay's house. They were there on a call made to Pool Creek that one of the neighbors had made. One of the officers went to the door, and Ms. Cheryl answered.

"We're looking for Shawnie Benton," the officer said, loud as hell.

Shay, Cheryl, and I walked over to the officers. Ms. Cheryl tried to explain to them what had happened. Then, my grandmother called. Ms. Cheryl then tried to explain to her and Aunt Lily that I needed medical help and asked if it was okay to stay with them for a while. Grandma cussed Ms. Cheryl out.

Ms. Cheryl was not a fast talker. So while she was still trying to explain herself to the police, they cut her off, saying, "Lady, go back on your porch before we lock you up for housing a runaway!"

I thought to myself, "A fucking runaway?! She told me to leave!" I even left them Ms. Cheryl's name and address so she'd know where I'd be! But to tell everybody I ran away from home was so that she could put everything on me!

The police officer escorted me to the car. I was brought where the old Atlanta Braves stadium used to be. There was another police car, and Mama was with them. After we met up, I went from one police car to the other. From there, we were taken back to Lily's house.

When I walked through the door, I saw Ron sitting on the couch with this smirk that I wished I could smack clean off his face. Time Mama walked in, she took Lily's thick, janitor-type broom and beat me with it until it broke.

She threw it to the side and said, "I'll buy you a new broom Lily."

"She so damn fast," Lily said.

"Yeah girl," Mama agreed, "She was all in the back seat of the car throwing her hands up saying, 'yeah, yeah' like she bad or something."

Mama lied on me. And to this very day, I can't understand why. My arms, shoulders, back, inner legs, chest, and vaginal area were so inflamed that I couldn't even hold my arms up even if I wanted to.

I could barely lift my head, let alone my arms. While I was still sore, I walked around the house to look for Grandma. Later, I found out Grandma had gotten on a bus and went out of town to play bingo. So, I lay down in Grandma's bed and went to sleep.

The following day, I got up to use the bathroom. When I went, I saw that I had blisters everywhere.

Mom went to the local corner store and bought some Peroxide, Bactine, cotton balls, and some kind of cream. She laid me down on the bed and had me open my legs, and nursed me. She placed some cotton balls on me to keep chemicals out. Then, poured some peroxide and then some Bactine antiseptic liquid.

Eventually, I started to heal. A few days later, all of my brothers and I were in the car with her while we were parked outside of her house, "Y'all know the way I make money. And y'all also know I use the stuff when it's in my hands, so I can't have it around 'em like that. So Ron is all I got to help me keep food and clothes."

My brothers looked at me with an 'it's all your fault' look. Almost as if they were saying to themselves, "If we go hungry, it's your fault. If Mama can't pay the bills, it's your fault." Everything was always my fault!

After we left the house, Mama stopped and picked Ron up and took us to the park. When we got there, we made sandwiches and had chips with them. Ron sat down across from me and picked up a single chip, and ate it slowly as he looked at me. I was speechless. I had to sit there and endure it while fighting back the tears. It was so hard to swallow. After that day, I never bought those chips in my life because every time I saw them, it reminded me of how I was forced to deal with that boy! The boy that robbed me of my virginity!

As we were leaving and my mom's back was turned, he told me, "I told you your Mama don't care nothing about you! So you might as well…"

After we got back up, Mama took us to motel 6, where she bought two rooms to make some more money. She got a room for my brothers and me and one for her and Ron. Later that night, Ron woke me up and told me that my Mama wanted me. So I got up. The room was dark.

He grabbed me by the hand and led me around the room. But he didn't take me to their room. Instead, he led me to the bathroom. He opened my legs up and performed oral sex on me. Not only did he have sex with me for the first time, but he was also the first somebody who had oral sex with me.

Something that I was supposed to enjoy with Steve or somebody else of my choosing. All I could do was take my leg that he had a hold of and kick him off me. I didn't even bother to tell Mama. I just went back to the room and went back to sleep.

From then on, whenever we were in the house at the same time, I would turn the other way. When Mom's back was turned, he would look for me. Sometimes when he did, he would grab me and stick his fingers up in me, grab parts of my body while holding me down.

Mama was somewhere getting high, and that was his opportunity. Then he started putting money in my pocket. I either gave it to my brothers or bought food with it. In the meantime, Mama began to fall off badly. Her addiction was getting worse.

I later became numb to Ron with his shit! Who was I gonna tell? Dad left; drugs had him. Mama didn't care. Grandma defended her kids. Every time I did, she would make it seem like I was going against my mother. Lilly, for damn sure, didn't care.

Joey and Derrick were stone-cold drunks. Ronald didn't come around much, and Rich was full of shit! George was in Germany; Shane and Teddy were dead. Who was I possibly going to tell? I had nobody, no protector, no nothing!

Mama's addiction had gotten so bad that I had to take on the responsibility of raising my brothers. I had to talk to their teachers, fill out lunch forms, make sure the bills got paid, making sure the food stamps and checks didn't get cut off.

But Mama didn't want everyone in the family to know that she was on drugs. So I had to keep it a secret. So many lies were spread about me throughout the family, but it was all to protect Mama. Mama begged me not to tell Grandma and Lily because they would really mistreat her.

Whenever I had to pay some bills, I changed my voice to make myself sound older. But the accent came out very proper. After a while, it became a habit. I don't know what my voice would have been like as a growing young woman. I never had a childhood that gradually led to adulthood that came with experience and changes. Everything was forced onto me at once.

One day I remember I came home from school, and I found out that some of my brother's little friends had policemen come to their homes and remove them because their parents were on drugs. The teachers noticed that they were being neglected. After I learned about that, I knew I had to step up my game.

Mama didn't have a washer and dryer, so I had to take all of the boys' clothes that night and wash them by hand in the bathtub with a bar of soap. It was wintertime, and the gas was off; thus, the water was cold. But I had to do it.

After the clothes were washed, I hung them outside so they could dry. By the following morning, I went out to find the clothes frozen instead of being dry. So I brought them inside, sat some of the clothes down next to a space heater, and ironed the others dry like Daddy used to.

After I got them dressed and saw them off to school, my body would be in a ton of pain. I stayed in pain so much and missed a lot of days of school. Finally, my counselor told me to start school again.

But then Mama got really sick on that stuff. She still tried to sell it, but she was supplying herself more. Mama and Ron had finally severed their relationship, and he stopped selling for Mama. She tried dating other guys. I avoided them because I knew they had their eyes set on me.

One said that I had pretty little titties. Another one rubbed on my ass as I slept. Another guy said that he didn't want my mother, but me instead. What all of them didn't understand was that the shit that they were doing was old. Besides, I had to take care of my brothers and my mother.

When Mama ran out of dope, she went to Bowen Homes to buy some more dope to break down and sell it. But she came home and used it immediately. I saw that she could not care for herself, let alone my brothers and me, so I had to take full responsibility.

Nobody in the family liked me. They all thought that I was trying to be grown. What they didn't realize was that I had to be. Mama continued to tell me that her people would shit on her if they knew just how far gone she was. So I had to make things look good and take the blame for some things that I had nothing to do with.

Like one time, Lily hid an ounce of dope in one of my brother's pants and put them down inside of Grandma's grandfather clock. I knew Mama was pinching off that ounce the whole night. I even went downstairs to take a piece to hide it so I could sell it to buy us food and kerosene for the heater.

I did not need us to be out of kerosene because that was how I cooked and kept warm water to wash up my brothers and myself. When Lily came to pick up her dope the next day, Mama put the pants in the washing machine. She told Lily that I was the one who put the pants in the washing machine and washed away what could have made $3,000.00.

To make her story seem real, Mama broke up little pieces of dope all over the washed clothes as some type of evidence. All I could do was close my eyes and take the tongue lashing that was given by Lily. She cussed me out like a dog! Mama said nothing.

But that was how it was. Anybody could do or say anything they wanted about me or to me. Mama never defended me or protected me. When Lily was young, she was an okay person, but she became bitter, negative, and mean due to men breaking her spirit.

She had gotten into an argument with a guy she was dating. The guy had a gun and tried to show out in front of his friends. He aimed the gun and shot at her. At the time, I was outside playing. She ducked down behind me, grabbed both of my arms, and used me as a human shield when he shot again. Then she yelled, "Stop playing, boy!"

When he saw me, he stopped shooting. Then Lily got up and started hugging him while laughing loudly. They took their shenanigans elsewhere, not even considering that I could have been hit with a bullet. Again, no protection.

Sometime later, Steve and I broke up, and he started seeing another girl. My Mama, my brothers, and I all stayed at Lily's house. I rode in the car with Lily one evening when she wanted to meet up with a dude she had just met. His name was Ray. When we got to Taco Bell, he was there with his friend named Quint. Quint was a skinny boy who resembled DJ Quik. We exchanged phone numbers and got to know each other. He often told me how much he loved me. The sound of *that made me feel good.*

I didn't know what love felt like. I had never had it before. It made me wonder about Mama. If she had ever had love before. I know that growing up, nobody said it. I never heard Mama and Daddy say those words to each other. They never told us. And that was the problem. No love, just surviving on what we believed was love because it was better than not having anything at all.

Well, what if you didn't know the difference between sand and water? Somebody may have told you that water felt good going down your throat or that it quenches your thirst. But then somebody hands you a glass of sand, and you begin to drink it. You're not drinking the sand because you wanted sand. You're drinking it because you don't know the difference. Well, this was me drinking the sand.

Quint and I hit it off. Before I knew it, he had moved in with us. He was also a drug dealer, and he was selling dope for Ray. I really needed his help. First, to help me financially with my brothers and protect me from the different male friends who came to our house.

On that note, let me say this:

As the mothers and protectors of the children God has appointed, we know that we are special. God chose us to deliver His exclusive package to one of His most fabulous creations... the world.

Unfortunately, and very much so, men play on our vulnerable situations as either being gullible, weak, single, misguided, or misinformed.

The desire to want to be loved so desperately is a human thing, yet a Godly and a physical thing that draws the connection between you and the Creator. To witness that He, of all things, is real. The true and living God, we feel his love through others. But if we're not careful, we confuse love with infatuation or romance, which are two totally different things.

Our yearning for companionship, relationship, friendship, and in some cases, ownership in specific involvements with the other person is a need... a want... a desire. A lot of times that want and need become a desire that consumes you.

A woman could possibly go crazy if they don't have the attention they need from a man. The want for this affection becomes so desirable that God Himself is not put first in her life. In many cases, the children become collateral damage because their desire is so strong and selfish. They don't want to let that infatuation go. Maybe finances or how he pays the bills and puts a roof over the family's head. Still, that is not worth the sanity of your children.

We as mothers, or fathers, bring these people into our homes. Young ladies, you get these boys into your house, hoping that they can be a man for you. But he looks around your home and at your children. Little do you know he is sizing up your daughter or your son. Figuring you out, finding your weakness and all the time plotting in his head how he will have his way with your babies. You are introducing him to them not knowing that you're serving your children up as appetizers for this angry beast.

Some men are too much of a pussy. These men realize that they don't want a pussy and hide their sexuality from the world. Too much of a coward to tell the world he's gay. But guess what? Your innocent little boy is going to pay the price for that. Then he grows up confused about whether he should be with a man or a woman, all because a pedophile came along and scrambled his little world. No matter what happens, time will go on. The one who did it will go on to the next victim, but this little boy will never forget it. He will live with this for the rest of his life.

Our daughters' beauty reminds us of our days of the cat chased by all the dogs.

Now she's a cute little kitten herself, but Mama, nobody told you to bring your dog home and chase her. You got it him in the house; she didn't go out looking for him. See her tiny breasts coming in and her small shape trying to curve its way in her jeans? Yes, honey, he's looking. And every time he's in bed with you, he wants to take a peek in her room to see what she looks like while she's sleeping - imagining himself taking control of her. She needs you, Mama. But your boyfriend tells you that she's too damn hot, and she needs to sit her ass down. Really? Maybe he needs to sit his hot ass down, too! In the back seat of a police car! I hear they have good A/C.

However, in some cases, good men come along who can love your children as much as we do. My daddy did that for me.

Chapter Thirteen
Still Drinking The Sand

My Mom met another responsible man named Keith. Since I wasn't well-groomed as a child and wasn't taught well enough by my mother or any of my family, I had to learn how to do it independently. My hair was short but it didn't stop me from making sure that I was up to par.

One day I put my hair in a ponytail. I didn't have one of those hair donuts to make a bun, so I used an old, long sock. I twisted it and fixed it around my ponytail and shaped my hair over it. Apparently, I didn't cover the sock up good enough.

When Keith saw my hair, he asked my Mama, "Why is this child wearing a sock on her head?" I can at least say that he cared. In other cases, there are men like Ron who are just weak-minded. And instead of the mother defending her child, she takes the side of the man and begins to challenge their own daughter over a no-good ass nigga that she brought home.

Mamas! In this case, grab a belt and whip your own ass! When this happens, it means that you have failed as a mother or as a father. To look at your own child as a rival, like competition, is unfathomable and unacceptable. To compete with your own child is a curse! It has to be!

When I think about m mother, I never wanted anything but her love and affection. God knows I craved it. I needed her badly. But her mind was looking for something that I couldn't give her. I don't think she even knew what she was looking for.

When I sat down and thought about how old she was when she was with Ron, she was in her twenties while I was a teen. She looked about seventeen or eighteen. I can understand why Ron was attracted to her. She was gorgeous. He had the height and weight of a twenty-two-year-old, but that still didn't make it right. So there I was an appetizer. I was the steak on the string to a pack of wolves. But instead of allowing them to get to me, I took myself off the line.

All of the things about love and protection that I've mentioned before, I thought Quint could give them to me, so why not? However, his living with us was unacceptable on so many levels. For one, I was about thirteen or fourteen years old. No boy had any business living in our home even if Mama was okay with it.

She wasn't interested in him like she was with Ron. Quint had a handsome face, but a poorly skinny body. I didn't mind that he didn't brush his teeth or that he overlooked the halitosis that plagued his breath. His self-made remedy for that was to get up in the morning and drink a cup of Kool-Aid. It might have changed the taste in his mouth, but nothing was accomplished when it came to the actual odor that came from his breath. Different family members continually asked if his breath bothered me. Many things about him were a turn-off to me, but back then, I overlooked it. One day, I did see Quint brush his teeth. Usually, after you brush your teeth, you're supposed to rinse the toothpaste out. Quint did not do that. He brushed his teeth, but then he swallowed all of the toothpaste suds and left the bathroom without rinsing.

Still, he sold drugs. But he would get upset and angry at me whenever I solved a puzzle of The Wheel of Fortune or whenever I answered a Jeopardy phrase correctly. What angered him more than anything else was the proper way that I spoke. He would say things like, "You wanna be white so motherfuckin'g bad! You ain't white!" he said that often. Then his anger turned into slaps, fists that punched, kicks, pushes, and severe beatdowns.

He told me that he hit me because he loved me and that if he didn't put his hands on me, it meant that he cared nothing about me. The way that he beat me made me feel like he hated me, and the way that he said he wanted to kill me time and time again was his love for me.

It's the water and sand scenario. Holding me, hugging me, telling me he loves me; we're holding on to each other, telling each other how much we meant to one another. All of this was the sand. Meaning that this type of affection was not love. He called me names like dumb, drop-out, and stupid ass bitch, along with hits, punches, kicks, and all of the above abusive things, characterize water. Soft and needed to the soul because all of that equaled love.

I never had either, so how was I supposed to know which was water and sand? So then, after a while of him being around my family, he and

Aunt Lily would get together and low-rate me; they would talk down on me like a dog. Sometimes Mama would say nothing. Occasionally she chimed in with little remarks.

It wasn't long before he saw the same green lights like the other gentlemen friends that Mama brought around. They knew Mama didn't care and felt that they could do what they pleased. And now the green light said 'Go' for Quint as well.

He didn't beat me behind closed doors anymore. Instead, he unsympathetically beat me in front of anybody and everybody. Aunt Lily saw him do it and she let out a big, "You so stupid!"

Yeah. I was. Because I thought they cared. After the beating, Quint would do something nice for me. I used to be so hungry that I started to shake the same way I did in elementary school. That is when Quint bought something from Taco Bell or McDonald's, or some other fast-food restaurant.

I told my dad about Quint but only the good things. For example, him helping to buy groceries for the house, paying some of the bills, and purchasing kerosene for the heaters. I didn't tell him that he was beating on me. Dad was already dealing with his own unwanted demons, just like Mama.

That winter, I remember looking out the window and wondering what my life would amount to. According to the people around me, apparently, the answer was nothing. I felt like any hope or anything that I wanted was impossible. It was like every step forward I wanted or tried to take, I always got knocked backward. It felt like somebody somewhere didn't like me. Maybe the universe hated me. 'Why was I born into a family like this? I thought to myself. What did I do to deserve this?

The only person who hated Quint and wanted him out of my life was Grandma. It was also this time around when Grandma's house burned down a second time. This time, there was no more insurance to fix it up again. She was living with Aunt Lily full time now. How I wished I could go home to Grandma's house. From the first day I got into that car with Patricia, I held my breath and found out that she was my mother and had not exhaled since. Not only was Mom's secret a burden on me. I was burdened with everything, and I was just downright tired and tired of living.

Food was still scarce. Sometimes there would be days when there was no food in the house. Sometimes I was so hungry that I would take a piece of the end slice of a loaf of bread, put mustard on it, and eat it just to stop the hunger pains. When we did have food, we didn't have anything to cook it on. We had a single hot plate in the kitchen, but it would be too cold to go downstairs. One day, Mama sent me downstairs to light her a cigarette on the hot plate. I had to stand in the cold for a long time, waiting for the hot plate to turn red, which took forever. Once it was red, I took the cigarette and laid it on one of the red, hot rings. It burnt half the damn cigarette up before it was fully lit. I had to puff the cigarette a little while before taking it to her to keep the cigarette burning. When I got to her room, she looked at me and asked, "You been smoking on this?"

"Yes, Mama," I answered, "I wanted to keep it lit. It was trying to go out because it's too cold downstairs."

"Quint gon' beat your ass!" she said loud enough for him to hear.

Next thing I knew, he was storming in the room, "What she do?!" he shouted.

"She been smoking my cigarette," Mama said.

All I remember is his hands hitting on the top of my head. Then he grabbed me by my hair and pulled my face to his knee as he kneed me several times in the head. Three large knots quickly appeared on my head. When he let go of my hair, I fell to the floor.

Mama was laying in the bed while he was beating me. Then she crawled down to the foot of the bed and said, "Darn! I didn't know he was gon' beat you like that."

Quint later apologized. It was his regular routine. This time, I wanted to leave, but I had nowhere to go. Every time Quint beat me up, he would brag about it the next day. And like a fool, I would recall everything he did to me and wore it like a badge of honor.

I, on the other hand, started to suffer from more leg and body pains. The stress and worrying made it no better. Quint was not in the least bit sympathetic to whatever was going on with me.

Mama did, however, take me to the doctor once. The doctor said that I could have sickle cell. After that, she never brought me back for any follow-up appointments. So I had to just bite down on my teeth, the same way I did as a child when I endured pain.

Mom and Quint were the same kind of numb-hearted people. I guess they had to be to survive the streets. Soon, Mama told Quint to stop selling drugs for Ray. After that, she taught him the game. The little knowledge that I had about it helped him also. Because being the street runner and the one on top were two totally different things, and Mama taught him how to really come up.

She even introduced him to her connections and helped him to get customers. Before we knew it, Quint could buy a car and give me a little more money. As long as I could take care of my brothers, I didn't care. I took those ass beatings just as long they were not hungry.

Quint worked and did everything to stay on Mama's good side. But Quint started to change on me. At first, his Mom or Grandma didn't care where he was or how he was doing or living. Then they saw him coming up, and friends who were far and few between started to hang out with him more.

The beatings got worse, and he became selfish. One time, the car broke down, and he had to put it in the shop. The shop was within walking distance of our house. He asked me to walk with him to pick the car up. He had over a thousand dollars on him. I was on my period and I needed pads badly. We passed a couple of stores that sold sanitary products, but he wouldn't give me money to pay for a pack of two or three-dollar pads. I had on a piece of cloth to catch the blood, but it needed to be changed out.

When we got to the place, there were two women in their 30s or so. I saw them looking at each other with a look of disgust on their faces. Then, finally, one of them couldn't take it anymore and said, "I smell fish." Quint knew they were talking about me, but he didn't care. In fact, the more hurt and pain it seemed to have done to me, the more it satisfied Quint's selfish ass soul.

I didn't have money to pay for pads or have a way to take a bath. I would have gone to Aunt Lily's house, but she wouldn't have let me bathe. I didn't know what I'd ever done to make Aunt Lily hate me so much.

Whenever she wanted to talk down on me, she would get with Mama and they both did it together. Then Quint joined them. I had no way to win. Mama had poisoned everyone against me. She made it seem like I was being grown and fast by dropping out of school and allowing a boy to move in.

And she made it seem like I disobeyed her when all of that was far from the truth. I couldn't, in fact, tell the truth. If I told them that Mom was on drugs and that I had to step in, it would have been the perfect explanation. But Mom also told the family that I told lies.

Uncle Rich dressed up as Santa Claus with a huge bag full of gifts when Christmas time came around. He spent about 30 minutes digging in that bag and calling out names. I waited anxiously for my name to be called. As time passed, the bag started to get smaller and smaller. Still I waited and waited, and then finally he got to the last gift and it was Joey's. Uncle Rich could not stand Joey. He hated Joey for being gay. He even put on his hunting gear once and looked for Joey to shoot and kill him. That was the kind of guy Uncle Rich was.

His smile portrayed the good brother to Joey, Mom, and the rest of his siblings, but his heart was fucked up.

There I was, a little girl, having to become an adult before my time. Everybody depended on me, but that wasn't the story going around in the family. Their story was chapters of lies. Everyone opened their gifts as I watched, I received nothing.

Grandma told me that Uncle Rich said that I was too damn grown and that he wasn't gonna give me shit! Regardless of what the situation was, I had never done anything remotely disrespectful or hurtful to him. I only saw him like once every few years. But this was my story.

If someone had done that to one of my daughters, I would politely hand them their shit back. Of course, Uncle Rich came there to make a point to his family with his Family Dollar wrapped gifts, but still, it hurt me all the same.

After all of that happened, Quint and I caught a cab back to Mama's house. Instead of eating Christmas dinner, he opened up a can of spam and ate that. I should have known then what kind of person he was.

Later, Mama received an eviction notice telling her that she had to move. So, we packed our things and moved. I went to Quint's grandmother's place while my brothers went with Mama to stay with Aunt Lily. I wondered if anybody worried about me. When I got to his grandmother's home, she was nice to me initially, then the green light effect came. Quint showed her how to treat me.

While all of this was happening with me, Noah's mother was living a similar life elsewhere. She was unwanted as a child. When she moved to California as a girl, she lived in a transitional home for women. Martha's mother had remarried, but it wasn't clear how her stepfather treated her. Some kind of way she ended up in the home of Edward. Fortunately, he was run off by his older children while Martha's health declined over the years.

Because Noah was born at home, he was never issued a birth certificate. He hated that he didn't have one because without it he couldn't get a driver's license which also hindered him from getting a car. He often worried about Martha walking back and forth from the store at night in a dangerous neighborhood. She told Noah that she was protected by God, so she was just fine. Even so, Noah couldn't take watching his family struggle. It was affecting his studies at school and it was hard for him to stay focused.

"Ms. Amos," Noah said to his school counselor, "I need to leave school to get a job. My Mom is having trouble with my little brother, so I had to move him in with me, so I gotta do something," he explained. Ms. Amos looked at him and said, "I know your brother and sister dropped out, but I see how much potential you have. If I put you on the work program and you keep up your grades, can you stay in school?"

"Yes Ma'am," he answered.

Ms. Amos called the sandwich shop above Richie's Academy Alternative School and asked if Noah could work there. The manager at the place told her to go ahead and send him. Noah was starving. He had no money. He had been surviving on tuna, crackers, and noodles for days, and even that had dwindled.

Noah had moved out from living with Angeline to living with his brother Isaiah to renting a room from Mr. Harris, who opened up rooming houses. Mr. Harris asked Noah if he could afford fifty dollars a week. Noah assured him that he could. After that, he was on his own and had the struggles of proving for himself for so long that he was no stranger to hard work.

Mr. Mason, the restaurant manager, said to Noah, "I can pay you ten dollars a day or I can hire you and pay you $4.10 an hour. Noah asked if he could get 10 that day and then get hired to work the following day. Mr. Mason was so impressed with Noah's cleaning and hard work that he agreed to his terms.

From then on, Noah started thriving in school. He carried a briefcase and was a part of all the student body gov. Every time the school had an event, Noah was always chosen to speak. By the time he came upon his senior year, Messiah had gotten so far out of control that Martha had to call for Noah. He had been hanging around with the wrong crowds in the bluff. When Noah got to his mother's place, he went looking for Messiah. He was told that Messiah had been around the wrong crowd and had been carrying a gun since he was 14.

Noah left the apartment and walked around the complex until he found Messiah walking back toward the apartment, "Messiah?" he called beckoning for him.

"Yeah?" he answered.

"What's going on? Why are you walking around here carrying a gun?"

"'Cause I got to," he retorted.

"No you don't! Go on back to the apartment and get your stuff."

"I ain't going nowhere."

"Yes, you are. You're gonna get your stuff, you're gonna go back to school, and you're not gon' throw your life away out here in these streets! Now, go back and get your things!" Noah said more serious.

Messiah shrugged, "You don't tell me!" he argued back.

Noah knew that Messiah was stubborn. So, he took Messiah by the arm and was gonna bring him back to the apartment himself. But Messiah resisted.

"Lil boy!" Noah yelled as he and Messiah got rough with each other.

Noah was pulling and Messiah was resisting.

Messiah made Noah so mad that he grabbed Messiah from the back and started lifting him up, "Since you wanna know what it's like to treat your life trash, I'm gon' let you see what trash feels like!" He carried Messiah to the complex's dumpster and threw him in!

Messiah crawled out of the dumpster with the smell of trash all over him.

"You didn't like that did you?!" Noah said, "If you don't, then why the hell would you treat your life like that?! Go in there, get your stuff, and meet me back out here in the car."

This time, Messiah listened to his older brother and went inside and got his things. Noah took Messiah back with him to the rooming house. When Noah asked Mr. Harris if Messiah could stay with him, he was told that the rooming house was no place for a child Messiah's age. So, Noah had to find an apartment.

That whole year, Noah made sure Messiah went to school. They both struggled it out together. In the middle of Noah going back and forth to school and work, Martha asked him if he could check on Mavis.

During this time, Mavis had two children of her own. Noah rode the bus to Perry Homes. When he got there, he found that Mavis and the children's father had been fighting. While Noah was checking on Mavis, his back was turned to Mavis' boyfriend, Fred, who was carrying a knife, and he tried to stab Noah in the back. Mavis saw this and jumped up putting herself between Fred and her brother. Fortunately for Mavis, she didn't get hurt. But that didn't stop Noah and Fred from getting into a fist fight. After the fight was broken up, Noah had to ride the bus home with blood all over his nice dress shirt and tie. On top of that, he also had to go and check on his mother and go back home to look after Messiah.

Noah's senior year got even harder. He had sacrificed so much for his siblings and his mother. During his school year, his academic progress earned him an award that was featured on WSB-TV special event covered by Monica Kauffman (now Pearson.) He was invited on the day of April 7, 1990 to the SCLC (Southern Christian Leadership Conference) where he was presented the SCLC Youth/Women Award by none other than Oprah Winfrey and Evander Holyfield. It was a Salute to Youth award for taking care of his younger siblings and being a role model for others. Later, Rich's academy held a graduation ceremony where he was presented with all kinds of trophies, plaques, and awards. Even though this was a huge deal in Noah's life, none of Noah's family were present to see him receive his accomplishments. Martha could not make it either. She was too ill.

However, Noah's best friend's brother, Malone, and his wife and daughter attended the ceremony. They took pictures and congratulated him. When Noah got home, Martha looked at him so proudly and said, "You did it," With a huge smile on her face.

"Yes ma'am, I did," Noah said.

After high school, Noah got a job at SunTrust Bank. After a few months of working there, he was able to rent a house big enough to move his mom and siblings in. Martha was so proud of Noah. Soon after that, Martha took her leave to be with The Good Lord. This old world had lost one of its greatest soldiers, but her soul was finally freed of her grief, pain, and suffering.

Martha had no life insurance, so her children raised whatever funds they could to give her a decent funeral. Noah made arrangements with the funeral home to pay monthly installments to fulfill the rest of what was owed.

After the funeral, Noah got on the bus and took a long ride until the bus had come to the end of its line. On the way, he saw some apartments and put in an application and was approved. He let his siblings do what they wanted with the house. Although he rented it, he had to go. He was just cut from a different cloth than the rest of his siblings. He loved them, but at that moment, he needed some time for himself.

As time moved forward, he began to go on with life. He was finally able to get a driver's license and bought himself a car. Everything that he was denied in life, he wanted it. He took the ridicule that could have broken his spirit and used them as stepping stones. He didn't want little things. He wanted big things. He wanted a beautiful wife, beautiful kids, a home of his own, his own business, and a lot of money. He had thoughts and fantasies. He went to strip clubs. It was okay to him, but not enough. He hung out with different people, but he wanted more. He wanted something that people told him that he couldn't have, and that was a drop-dead gorgeous woman on his arm that would give him everything he wanted in a woman and mother to his children. He knew in his heart that he was gonna be a better husband and father than what his father was.

Chapter Fourteen

A Brand New Day

Noah worked two jobs so that he could have the finer things in life. He knew where he had come from and where he wanted to go. When he separated from his family, he was able to get a mental break; however, Messiah was still living with him.

From time to time, he would take in Mavis's now seven-year-old son to help her out. Jamal had become a full-blown street dude. He made his own rules and didn't let anyone stand in his way.

At some point, Noah wanted to get on with his own life. I believe that Martha's spirit had attached itself to Noah and watched over him. As Martha's now free spirit traveled the universe, I was on the other side of town knowing and understanding what she had gone through. I was living with Quint and his grandmother. They were so cold to me. I constantly stayed in his bedroom, where he kept me.

Whenever I tried to go in the kitchen to make myself something to eat, Ms. Kelly would say, "Stay your ass out of my damn kitchen!"

Then, I would tell Quint that I was hungry and ask him to buy me something to eat. The moment he bought me something, she would tell him, "Stop going to those fast-food places to get her food. Give me the money so she can eat healthy." 'Yeah, right,' I thought to myself. She put that money in her bra, and my breakfast, lunch, and dinner was a bag of popcorn and some Kool-Aid for months. What was worse than that was that I was pregnant at the time.

Quint came up in the world because Mom and I helped him, and he shitted on me like a toilet. But one thing Mama told me to do while I was there was to read the bible. She said, "Baby, I want you to read Psalms 27-35 every day, and I want you to pray."

I was getting dogged out on one end and Mama was getting dogged out on the other. She told me that she was working on getting us an apartment so that I could come home. Mama applied for an apartment where Aunt Lily lived. Every day Mama called for me from Quint's phone and they would lie and tell her that I wasn't there.

Quint left home when he wanted and came home when he wanted. One day, he was taking a shower and his underwear was on the floor. Green puss was all through his underwear. I found out later after a visit from the health department that Quint had been given Chlamydia. I had to get shots in my ass with a huge needle. First, he beat me, then starved me, and now he had given me an STD. I had all I could take. I tried to kill myself. My childhood friends were all on the phone talking me out of it while Quint and his cousin overheard and laughed the whole time. Finally, he came into the room, insulted me more and beat me again. A few days later, I was sitting on the bed when the phone rang next to me. I picked up the phone, "Hello?"

"Shawnie?" Mama said.

"Yes?"

"Baby, come home. I got the apartment. You need to leave now."

I didn't pack my clothes. I slung them into bag after bag. Quint walked into the room and asked if he could take me to Aunt Lily's house. Mama told me which apartment it was. It was right up the stairs from Aunt Lily's. While he was driving, he started cursing me out, saying, "Don't get your ass over here and call me for shit! You wanna run your ass over here knowing they don't give a fuck about you!" And blah, blah, blah, he went on and on.

When I got to Mama's, I got out and started getting my things. He brought my bags upstairs, and when I opened the door, he told my Mama, "Here! Get this bitch!" "I got her," Mama said, "You can leave."

I went back to the car to get the last few bags. As soon as I got them out of the car, I said, "Nigga fuck you!" He ran after me. He caught me before I could get up the steps good and beat me - again. I didn't see him for a while after that. I don't know what the hell I missed about him, but I did. Although Mama had us in a new place, the financial circumstances were still the same. I ended up getting back with Quint, but I hardly went to his house. Something about it had changed. When I walked in there, the energy, the spirit, and the smell pushed me right back out.

I wanted to cry when I went back to his house. I made up every excuse in the world not to go back over there. But one day, I was happy

I was there. I got a call from Lizzy, Uncle Teddy's daughter. She told me that they were hungry. It had been years since I last saw them. So I asked Quint to give me a ride to Dixie Hills. It was freezing cold outside. We rode around the apartments over and over, but the little girl I knew as Lizzy wasn't out there. As we were about to leave, I saw what looked like two people snuggled together. I got out of the car and asked, "Do ya'll know Sandy?" as I got closer, what I thought was two people were actually four little girls. Their hair was so severely damaged, and malnutrition had caused their stomachs to round out. They were very thin and neglected.

One of them said, "I know you! You're Shawnie!" "Lizzy!" I shouted. They all ran up to me and hugged me. Then they took me to the back of the apartments to a shack that was no bigger than a bathroom. They were living there with a one-legged man named William. Sandy was nowhere to be found.

I had the girls pack their things and tell William goodbye for good. Then, I brought them home where they ate and got a bath. The next day, Mama said, "I gotta take them back. They have to go to school."

"No, Mama," I said, "They need to stay with us. We'll do this together." So we kept them. A few weeks or so had gone by, and Sandy had come to the house with a social worker. DFACS were set to get the kids a day or so after I got them. Sandy told them, "Patricia is my sister. I know she can take better care of them than me." Later on, me, Mama, and somebody else had to go to court to fill out the necessary paperwork so that Mama could have full custody of Teddy's children. Still, money and food were an issue for us. When we got on the Marta bus to go home, we hugged each other and cried. I prayed for her. I didn't know how we were going to make it.

Aunt Lily started selling drugs stronger than ever. She had money but wouldn't help us. Grandma took twenty dollars worth of food stamps from Aunt Lily's food stamp book and brought it to me.

My cousin, Mark, was at our place visiting that day. He took me down to the grocery store. I was able to get chicken leg quarters, noodles, bread, and other things to stretch. Mama put in food stamps for everybody, but her case was backed up.

I asked one of my brothers to call Quint to see if he could loan me five dollars or something. Instead, he told my brother to tell me to leave him the fuck alone. And so I did just that.

I sat outside night after night once I had put the kids to sleep. There were two ladies that lived in the apartment underneath ours, Ms. Shariff and Ms. Thompson, who heard me crying one evening.

"Little sister," Ms. Thompson asked, "Are you ok?"

"Yes ma'am," I replied.

"Baby, you are a strong young lady. I see you helping your Mama to raise your brothers and sisters. One day, God is gonna bless you with a good man. I see that little skinny motherfucker who beat on you, and baby, I want to take a broom and beat the shit out of him."

"Little sister," said Ms. Shariff, "You are a beautiful girl. I wish I could let you meet my brother. I would love to introduce you to him. He works hard and he has a good job. He'll take care of you," she said, trying to calm me down. "Ma'am," I said, "Guys like him that have a good job and good education, they don't date girls like me."

"Little sister," said Ms. Shariff, "Your self-esteem is so low. That no-good dog has beat you down so badly that you can't see the good in yourself. I'm gonna be praying for you."

As the days went on, I sat outside wondering how Mama was doing. She had to stay in rehab for thirty days. All I could do was pray, read the bible, and hope. Ms. Shariff continued to tell me how good of a man her brother was and how much she wished I could just talk to him. Then I thought about my Daddy and how he gave up his education and didn't live out his dreams. I wasn't going to do to a hard-working man what my Mom had done to my Daddy. So, I didn't want to meet him. I wasn't going to be responsible for bringing a man down. I even thought about ways to hurt Quint, but again, I thought of my Daddy and the promise that I made that I wouldn't hurt a man. I was filled with all kinds of emotions. I sat outside almost every day with the worry of how I was going to buy us more food.

I looked across the street to see that the mailman had passed. It was unusually early. I got the mailbox key and went across the street to check the mail. It was only a single brown envelope lying in the box by itself. When I opened it, it was our food stamps! Over eight-hundred-dollars-worth! I ran back across the street and saw Grandma was sitting in a chair in front of Aunt Lily's apartment. I waved the envelope in the air as I called Grandma, letting her know they had come. Grandma got up quickly to go get dressed. She and I walked down to Marietta Blvd. to catch the bus. While we were waiting, a lady in a car pulled over and asked us if we needed a ride. We told her we were going to Bankhead Food Court to cash the food stamps. All she wanted was the money that we were going to use for bus fare. She needed it for gas. When we got to the store, I cashed the food stamps and bought so many groceries. When I got home, all the kids had a field day!

Two weeks after that, Mama was released from rehab and was allowed to come home. I was so happy to see her. She called Quint and asked him about the car he had let go back to the dealership (before, he bought a Cadillac while getting the other car fixed up). He told her that all she needed to do was to pay what he didn't pay, and they would let her get the car. So, she and I walked down Marietta Blvd. in the rain. My feet were swollen so bad that I had to wear house shoes. We went into a store where Mama sold some of the food stamps. Then we got a ride to the dealership. The very same lady who once said she 'smelled fish' started talking to Mama. She told her she could tell that Quint was low down and how I carried myself that day. Mama told her that he was beating on me and that she had just gotten herself together. The lady told me to stop Quint from dogging me and that I could do better. When Mama and I got the car, she and I had a talk, "Shawnie," she started, "You know, hustling is the only thing I know how to do. So, me and you are going to do this together. We're gonna buy some dope, and we're going to come up together. You hear me?" "Are you sure, Mama?" I asked worriedly, "You sure you're not gonna use this stuff again?"

"I don't know. But I'm gonna do my best."

Mama and I went back to her old connections and then we started selling. Quint didn't know how to start a trap. He was selling out of

Mama's house. When I first moved with him to his grandmother's house, he had so much dope, but he had no customers. One day I said, "Watch this." I called a guy from across the street, "What's your name?" I asked.

"CJ," he said.

"CJ, do you smoke?"

"Yeah."

"Here," I said while handing him a dime sack, "I want you to try this and tell me if you like it." He got high off the dime sack and then said, "Yeah. Yeah, I like it." "Alright. For every customer you bring me, I will give you one for free." I made sure he was motivated by getting him high because now, he was chasing a ghost and wanted to stay high. Before the day was over, Quint's backyard had a line. He sold out several times. Before he knew it, he was on. I showed him straight out of Shane's "How to Sell Dope" playbook.

I wasn't in the game, but I watched the best play it. Quint's cousin that barely had anything to do with him, became his friend. Even his Grandma liked the dope money he was making. But he did what most ungrateful assholes did by turning on the very people that helped them to get places. He started to act as though Mama and I never did anything for him. He saw me read the bible all the time. He would just come up and knock the book out of my hands and say, "That shit don't work!" He turned all kinds of cold-hearted that I didn't think he was capable of. He started cheating on me with several women on dope and became very disrespectful.

Mom and I knew the game. We taught it to him. Well, at least some of it. But Mama was about to change the game. Quint came by Mama's apartment one day and noticed brand new furniture. I told him that I bought it with my own money. When he asked me how I told him I was serving. Then that turned into a beat down. But I started to hit back. Then he said, "I don't want you selling drugs! I don't want the woman I love in jail." That lil' nigga didn't want me to make more money than what his pussy ass did. Mama and I were pushing so hard and making so much money that she decided to go out with Aunt Lily and enjoy herself. She deserved it because she had done so good. I didn't want her to drink because I was scared that it would trigger her to get high. I could barely sleep when she came home from rehab. I kept watch on the bathroom to make sure she wasn't in there getting high. For some reason, she always locked herself in the bathroom, which was where I found out she was getting high before.

I remember that I was rushing to get to the bathroom and smelled something funny on the side of the toilet. I saw smoke coming up from behind a shirt that was put there to hide the paraphernalia. My brothers tried to tell me earlier, but I didn't believe them. When I saw it for myself, I started screaming and crying. Mama cried with me. I knew Mom was weak, and I knew we had no other way of making it financially. Now that she was fresh out of rehab, I was still on edge. Every time I dozed off and heard what sounded like the bathroom door closing, I would jump up. This happened for a long time. I was happy that she wanted to go out because I didn't have to watch her all night. I also needed a break. I slept through the whole night.

When I opened my eyes, I woke up to Mom talking to a guy that she had met at the Tasty Dog on Simpson after she and Aunt Lily left the club to go and get something to eat. His name was Curtis and she invited him over. He was tall, dark, and not really her type. But to be honest, I didn't know what her type was. Mama didn't seem to discriminate. Maybe it was just me, but Mom liked hard, dope-dealer-type guys, and Curtis didn't fit that profile. He looked more like a college student. Then I found out later on that Curtis had just been released from prison for violating probation months ago on old drug charges. They began to get close. Then, Mama let him move in. She told me that she didn't want me selling anymore and that she would provide for me. During this time, I was pregnant. Mama wanted me to stay focused on taking care of myself and didn't want anything to happen to me. So, Curtis started to help her.

Quint noticed that our lives were getting better. I had better clothes, shoes, my hair stayed fixed, and so did all of Uncle Teddy's girls. Even their health had gotten better. They picked up a healthy weight, and their hair had grown down their backs. I kept them neat and clean so much that other family members were jealous of Mama and they took it out on the girls. They were being threatened with going back to Dixie Hills to their mom. I assured them that it was not going to happen. I didn't look at them as cousins. I looked at them as my little sisters because Mom had made them her own.

My baby sister, Jay, my little songbird, followed me everywhere I went. She bathed with me, slept with me, went to my doctor's appointment with me and everything. That little girl stuck to me like glue. I taught her how to read, write, spell, and everything before she started school. Although I only had an eighth-grade education myself, I was gonna make sure the girls got their education.

As I was helping Mom to get her back on her feet, her attitude towards me changed back to how it was when I was little. Before I knew it, Curtis recognized the green light and started telling lies on me, and Mama believed him.

One day, he saw me cutting up some paper with a pair of iron scissors. He grabbed my hand while they were still gripping the scissors and squeezed my fingers against the finger handle. He, as a grown man, put all of his might into squeezing my hand until tears started to flow from my eyes. I was wearing a pair of clogged heels when I kicked him in the leg several times as hard as I could.

Mama was sitting right next to him. I started to shout her name and she did nothing. Then he finally let my hand go. When I looked at my fingers, my skin had become dented with the print of the scissor handles. Later the same day, knots had begun to form on his leg where I had been kicking him. Mama came outside to where I was and approached me, saying, "Look at what you did to Curtis' legs. I might have to take him to the hospital!" I yelled back at her, "Look at what he did to my hand! You already know how much my body hurts me!" I started to cry those hurtful, salty tears. The kind that leaves a stinging knot in your throat. It hurt because I knew she cared more about him than she did me.

My body was already riddled with God knows what and there was no pity from her at all! But, despite all that, we were all doing well financially. Life for us had gotten so much better that Mama bought a

Jaguar. When I went to Quint's house over the weekend, he got all up in my face while counting money, "You'll never see this much money!" he bragged. I rolled my eyes at him and said, "My Mama got way more money than you!" That offended the hell out of him. "I got Thomasville, the Westend, and Bowen homes on lock. And yo Mama got way more than me? I don't think so!" he replied.

He got nose to nose with me, hoping that I would say something wrong so he could hit me. The jealousy was truly real. Then I said, "You may have Thomasville on lock, and you may have the Westend on lock. But Bowen Homes? Nigga, please! You would get yo ass shot up talking 'bout you trappin' in Bowen Homes! You still on nickels and dimes while my Mama pushing weight! Don't forget, she know the game. She got knocked down in it when I met you, but she got her shit together."

He got closer in my face and started talking a lot of shit while slapping me in the face with the money that he was bragging about earlier. "Quint! Get out my face before I have yo ass knocked off! I'm dead ass for real!" After that, I went home and told Mama what Quint did. Mama got to the point where she couldn't stand him. He was so envious of us that I had to stop talking about the going's on with us. He was even threatening to break up with me because he couldn't keep up with us. Soon, I got to a point to where I could go to his house on my own because Mama had hired people to drive me around. One night, Mom and Curt picked me up themselves. When I got in the car, there was a guy in the back seat. He introduced himself. "Hello, sister," he greeted, "My name is Jap." He was a bit on the chubby side and was very dark-skinned and very nice. Mom told me that Jap was going to serve at night so she and Curt could get some sleep. After about a month or so, Mom and Curt were together, she decided to throw a birthday party. She spared no expense on him.

Mom told me to go downstairs and invite Ms. Thompson and Ms. Shariff. So I got dressed and made myself look really cute. I wanted Ms. Shariff to know that I was doing much better. Still, she was really hell-bent on me meeting her brother and leaving Quint alone.

She had seen me crying for so long I wanted her to see me happy and smiling. So, I was happy to go and invite them to the party. So many people started to come in - everyone looking so nice. Then Jap walked in sharp as hell! Earlier that day, he wore the same raggedy clothes that he always wore. But he cleaned up nicely. As the party got going, people started to make their way in and out of the apartment, enjoying themselves. Mama also had the mood on the inside of the apartment set by dimming the lights down. It was darkish, not too dark, but like a party-type of dark.

Soon, Ms. Shariff and Ms. Thompson walked in the door dressed nicely. I noticed that Jap and Ms. Shariff were heavy in conversation. Ms. Shariff was turned facing forward while sitting in a chair. Jap was standing behind her and talking to her over her shoulder.

Later into the night, more beer was needed. My mom asked some guys who were outside to bring in another keg of beer. There wasn't enough light for them to see when they got the beer in, so somebody flipped the lights on. I was sitting right in front of Ms. Shariff, looking at her when she turned around and said, "I'm gon' get a good look at you with the lights on so I can see who I'm talking to." When she turned around, Jap was looking the other way to see if the guys could get the keg in. When he turned back around, he saw Ms. Shariff looking right at him and shouted, "ANGELINE?!"

"JAMAL?!" she yelled. Everybody stopped what they were doing and looked at each other and then back at them as if they were saying, 'Like…. ya'll know each other or something?' Angeline quickly explained, "That's my brother!" "That's my sister!" Jamal said at the same time. She looked back at Jap or, as we knew now, Jamal, and said, "I thought you were in Texas!" Then someone asked, "Ya'll must have different moms or dads or something?" "Naw! We have the same mama and daddy!"

Angeline started crying as they were hugging, "I didn't know what happened to you. I haven't seen you since Mama died," she cried, "You told us you were going to Texas." So, this was why everyone was so confused. Jamal received the name Jap because his eyes looked like Japanese eyes. Also, he didn't go to Texas. Instead, he went to Techwood so that he could hide his drug addiction. He didn't want his family to know that he had fallen from the grace of their family religion. Therefore, he told them that he was leaving Atlanta when all the time he was hiding in plain sight. To add to the shock, Jamal found out that his sister's apartment was right beneath our very home. A lot of people teared up when they witnessed their unintentional reunion. But, I was happy to see them happy.

Chapter Fifteen

A Brand New Day

As time wound down, I called Quint to see how he was doing. He told me that he wanted to see me. So he picked me up, and I spent the night at his house. The next day, Quint took me home. When I got there, I saw a group of men gathered outside. They were guys that I had never seen before. When I got out of the car, one of the men caught my eyes. He was medium height, had a nice build on his chest, was dark-skinned, and had his hat turned backward on his head. For some reason, the sun seemed like it was shining only on him. I saw him flash a smile as he spoke and saw nothing but pearly white teeth. 'My God, he is fine as hell!' I thought to myself. I had never looked at a man and actually felt horny in the first few seconds of looking at him. I started making comparisons in my head; He was thick, Quint was skinny. He had a build. Quint had the body of a ten-year-old boy. His teeth were white, Quint's teeth were yellow; He looked like a man, Quint looked like a minor.

We stood there, staring at each other. Quint quickly blew the horn,

"Take yo motherfuckin' ass in the house!" he yelled. 'Boy, Fuck you,' I said to myself. I was still taking my time and walking slow. My little sister was outside playing, "Lizzy!" I said, "Come here." When Lizzy came, I got close to her ear, "Who is that talking to Jamal?"

"Oh, that's Noah. Jamal's brother," she answered. "Well, damn," I said, "What the hell happened to Jamal?" I replied out loud.

Noah watched me as I walked up the steps. I heard him ask Jamal who I was. And Jamal's response was, "Sheerk," he said as he held his hands up like cat claws, "Man, she is mean as hell!" Yeah, I was mean. That's probably why nobody liked me. I wasn't mean because I had nothing better to do. Life had made me that way. I was angry, mad, hurt, and I had a very foul mouth. I was not going to be Patricia. I was not going to allow anyone to do to me what they wanted and get away with it.

I had begun to get to a point where I would make a person sorry that they ever hurt me. I had become borderline bitter. Nobody would fight or stand up for me, so I had to stand up and fight for myself. But it had become irritating and a burden. I had been serious for so long that I didn't even know how to have fun. As I turned to the bible, I realized that God didn't want me to be that way. Months had gone by and the swelling in my feet and everything had subsided. The next time I saw Noah. I was about fifty pounds smaller. He didn't recognize me. I walked in the kitchen where Noah and Jamal were. Noah saw me come in, "Who is she?" he asked.

"That's Pat's daughter."

"She looks different."

"Yeah, she lost weight after she had the baby," Jamal explained.

"Hello," Noah greeted.

"Hello," I said before leaving to go back to my room. Then, I walked back out quietly to overhear them talking. The sound of his voice was the vocal of a man. I said to myself, 'I bet he would make a great father'. I stood about 5'0" even to his 5'5" or 5'6" height. Again, I said to myself, 'how I wish he could be the father of my children.' Somehow, I felt like he could be the best daddy in the world. Well, that was what I thought of him that night. I went back to the kitchen and Noah said, "Can I see the baby?" I said, "Sure," then I went back to my room and got the baby. I walked over to Noah and gently placed my son in his arms. Noah removed each layer of the blanket away from his face slowly and said, "Look a' there. Awe, look a' there," with a gentle smile. The way he was holding him was as if he was holding his first-born son.

The next day, he was outside talking to Aunt Lily. She was always somewhere trying to be the first one to get with somebody. Oh well, that ruined my chances with him. I didn't want to talk to anybody my mom or aunt had anything to do with. So I went back into the apartment and back to my room. Soon, Noah came over almost every weekend. I noticed him but didn't notice him. I was all about me at that time. Quint and I had broken up and he was in jail on drug charges. I was so happy! And free! Free from the responsibilities of my brothers and sisters, free from having to take care of Mom, and free from having to worry about money.

For about a year, I started to find myself. The little knot that people knew as 'Shawnie' had lost fifty pounds. I continued to keep my hair fixed. And the skirts that I wore got shorter and my shirts got lower. I went from sneakers to stilettoes. I wanted to be a stripper like some of my homegirls. I was able to look like a stripper, but Patricia wasn't having no daughter of hers flying off of anybody's pole. However, the sexier I became, the more attention I got. And I got a lot of it. There were so many boys after me that I could make them do whatever I wanted them to do. I didn't even want those boys, but they would have gone to the moon and back just to be around me. I could get any boy to let me have my way with them. Even some men that we knew let me have my way. I got what I wanted, whenever I wanted it, and didn't even have to sleep with anyone, kiss, or sell myself for cheap or for free.

I mainly asked for things from people I knew would give them to me with no questions asked. Then one day, I was outside sitting on Noah's car. I thought it was okay since he was there to visit Jamal. Noah and Jamal walked downstairs while engulfed in a conversation.

Suddenly, Noah saw me and said, "Um, you can't sit on my car."

I got up and looked at that man and thought to myself, 'Your car looks like it was painted with shoe polish, sir'. I wanted to tell his arrogant little ass that so badly. But I didn't say anything. Then again, I thought, let me tell him what he can do with his piece of car. Then out of nowhere, "Shawnie?!" Mom called.

"Ma'am?" I answered.

"Come here!"

I went to her, "Yes?"

"Go and ask Jamal's brother if he can give you a ride to the store for me and pick up a few things," she said while handing me a list.

I was looking like, 'I'm not going to ask that little prideful bastard shit!' Then, Mama went back in the kitchen. I saw her trying to cook. I knew she needed the things she had written down. I had to build up my confidence and gather my own pride while staying humble at the same time.

So I walked up to Noah and said, "Excuse me, sir. My mom said, could you take me to the store?"

"Take you to the store? What am I gonna get out of it?"

'You little fucker, you!' I thought to myself. I shrugged my shoulders and said, "I'll buy you a drink."

"A drink?"

"Yes, a drink."

On the way to the store, he asked me my name. "Shawnie," I said.

"You got a boyfriend?" he asked.

"No, sir."

He continued to ask questions as he drove. Then I noticed a shingle-type string thing hanging from his rearview mirror. It was made from yellow and green strings with the year 1990 on it. "What's that?" I asked. "That's my tassel. That was on my graduation cap when I graduated high school." 'Damn, I need your autograph,' I said to myself. I had never seen a high school graduate before. Although Quint said he graduated, I didn't see proof. Then, Noah started telling me things that I had never heard of, like the movie "Roots" and the different meanings of things. Then he'd finish his sentences by saying, "Oh, I'm so intelligent." Now, that shit pissed me off!

When we got to the front of the store, I looked at him and said, "Does a dime tell you how shiny it is? Or better yet, does a flower tell you how pretty it is?"

"No," he replied.

"How do you know that the flower is beautiful?"

"The flower doesn't know. You tell the flower how beautiful it is," he said.

"Then why don't you let somebody tell you that you're intelligent? Because if you really are, they will be sure to tell you," I said as I got out of the car.

As soon as I was out, guys riding around in other cars started honking their horns at me. Trying to get my attention. I looked back to see where Noah had parked. I saw a smirk on his face - proud that a lot of attention was directed towards his car. He had something inside that everybody wanted.

It was me. And I was right beside him, riding with him in his car. From the conversations that we had on the way there, it was apparent that he was cocky and very egotistic. With all of the attention that came my way, it was clear that his ego was off the chain!

I went inside, I shopped, and then came back out and got back in the car with him. I gave him his Mountain Dew. On the way back, he continued to tell me how intelligent he was. He had told him shit that so much that it became a habit. So much that I didn't see an intelligent person. Instead, I saw an asshole. A big, giant asshole that I was quickly losing respect for.

"So, what's Roots all about?" I asked. Anything to keep him from talking about himself.

"Do you want to come to my house this Wednesday and watch it? I have it on tape."

"Sure," I agreed, "Noah, can you help me get the groceries out of the car please?"

"Uh, do I look like Jamal? I'm not ya'll's flunky. I don't care how much money ya'll got!"

'Oh! So that's what it is!' I said to myself, 'You don't want us to think that because Jamal is on drugs and he chose to be out in a position to be slaved around for it, you want to make damn sure that we know that you're not like him. So, we don't need to get it twisted. Well, don't blame us because dop turned him into a slave. He was already that way when we met him.'

Although I was thinking that, I got to the point where I said, "We didn't always have money. I know what it's like to be hungry and homeless. Even though your brother chose to mistreat himself, God would punish us if we decided to help him. Yes, my mom sells drugs, but she never put a gun to his head and forced him to buy them. On top of that, you see all these kids with decent clothes and shoes? Not my siblings, but the neighbor's kids whose parents are on drugs? My mother takes the money that their parents use to buy the drugs and make sure that their kids have food, clothing and that their rent is paid. I guarantee you that the niggas down in Pepper Mills in 1020 ain't doing shit for the kids in the community.

My Mama bought these children their Christmas and back-to-school clothes and put money in their pockets. She puts back into them. It doesn't make selling drugs right, but their parents are gonna get high somewhere. We've been there and nobody gave a fuck about us!" I grabbed the groceries, closed the door, and walked up the stairs.

Meanwhile, Nixon saw Noah and me exchanging words. He lived across the hall from us, but our families grew up together. My mom went to school with his mom, Louise. They were very close when they were teens. Then, Louise ran away from home and married an older white man. My mom and Grandma stood by their sides to protect them from ridicule for them being together. Interracial marriages in Georgia back then were a huge issue at the time. But Louise didn't want anything to do with Mama when she was a drug dealer. She would speak to her, but she kept to herself. On the other hand, Nixon was a wild one, and he was my jump off when I wanted to have sex without any emotions attached. Noah left while I was going into the apartment, and Nixon came behind me, "I saw you fussing with that nigga," he said. I didn't say anything. I just pretended that I didn't hear him.

About three days later, I got a call from Noah, asking me if I still wanted to watch Roots. I told him that it was fine. I wanted to get out of the house anyway. Wednesday came and I dressed really nice. He came to pick me up. I was waiting for him to open the door, but he approached me and said, "Check your pockets to make sure no dope is in there." When he said that, I said to myself, 'I'm just gonna keep my ass at home.' Then he said, "I'm just trying to make sure you didn't mistakenly have anything on you." I didn't have any drugs on me. After that, I got in the car. When we got to his apartment, he opened the door and I saw it on the inside. 'Wow,' I thought to myself, 'This is very nice!' He had a nice townhome. His trophies, awards, plaques, and medals were everywhere!

I was proud to be on a date with a smart, high school graduate that had his own place and a job at the bank. While I was reading one of his awards that said SCLC, he told me that Oprah and Evander Holyfield were at the event where he was honored. He even had taken a picture with Raven Simone.

'Wow! Quint, eat your heart out!' I thought to myself. I remember Quint used to brag to me about what all his new girlfriend had and what I didn't have. Noah had done everything that I wanted to do and was everything that I wanted to be. A smart, sophisticated person with a good job and money. Quint paled in comparison. He bragged about his education. Then I found out that he didn't graduate high school and his Grandma wanted him to go back for his GED. When I asked Quint what a GED was, he told me it was a step higher than a diploma. Even during the summertime, he bought an expensive fur coat. Since it was too hot to wear, he turned the A/C on in the car on full blast. I said to myself, 'No wonder you beat my ass'. He was dumb and wanted me to be dumb with him.

Noah's friends were the same as he. Hard-working and high school graduates. That was the circle I wanted to be in. Noah turned on the Television and put in the first tape of the movie. We both watched Roots together. "Noah," I said, "Can you get me something to drink, please?" "Get it yourself," he replied, "I'm not Nixon and those other folks that you boss around." 'This smart-mouthed fucker has it in for me!' I thought to myself. I didn't understand why. I had never been to his place before. I didn't know where he kept his cups. I didn't even know my way around there. I just forgot about it. If only he knew how impressed I was with his accomplishments. Maybe he wouldn't be so damn nasty to me. He had no idea who I was or where I had come from. To be honest, neither did I, really. Roots opened me up to a whole 'nother meaning of 'Where did I come from?'

After seeing the movie, I wanted to know more about myself. His nasty-ass attitude was far less important than me going home and calling Big Ma - Grandma's mom - to seek more information from her.

And speaking of calling Big Ma, I had to call my mom to tell her where I was. When she picked up that phone, I said, "Ma?"

"Where are you?!" she yelled.

"I'm at Jamal's brother's house watching Roots," I replied.

"Bring your ass home right now! That's a grown-ass man and you don't have no business with no grown man!"

"Yes ma'am," I replied. Noah turned off the TV. I hated that because I didn't get to see the other parts of the movie. When Noah took me home, I was on cloud nine. I couldn't believe somebody like him went out with a girl like me.

When I got home, I went straight to Aunt Lily's apartment to get Big Ma's phone number from Grandma. When I called her, I told her all about Noah, his awards, his apartment, and how smart he was. When I finished talking to her, I ran upstairs to Mom's apartment so that I could see Noah off before he left. As I was walking toward my brothers' room where Jamal and Noah were, I overheard Jamal asking Noah, "So, you and Shawnie hit it off?"

"Man, please," Noah replied.

"What' chu mean?"

"Man, you know I'm not with that!"

"With what?"

"I'm not with dating a girl like that. Too much baggage."

My heart dropped. I knew it was too good to be true. I knew a person like me was destined to be on Section 8, welfare, food stamps, and having a boy like Quint. Well, anything better, I guessed that God made it easy for some people and difficult for others.

I've had it hard my entire life, and that was one of those reminders that I had to stay in my lane. When Noah walked out of my brothers' room, he saw me standing outside the door, "I'll see you later," he said. "Okay," I replied without looking at him.

"What's wrong with you?"

"I'm good, Noah. You're not with dating a girl with a lot of baggage, so you can leave." He walked off and left.

Later that night, I was still thinking about all the things I learned from Big Ma. First, I learned that her real name was Elaine Dobbs-Hull. She was born a Dobbs, and so was my grandmother, and by blood, so was I. The Dobbs are related to John Welsey Dobbs, who is also related to the first black mayor of Atlanta, Georgia, Maynard Jackson. I was wondering why my grandmother never spoke about it, so I asked her. Grandma told me when she was fifteen years old, she had Uncle Richard out of wedlock. Her parents were upset because she wasn't in what they called, "The family way."

My great Grandma and the rest of the family didn't want shame because the Dobbs' were making a huge name for themselves in Atlanta. After she had given birth, she started dating one of the Bronner brothers for a short period of time. I guess his family didn't want their son with a girl who already had a child. Even though Grandma had given birth, she was supposed to give her child to her aunt, but she wanted to keep her baby. So Big Ma took her son and raised him as her own, which was why Rich had no respect for her.

When it came to Granddaddy,… well,… he was a boy that Grandma really didn't know. But Grandaddy liked Grandma a lot! Big Ma knew this too. So she asked him if he liked her daughter and he said yes. Big Ma then made Grandma marry him. She didn't want the embarrassment of her daughter having a child without being married. Poor Grandma. She married a man that not only did she not know, but she also didn't love him. Grandmother did everything her mother told her to do. Obeying your parents was part of the good ole' Christian culture in the South. Plus, Georgia was neatly nestled in the crevice of the bible belt along with racism, Christianism, and fascism.

After Grandma and Grandpa were married, she quickly found out what kind of man he was. He had a third-grade education and broke into people's houses. He couldn't read, write, or spell. He was a serial adulterer and constantly stayed in jail. All of these things brought more embarrassment to the family. So Big Ma told Grandma one day to call the KKK so that they could come and hang Grandpa. Like the obedient young lady my grandmother was, she called. They told her that they 'didn't do things like that'. Yeah, right. My first question to Grandma was, "How the hell did your mother get the number to the damn KKK? And second, why the hell did you call them?" Then Grandma said the words, "Mama made me."

Big Ma was a fair-skinned lady with beautiful curly hair. Her mother was also fair-skinned. She was nicknamed "Mutt" because she was Mulatto. When Mutt was pregnant with Big Ma, white people burned a cross and a casket outside of her and her husband's house because they thought Mutt was a white woman having a baby by a black man.

I listened to Grandma tell me the bits and pieces of her part. As sad as it was, I was wondering why she would stay in a loveless marriage. So I decided to ask, and she said, "I had no place else to go. Where was I gonna go with nine children?"

I came to understand that Grandma suffered in silence, and she did what she was told on both ends by her mother and husband. I actually watched Grandma adhere to her mother, right or wrong. When Big Ma called, Grandma jumped.

Around the time when Maynard Jackson was running for Mayor, Grandma got out in the cold to go vote for a cousin that not only we had never met, but didn't bother to have anything to do with her or her children, all in the name of obeying her mother. I felt like if she wanted to vote that she should vote because she wanted to no and not because somebody is so-called related to you. That's when I learned the difference between family and relatives. Family is someone who loves you, and you love back. Blood never made anybody family. Blood relatives could be less associated with you than a person on the street.

Your relatives are just a part of your family tree, and neither one of them is obligated to the other. I went home thinking about what else I didn't know about my family. All I knew at that very moment was that I wanted to be loved.

Grandma was in her sixties at that time. I didn't know if she ever had the experience of a man loving her, kissing her, and telling her how much he loved her, a genuinely romantic man. Quint was not the romantic type, and Nixon was a fill-in whenever I needed to get my rocks off. And he was way too young to understand the concept of romance. But, on the other hand, I wanted love, and I wanted it badly. I wanted it so much that I was willing to just keep myself from allowing myself to be all worn out down there. I wanted to save what was left of me for that special guy.

After Grandma told me what she told me, I often thought about her, and I wanted to be with somebody who I could see myself being with for the rest of my life. Then out of nowhere, Quint came back into the picture. Once he got out of jail, he started telling me that he missed me and that he wanted to be a family with me and so on. The words that I overheard Noah telling Jamal - that he didn't want an instant family and the baggage that I came with - made me think of something that Quint once told me before. He said that a man don't want a woman that has baggage or children. I felt that Quint was right after the way what Noah said made me feel. I thought I might as well be back with him. Of course, everyone said that I was stupid. But I wanted Quint back also. ...Or so I thought.

This time around, Quint's mother and grandmother had moved to a different house. That summer, I went to his house and spent a month with him. The girl that his Grandma had last seen in me was there no longer. I had a bit more spunk and confidence about myself. After being at his house for a month, I wanted to go back home. When he saw me packing our bags, he got angry with me and told me that I could leave, but that I was going by myself. I didn't trust this boy to leave my precious baby with him. I knew he wasn't interested in my son. He was interested in misusing my son to get what he wanted. I packed up my baby's things also. I had some more clothes in the dryer, so I went to the laundry room to get them out. He walked into the laundry room while I was getting the clothes and kicked me in the face as hard as he could with his high-tech boots on. 'Here we go again,' I said to myself. I went to the bathroom to go look at myself in the mirror. I said to myself, "Uh-uh, I can't do this anymore."

When I went back to the room, he pulled a gun out. I stopped in my tracks. I didn't want him to shoot me. He had become even meaner. Even my baby didn't like him. The only man my baby had any connections with was Noah. I dared not to mention him because the last thing I wanted to do was ruin Noah's good life by a having-nothing-to-lose ass nigga try to hurt him. So I made the decision to be back with Quint. During that same month, my mom had constantly been calling me, telling me to come home. The only reason I didn't leave was because Quint was practically holding my son hostage, forcing me to stay there. Noah tried calling to tell me how sorry he was. He worried about Que and me and wanted us to come home. After that, I didn't accept any more phone calls from Noah because I didn't want to put him in the middle of what was going on with me.

Then Mama called again. This time, she called with Noah on the other line. When he started talking to me, I started crying because I didn't want to do to him what my mother had done to my dad. Noah had a good life, and I was not going to let history repeat itself. So, I hung up the phone. I continued to put up with more of Quint's abuse until he hit my baby in the back as hard as he could. Que was hungry. Quint tried feeding him eggs, but Que didn't like eggs. There was a pack of donuts on the bed, and Que tried to reach for them. That's when Quint hit him as hard as he could. When Que cried, he didn't let out a whiny baby cry. It was like, 'I'm tired, mommy. I'm tired'. When Que looked at me, I could see the fear in his eyes. Later that same day, I told Quint that I had to go to the WIC office and take Que for his shots. Now, Mama had bought me a car from the auction maybe a few months before. It was an old Chevrolet. I told Quint to keep the car so that he could have a way of getting around. I also wanted him to assume that I was coming back. I called a cab and me and my baby slowly got in. Quint looked at me and said, "I think you're lying about that appointment. And I don't think you're coming back." "I'm leaving my car here, and my welfare checks get mailed here. So I have to come back," I said before closing the door.

Once the cab driver put the car in drive and drove away from Quint's house, I kissed Que on top of his head and said, "We're free, baby."

The cab took us back to Mama's apartment. When I got home, I saw Mama sitting outside. Once we got out, all of my sisters ran to the car and got all of our stuff out. They were so happy. Mom came over, too. I looked at her and said, "I'm home, Mom."

"You not going back there, and I mean it!" she said.

I was happy to be back at home. I was happy to be with my family. But I was sick as a dog. A few days had gone by and Noah came to visit Jamal. When he came, I was standing in the kitchen, cooking. When Noah came in, he stopped in the kitchen and just stared at me, "Shawnie?" he asked.

"Yes?" I said.

"I'm sorry. I didn't intend for you to hear that," he explained.

"Noah," I said while shaking my head slowly, "the damage has already been done. I didn't want anything from you, and I didn't need anything from you. I've never asked you for nothing."

"I'm sorry, Shawnie," he apologized again.

"Ok," was all I said back.

"What are you cooking?" he asked.

"Fried green tomatoes."

"You better stop eating like that. You're getting chubby around the waist." I looked at him and he looked at me, "Are you?" he asked. I didn't say anything. "By who, Shawnie?"

Still, I said nothing. Noah dropped his head and left. What was I supposed to do? I just had to deal with it.

Months had gone by. Neither Noah nor I called each other. Before I knew it, Christmas had come. It was wonderful. My cousins from Decatur, Georgia, came to visit. Later that night, Quint came bursting in the door asking for Que. I didn't want Mama to hear him because she hated him. Quint had on a wifebeater with a coat on in the middle of the cold weather, looking like he was ready to kill or be killed. I got out of bed when I heard him storming in the house and pulled him to my room, "What are you doing?"

"I came to get Que."

"You know damn well you didn't come here to get the baby! You came for me! He's with Mama in her room, asleep. I don't want to wake everybody up. Let me get some clothes so I can leave."

I knew if Mom and Curt got out of bed, Quint's brain would be splattered all over their house. They had tons of ammo and the right to kill him because he was trespassing. To save Quint's life, I went with him.

I started to hate Quint. He wanted nothing out of life. And all because I wanted something out of life, he started calling me Ms. High and Mighty. He told me I thought I was better. I knew I wanted better, and he wasn't it. When I got to his house, I told him that I wanted to leave. He took out his gun and told me that he was ready to kill me and himself, saying that at least he knew that we would be together. I told him if he killed himself and me, he would be killing three people. My baby and I would be together and he would go to hell. As fast as I could, I ran into the bathroom and locked the door. He kicked the bathroom door open. The door busted me in the head. Blood splattered everywhere. I looked out the window to see if I could fit, but my stomach was too big. Soon, his mom and Grandma ran out of the room after hearing all the noises. They saw Quint with a gun while yelling that he was going to kill himself and me.

Together, they tried talking him down. Then he started crying, saying that he had never been in love like that before. I knew that his mom and Grandma hated me for not wanting him. But I just couldn't do it anymore.

As much pain as I was in, I started to talk to Quint to get him to calm down. Eventually, he calmed down. It was such a long night. After his mom and Grandma took him back to his room, I stayed in the bathroom to treat the wound on my forehead. The next day I asked him to take me back home to get my baby. When I got home and went into the house, Mom saw where I had a gash over my eye. Her face turned blue. She saw dried blood in my hair and where Quint had hurt me. She jumped up out of her chair, and I started yelling, "Mama! Mama!" She went and grabbed her gun, "I'm tired of this little motherfucker putting his hands on my child!" she cried as she was rushing out the door.

"Curt!" I yelled, "Curt! Help! Hurry! Mama about to shoot Quint!"

Curt came from the back and ran out the door after Mama. He jumped down the stairs while Mama aimed the gun at Quint while he was in the car and was about to pull the trigger. I was right in front of Curt, and I jumped in between the gun and Quint, "Mama, no!" I cried, "He's not worth it!" Then I turned around toward Quint, "Go, Quint, Go! Just leave!" I said. Quint took the fuck off. "You should have let me shoot him!" Mama yelled, "You never take a gun out on somebody and not use it! They'll never forget it and will come back and try to shoot you!"

I was not going to let my mother go to prison for killing Quint. He was not worth someone spending their life in jail because of him. I was happy that he was gone, but I wasn't happy with Mama putting her life on the line. So now, I was free from Quint and free from Noah having to see Quint at my Mama's house. Noah had no respect for him. He didn't even care if I was with Quint. He told me that he would have backed off if I was in a committed relationship. When I told him that I was committed to Quint, he said, "Yeah, right."

Noah and I were seeing more of each other. But the arguments between us were nonstop, so I didn't see him for a while. At the same time, Mama had broken up with Curt, after which he had stolen twenty-thousand dollars of her money. When he got caught, he was with a drug-addict female who had bought dope from them. They were both in a hotel getting high. Jamal was also with them and that pissed her off.

I wanted to call Noah, but I thought that he might have already moved on. In the meantime, I started seeing a boy named Danny. He was from Louisville, Kentucky. Months later, that winter, we saw Jamal again after a while, and he apologized to Mama. He told Mom that Curt forced him to go with them after he told them that he wanted to stay with Mama. Mama had a new boyfriend by then. After Curt left, Aunt Lily introduced Mom to a man named Drew. Drew was working on Fulton Industrial and he had an old run-down car. When he got with Mama, he knew he had hit the jackpot, and so did his parents. They didn't care that Mama was eighteen years older than their son. To them, her age was 'Rich', her race was 'Rich', and her name was

'Rich'. In no time, Drew went from driving that broken-down car to driving an Expedition, Jaguar, and any other car he wanted because Mom owned a car lot, a restaurant, flea market, and boarding houses. He quit his job and moved in with her. My brothers, now older, were the ones getting out and risking their lives while he walked around with the keys to everything like he owned it himself.

One night, Danny and I got into a really bad argument. We broke up after that. Drew and Mom had been drinking when they heard me crying. Drew was the one to come to my room and tell me that everything would be alright. That was fine and all, but when he started trying to talk to me and kissed me several times on my damn neck, that wasn't the move! "Move!" I yelled. He got up as if he was only joking. I didn't play those games. I had already gone through hell. I really didn't care anything about Danny. He was there to comfort me when Quint and I broke up. I think he knew that, which was why he wanted to go back and be with his baby's mother. So him leaving didn't hurt that bad. He had given me a ring before and told me he wanted to marry me, but we were both dealing with hurt, so the feelings weren't real.

Chapter Sixteen

Unwanted Adversary

Over time, Drew learned more about what I had gone through and was more sympathetic than Curt was. When I showed Drew where I stood, he never disrespected me again. In fact, he turned out to be my biggest advocate. Especially when it came to how Mom treated me. Even though I helped Mom back on her feet and all the kids in the house, I still wanted to live out my dream of being a recording artist. I wanted to be that so bad. I had contacted several studios to see which one I could go to. I was eventually invited to a studio in Atlanta that next day. I was told that they could help me depending on my material. Mom knew that Drew, my brothers, and I were excited to go. I wanted a deal so that I could buy my way out of her house.

The next morning as we got ready to go to the studio, Aunt Lily came by and told Mom that she had gone to a fancy restaurant the night before. Aunt Lily glamorized it to be something amazing. Then Mom said, "Drew, I'm about to put on my clothes. We're going to that restaurant now!" Drew said with quizzical brows, "Pat? You know Shawnie has to meet people at the studio. We were preparing for this all day yesterday." "Why does she always have something to do!" she yelled, "I don't care what she wanna do. I told you what I want to do!" "Pat? Do you know how many of those restaurants you could have if your daughter makes it?" he yelled. Mama didn't say anything. She just continued to get dressed while ignoring Drew's plea to her. Then I said with bitterness going down my throat, "Drew, it's okay. I'll be fine. Y'all go ahead and have a good time, okay?" I had chills going down my spine. She was heartless towards me as always. "Zay, I want you to go with us," Mama said.

"But Ma, I don't wanna go," he said.

"You *are* going! If you don't go, I'm not going!"

Drew looked at Mom and said, "Pat, why you do that girl like that? God is gonna punish you! While you sittin' around here breaking your back for these other girls, they are gonna give you their asses to kiss. You're gonna need your real daughter one day."

Drew got very emotional. They all gave in to Mama and went out with her. While Drew was out, he bought me an outfit because he said that we were going to set up another meeting and he wanted me to look nice. The outfit that he bought for me was the only outfit that I had. In fact, I went most of the winter with hardly any clothes. I didn't even have a coat. I almost had one when a guy on drugs came by the house with some Olympic jackets and coats to sell them. Zay bought a coat from the guy and handed it to me, "Here you go Shawnie. I know you don't have a coat." I thanked him and took the coat to my room and put it in my closet. I was so happy that I finally had a coat. When Mama got back home, Zay gave her her package back and the money he had made from the sales.

He told her that he used a couple of dime bags to get coats from a guy. I heard her say, "What coat?"

"Well," Zay said, "I got one for Shawnie because she needs one and it's cold outside."

"Bring 'em here. Let me see 'em."

I went upstairs and got the big, thick green and white coat and brought it to her.

"Ooh, those are nice!" Mom said, "Reshad!" she called to my baby brother, "come here and try this coat on!"

"Mama, I got a coat," Reshad said, "Shawnie don't have one. She needs it," he said as he obeyed Mama.

"What I say?!" she yelled. Reshad put the coat all the way on, "Yeah, that looks nice on you. You keep that!" she demanded.

"Shawnie, you can just get it out of my room if you need it," he said sadly.

As heartless as Mama was, things didn't get any better for me. She started treating Sandy's girls like the Golden Girls. To her, they were her new beginning. It was her turn to hit the 'parent the right way' reset button. Sandy even had twin boys, Ashford and Allen, that she had given up at just a few months old. Mom and Drew adopted them.

It wasn't long until even my brothers started to pick up on the green light and treat me the same as Mama did. Whenever I needed socks, I had to search for them because my brothers would hide them from me. Whenever I needed extra money for Que's diapers, I had to wash everybody's clothes, including Drew's underwear (Drew was about four hundred pounds.) About twelve people lived in the house, and I had to wash and dry everyone's clothes as if I was a maid.

Every time the house got dirty, my name would get called. I didn't go anywhere because I didn't have any money. One time, Mama told me to come to the Atlanta fair and that she would pay my way. When we got there, she paid for everybody, and when she got to me, she said, "You shouldn't have come." Then, she bought everybody a gold tooth and bought me one from the flea market. Everyone else had their gold tooth put in professionally by a dentist. I put mine in with superglue, which eventually rotted out my teeth.

I even tried to go to school to become a nurse. I went down to Georgia Medical Institute of Atlanta. I took a test and made a 12. The passing score was 7. I was proud of myself. I was able to get into the school, but I couldn't get financial aid because she put a gas bill in my name the year before. The school told me if I could pay seventy-five dollars that day, they could work with me and allow me to make monthly payments from my welfare checks. I didn't have any money, so I called Mama to see if she could help me. She told me that she didn't have it. The counselor at the school was my old high school counselor. He and his assistant told Mama about the nursing program, and she told them that she didn't have the money. Mama had thousands upon thousands of dollars. When I got back on the phone, she could hear my heart breaking and told me if I didn't like it, I could leave. When I got back home, I found that she had taken Lizzy and her sisters shopping and had bought a brand-new dining set. The cold chills ran from my jaws to my throat and down my spine. That feeling was not new. It was a common emotion that I had become familiar with.

I went downstairs later that day to see her laminate the girls' report cards because they had done well in school. I had the score papers from my school that showed I had at least part of the test, and I asked her if I could Laminate my paper so that I could at least have it to remember that I made an effort and passed. She said, "That's really nothing to laminate, so no. I mean really, it's nothing at all." Regardless of if it was nothing to her, it was something to me.

Another time, I went into the kitchen where Mama had laid out brand new outfits for the girls all over the deep freezer, " Wow, these are nice," I said as I picked up a shirt and looked at it. "Don't touch their stuff!" she demanded. So I put the shirt down and went back to my room. Drew said, "Pat, why you do her like that?"

I didn't hear a response. The following day, I asked for a ride to the WIC office. I knew they were going that way because it was the same way as the flea market. Then Mama told Aunt Lizzy and the rest of the girls to get dressed because she was going to take them to get their nails done.

"What about Shawnie?" Drew asked.

"What about her?" she asked.

"Are you gonna get her nails done, too?"

"Shawnie is my child!" she yelled back.

"I know she's your daughter. That's why I asked."

Mama didn't say anything to Drew's plea. He stood there, waiting for her to say something. But she continued to ignore him and told Aunt Lizzy and the other girls to get dressed. All I wanted to do was go out and get my kids' WIC vouchers. So I got in the car with them. While we were on the way to the nail shop, Mama yelled, "You want your nails done?" "No ma'am," I responded. But I really did. It would have been nice. But my pride wouldn't let me. Just like the other time, my pride didn't want to ask her for help.

I had dropped out of school and stood by my mother to help us as a family. I can't say that she turned on me. What I can say is that her true feelings stayed the same. Of all the sacrificing I had done, everybody else reaped the benefits. I watched as everyone got what their hearts desired while I had to pine for my baby and me. I had even decided to go to a shelter, and Drew wrote a letter for me to take. I had a pack of old pampers that was for a newborn, and I was using them for Que, who was nearly a toddler. As cruel as they all were to me, I couldn't be as cruel as they could. Even when Lizzy got her eye shot out by a BB gun, I stayed with her in the hospital for weeks, leaving my own baby at home. While I was there, I was pretending to be happy. But, in truth, I had nobody. Until the night I was standing outside looking up into the sky, and I spoke to God, "God? Please. Send me one of your angels that can help me, and I can help him. I promise, God, I will take good care of him. I will never hurt him."

By the end of winter, Noah started to come over a lot. I told him that I didn't want him; I didn't want to ruin his life. He said that he didn't come to see me. He came to hang out with Zay. The more Noah came over, the more I found out about him. I even found out that he was a DJ. He was shocked to find out that I could rap. He didn't believe me until he asked the kids in our complex which of them could rap, and they all pointed at me and said, "Shawnie know how to rap." Then Noah looked at me and said, "Lil girl, you can't rap. Let me hear you."

So I showed him,

Here's a situation that happened at birth

When I raped the doctors and killed a nurse

I was living my life like a Bebe kid

Hard-life female from the pull-pit

Because a girl like me, I don't give a fuck

Put a nine to your head. Nigga give it up

'Cause a girl like me, I'm down with it

And guys like you straight bullshitting

Living a life like mine ain't swell

'Cause I'm a down for it hard core female

A life like yours ain't nothing but whack

I got a nine to my side, gotta watch my back

This is my world, straight kicking smooth

` And this is how it is when you're down for a gank move

Noah's mouth dropped wide open. He told my brothers and me to ask our mother if we could go to his studio. The first time I went to his apartment, I recalled that he did have a small studio. The second time I went, he moved to a bigger apartment where we finished watching roots. Nixon felt like Noah wanted me then, but I was not

Nixon's girl, so he didn't have the right to check anybody about me. Since then, Noah and I had grown to know each other more. If I wanted to be with Noah, I would have done that a year ago. Noah's smart ass, egotistical ass mouth ruined that.

Although Noah's smart mouth made me sick, for some reason when he came over, my sibling would say, "Shawnie! Noah's here!"

Then I would yell, loud enough for him to hear, "Why do ya'll always tell me when he's here?! So!"

"So!" he would say back, "I didn't come here to see you!"

"I didn't say you did!" Then, like always, he'd just walk right into my room after I had just made up the bed and lay on it.

"Why do you come in my room and lay on bed every time you come over here?"

"You don't pay no bills," he said.

"Fuck you!"

And this right here always happened every time we saw each other. It was like Shawnie vs Noah.

"Fuck you more!" Noah replied.

"Kiss my ass!"

"Kiss your own!"

"You kiss your ass! You sleep with it! Now go to hell!"

"You meet me there!"

"You beat me there!"

"Crazy ass lil girl! Leave me alone!"

"Go to hell!"

"Go there faster!"

"Fuck you!"

"Fuck you even more!"

"Buy me something to eat."

"I ain't your man!"

"But I'm hungry, Noah. and my feet hurt."

"Come on, let me mash 'em."

I sat down on the bed and raised my leg so he could mash my feet, "Kiss me," he said.

"No," I replied.

"When you gon' be mine?"

"I'm in a relationship,"

"Fuck him! He ain't nobody."

"I'm in a relationship."

"No, you are not."

This shit went on and on and on. Noah asked me to be with him and I said no. He left, and after that, I didn't see him for a while.

Then we moved from Bolton Place over to Wadly street by Dixie Hills. Soon, Jamal started acting weird. He went around starting fights with people, and that was something he usually didn't do. So I called Noah to tell him about Jamal. When I called, he hung the phone up in my face. I said to myself, 'Yeah, he got somebody else'. All of a sudden, after Jamal was acting erratically for a few days, he left. When he left, here comes Quint trying to make amends. I didn't stop him from coming around. And it was almost time for me to give birth to my daughter, Angelica.

When I went to the hospital, Quint showed up with roses in a glass vase, but that anger of his couldn't stay suppressed for very long. He sat the vase by the window at the hospital. When he left, a strong gust of wind blew against the blinds, knocking the glass vase onto the floor; it scattered the broken glass and roses everywhere.

I took it as a sign telling me that it was all fake and if I didn't leave him alone, my life would be as shattered as the glass. So when the birth certificate people came into the room, I didn't give a name for the father. Instead, I followed my first mind. When Quint came back to the hospital, he asked me what name I gave the baby. I told him that I had given her mine. He got so upset, just like he did with Que. But with Que, he tried to fight me in the hospital shortly after I had just given birth. This time, he tried to suppress his anger, but I knew it was a lie. He was just as fake when he bought those roses. He was fake as hell and the real him was waiting to come out. He knew I wanted nothing to do with him. Again, I was just holding on. What I couldn't understand was why. What had a hold over me?

As soon as I got home from the hospital, he started roughing me up. Playing with me but trying to hurt me at the same time. I tried to distance myself again. He had also weaseled his way back into Mom's good graces after she kept saying she wanted us to be together and to move in together. I didn't want that.

He was unstable and unreliable. Well, Mom saw that when the fourth of July came. I rode with Mom and her new boyfriend, Drew, to Alabama to get some fireworks. Quint was supposed to go with us, but he took forever. So we went ahead and left. When I got home, he was there. I tried not to notice him. He followed me back to my room, already enraged. All he needed was a reason. When he asked me a question, I halfway answered him, and he slapped me so hard that his fingerprints were melted into my face. The last time he hit me like that, he took some skin off. I thought he would have learned a year ago after he hit me. I busted him in the head with a glass sparkling water bottle. But no. He just wouldn't stop. I tried to walk off, but he wouldn't let me, and company was filling up the house to celebrate the fourth with us.

Unbeknownst to me, Zay invited Noah. Everyone was outside at first, so I went into the kitchen. Then they all came in to get a plate of food. When I saw Noah come in, I ducked and hid behind everyone else who had come in before him. We did manage to catch each other's eye, but I put my head down. I knew he was trying to get to me, so I kept on dodging him and losing him in the crowd slipping from the living and then to the kitchen and so on. Noah came out of the kitchen and then to the living room, and that was when I slipped right back into the kitchen. While I was trying to dodge Noah, I ran right into Quint, "Why every time that nigga come around, you act like you don't know me?" I did not want Noah to come into that kitchen. I could see that he was still looking for me. Noah, at that point, didn't care anymore. With the small glance that I did get from him, I could tell that he knew something was up. He was going to risk everything, even if it meant his life or going to jail. All I had to do was say the word. Que saw Noah and was happy. But Noah was on that 'I'm gonna kill that nigga' type shit. I didn't want Noah to get involved. He had too much going for himself. Noah wanted to take the babies and me away, but I couldn't let him do that. It was too much, and I didn't want to be a burden.

He had no idea that I was breaking down on the inside. I wanted him just as much as he wanted me. Then I thought, 'I have no money, no job, I'm sick with something that makes me hurt badly, and a lot of other things. I couldn't let him take the risk that he was going to take, so I slipped away through the living room while his back was turned and ran up the stairs and faded into my mom's room so he wouldn't see me. I stayed there and didn't come out until everybody left. Quint and my brothers went riding somewhere that same night. I didn't care. I just wanted him away from me. I called my daddy, and I broke down crying, finally telling him how Quint had been treating me. Apparently, he thought that Quint was a stand-up guy. He didn't know that he had been beating me. Then Daddy said, "Shawnie? You need to let him go. You need to make Quint a part of your history. Let...him...go." Suddenly, that stronghold over me lifted. That thing I couldn't shake that kept me holding on had suddenly disappeared like magic. I believe I needed my father's permission to let him go. And like magic, I did. I thought I loved him at one time. I thought I wanted to be with him, but it was really like walking through a fog.

Later that week, my brothers came and told me that Quint was cheating on me with a girl he just met. They told me that he bought her a watch and a necklace. He had even gotten her a car painted the same color as his. He couldn't help me financially, but he did something for a girl he had just met? When I did see Quint again, I told him that he was free to go. Still, he would call and tell me how he and his girl were about to buy them a house. He even came to Mama's house bragging and shit. He was bragging about shit that wasn't even his! That was his girl's car! Quint was too fucking sorry to try to have something in life. Then a few months after we had broken up, he went right back to jail. He called my Mama, telling her what happened. Come to find out, the same girl whose car he got painted turned out to be her boyfriend's car. Oh well. If I could see that girl today, I would thank her for helping me to move the stumbling block out of my life. I would like to say 'Kelly, whoever you are, thank you, girl! You did me a favor.'

I dated a bit to try to clear my head and get on with life in my free time. Noah considered himself tired of trying to be with me. I understood if he had moved on. He needed to be with a woman who was his speed, someone who was classy and elegant.

I only dreamed of being that one day. That kind of life was so far out of my reach I couldn't think about it. After that winter had gone, spring started to make its way in. Over that period of time, I had become more involved in music. I started going to studios to get my music out there. Still, I didn't know why I had Noah on my mind so hard. I had imagined sending him a ticket to come to L.A. should my career have taken off. That would have been my appreciation for him being a good friend to me. Suddenly, my pager went off with "911". I called home, "Shawnie!" Mama cried on the other end, "You need to get home now! Jamal is in the hospital dying! Noah just called."

I told everybody at the studio that I had to go. Even though I thought about Jamal, my heart was on Noah. Knowing how hard he had taken his mother's death, I got home as fast as I could and ran straight to the phone.

I called Noah, but his older brother Samuel answered the phone. My heart was pounding because I didn't know if Noah had somebody or what. But I didn't care at that point. Jamal was like family. When I asked Samuel for Noah, he told me that he was asleep. I hung up the phone and then sat down. About five minutes later, the phone rang. I picked it up, "Hello," I asked.

"Hey, this is Noah. You just called?"

"Yeah, this is Shawnie. What's going on?"

"Jamal is sick. I told Pat everything."

"Well, are you going to be alright? I mean, who's gonna take care of you?"

"I'm grown. I can take care of myself," he said.

'YES!' I screamed to myself, 'he's still single!' "Well," I said out loud, "I'm going to the hospital tomorrow."

"Okay. I might meet you there."

The next day I went down to Grady to see Jamal in a coma-like state. Noah and Angeline were already there. I could tell that he had been crying. I called Mom, and she told me to take all of his siblings by the hands and pray over Jamal. I had been standing for a while. Angeline looked at me and said, "Sit down, Shawnie. I know you're tired of standing." I looked around and told her, "There's nowhere to sit." Noah lightly slapped his knee for me to sit there. I sat down on his lap comfortably. Days of going back and forth to the hospital had allowed both Noah and I to let our guards down. The insults stopped, and the conversations started. We were getting closer than ever. That was until about the fifth night when we were riding in his drop-top Volkswagen on Moreland Ave. and his pager went off.

He and I froze up every time that happened because we thought the hospital was calling with bad news. This time, he looked at the pager and said, "Oh, ok."

"What?" I asked.

"This girl I'm dating fried me some chicken for dinner tonight."

"Some chicken?" I said with the most fucked up-est looking face, "I thought you said you didn't have nobody."

"We're just kickin' it to see where it goes."

I just looked, "So, not only was Quint's ass trying to come back in the picture. I'm dating another nigga, but I put you first!" I yelled.

"So, you got somebody?" he asked.

"NO!" I yelled. "Pull over, Noah! Pull the car over!" I yelled. Everyone who was around could hear us yelling.

He pulled into a BP gas station, "Why do you want me to pull over?" he asked.

"I'm leaving. I'll walk home!"

"Why you getting mad? You don't want me! So now you getting' mad that another woman is frying me some chicken?" he yelled.

"Fuck that motherfuckin' chicken!" I yelled back.

"Come here Shawnie! Come here!"

"Naw! Go get that nasty ass chicken that bitch cooked you! Have you had sex with her, Noah?! Have you?!"

"Yes, I did," he answered.

"Then what is all of this?! Take me home! Please!"

I told Noah that me and the babies were gonna spend the night with him that upcoming weekend. I knew he was attached to the kids, and they were attached to him also. Noah had been around since they entered the world. He was the only man I allowed to interact with them. I even kept them from Quint because Quint was a user. He wasn't interested in being a dad. He was interested in coming up in the dope game and using the babies and me as pawns to do it.

Noah brought me home. When I got out of the car, Noah stopped me and said, "Shawnie? Are you still gonna spend the night?"

"I don't know. I'll see." When I came home, I had a lot of bags in my hands. Mama saw and asked me what all I had. I told her that I had been out and that Noah was my sugar daddy. Mama looked at me and said, "Y'all young girls don't realize when y'all got a good man. Y'all call 'em sugar daddies, cake daddies, and paymasters. You let these no-good-ass niggas beat y'all asses and black your eyes, and you love 'em. But a good man that try to do for you, y'all wanna use 'em and then get mad when another woman sees the good in 'em."

Mama was on point and 100% serious. God almighty guided Mama's words that night. When Noah got home, I called him. "Noah?" I started, "I got something I need to tell you. Well...ask you. I need your opinion. A friend of mine called me and said that they needed some advice. So, here's what she asked me. She had a friend and her friend is a man. She's been knowing him for a long time. She really wants to be with him, but she's scared that she's gonna mess up his life. My friend also has a boyfriend, but she really don't want the boy because, in truth, she wants to be with her friend. But she don't want to mess up their friendship or his life." Noah didn't say anything for a minute. Then, when he did, he said, "I'll call you back."

"Alright, see you. 'I shouldn't have said nothing,' I thought to myself.

Then, the phone rang. I picked it up, "Hello?" "So, " Noah started, "You a have a friend. Your friend has a friend that's a man. And she also has a boyfriend that she don't want to be with. She really wants to be with the man but scared that she's going to mess up their friendship and his life?"

"Yeah," I agreed after he repeated everything almost word-for-word.

"Are you talking about us?" "No!" I said aloud.

Then Noah went back over the whole story again and again and said, "Yes, you are! You are talking about us!" he yelled.

"Bye, Noah," I hung up the phone. Right when I hung up, he called back again, "It's about damn time!" he yelled out of happiness, "When are y'all gon' move in?" "Noah! I don't wanna mess up your life! I don't wanna bring you down!" "Shawnie? Do you know how long I waited for you? Do you know what it felt like to want to pack up the babies and bring y'all home with me? Those are my babies. Y'all are my family. Shawnie, come home. Baby, please come home. I love you," he cried.

"Nobody has ever really loved me, Noah," I cried, "You don't understand. It's complicated, and I don't want to ruin you!"

"Where did this 'ruining my life' thing come from? What if you made my life better?" I had no words. Noah couldn't wait for the weekend. When it came, he had come over and picked us up and brought us home with him. The first two nights, we tried to have sex, but he was nervous and so was I. We were friends crossing the line that could blow up our friendship for life. The third night, he touched my breasts. That was my hotspot. Then he started to rub all over me. The way he touched me was different. His grip was different. He was different. He was older than Quint. He was a grown man and not a little boy. His embrace was different. He knew what to do, where to touch, and how to touch me as if he was reading directions from my mind. Damn! What the hell was I feeling? Things were happening to my body that had never happened before.

Oh my gosh, his penetration was different. His thrust was different. I was asking myself, 'how in the hell can you kiss and lick my body at the same time you're inside of me?' There was so much compassion I could have cried. I could tell that he loved me through every touch, feel, kiss, and whisper. "I love you, Shawnie," he whispered, "I love you so much. Why'd you make me wait for you? I craved you. I dreamed about you." Suddenly, my ears stopped up and my body wanted him harder and faster, harder and faster. My heart started racing. Something I had never felt before. Then something happened to where I grabbed him. Then, I was relieved. My body started to tingle. I found out later that my body climaxed. That had never happened before even though I wasn't a virgin, although I felt like it.

Instead of being on my body, he was in my head touching parts of my soul that had never been explored. 'What is virginity really?' I wondered. Is it really where the skin is broken and the hymen is removed? Well, an unfortunate fall can affect the hymen, amongst other unfortunate things. A virgin can be said to be a virgin as long as a man has never penetrated her. But... penetrate her where? My body was taken by Ron. Quint had sex with me. Nixon got my rocks off but none of them - and I mean none of them - had ever penetrated my soul and received a reaction from my body in response to everything that had happened to it. This man... this grown man whose entire body says he's a man; this man whose life confirmed that he is indeed a man; everything he has is his. He wasn't living with anybody that could control his life. And the most remarkable thing about him was when he got up the next morning, took a shower, put on his bathrobe, and prayed. When I saw Noah pray, I knew he was a man of God because nobody who was supposedly Christian in my family prayed in front of me.

Chapter Seventeen

A Knew Life

The next morning, he ran a shower for me. I got in and showered for about five minutes. Noah looked at me when I got out and asked, "Are you done that fast?" I didn't know what to say. "You can't be done that fast." I didn't have an answer, so I said the first thing that came to mind to keep me from looking like an unclean girl, "The hot water is…" I stalled. "Oh! The hot water!" he cut me off, "Yeah, come on I'll fix it for you. I have trouble with this myself." After he 'fixed' what didn't need to be fixed in the first place, I got back in the shower and stayed a little longer that time. When I was done - for the second time - Noah came back in the bathroom to brush his teeth. I wasn't used to brushing my teeth. I only packed a toothbrush to make me look good. I went and got my toothbrush and started to brush my teeth as well. The way I brushed made it seem like I brushed my teeth every day. I also found out that Noah didn't eat unless he brushed his teeth first. It made me think of the times when Mama would tell people that she made me brush my teeth every day. That wasn't true. Noah taught me how to brush every morning and every night.

One day, after being with him for a minute, he told me that he needed to go to the ATM machine. I had never used an ATM card. I had never done a lot of things. I hadn't even been kissed by someone who was supposed to love me. I didn't dare kiss Quint because of his yellow teeth and bad breath. When I did have sex with him, he would tell me how good it was and that he wished I was deeper. But he seemed to be satisfied. I didn't know I was supposed to get anything out of it. And as for him wishing I was deeper, I was not going to allow him to wear my body out. To be honest, I shouldn't have been having sex at all. I should have been somewhere in school and being raised. That wasn't the case though.

Instead, my life was changing right before my eyes. Noah had taken up every available space within me. I couldn't get my day going without touching myself in the places where he had touched me the night before. My mind was blown. It was as if I had experienced something more, and I couldn't go back to nothing because Noah was the complete package.

Although I still lived with Mom, Noah came to see me almost every day, and most of the time, he would pick us up and take us home with him. He didn't want us to leave, but I was still young, and I needed my grandmother's help from time to time. Mama started telling people that I was changing, and then before I knew it, I was being told that I was on my high horse because I was with a man that worked at the bank and had his own. Of course, it was more lies. In truth, I really didn't know Noah on a relationship level very well. I was scared to tell him about Mama, about my body hurting all the time, money problems, and my education level. But, I figured that I'd better tell him before we got any deeper. I didn't want to surprise him later on. And if he wanted to cut ties with me, it was better to do it then. That way, we wouldn't be too attached to each other.

We were both at the wash house having a random conversation. First, we spoke about topics relating to school. That was when I admitted that my education had only gone as far as the eighth grade. I also told him that I would have dropped out in the ninth had I not been kept back from being absent from school so much as a child. As of that moment, I should have been graduating high school. When he sat down, I said, "That's not all. I don't have money. All the people who think that I do, I don't. It's not mine. It belongs to my mom."

"But she does help you, right?" he asked.

"No. I get a welfare check for $284 per month, and I get about $200 in food stamps. I tried to get a job, but my body hurts something really bad, so bad that I can barely stand on my feet. With my education, I really can't get a good-paying job."

"Why doesn't your mom help you?"

"Mama never liked me. I didn't grow up with love. Nobody cared for me until my children were born." Noah raised a brow, "That doesn't sound realistic." "Well, she don't. I have friends that I can call, and they will tell you the same. My grandmother raised me," I explained.

"Well, I see you at her house always happy. It didn't look like you didn't have love and support." "Trust me, Noah, I'm telling you the truth now, and if you don't want to go any further, I'll understand."

"First of all, lil' girl," he spoke in a demanding tone, "you are going your little ass back to school, and you and the kids are going to move in with me!"

"But Noah, I'm not ready yet," I said.

After that conversation, we got in the car and went back to his place. When we got there, I fell asleep. I slept the whole night, then the whole day, and then another whole night. My body became feverish. I grew very thirsty. I told Noah that I had Sickle Cell. Well, at least that was the last possibility, according to the only appointment I had as a child. I really didn't know what was wrong with me.

I became very tired, too tired to even take care of the kids. Finally, on the third day, my strength had returned. I was able to go home. Noah dropped the babies and me off and went to work. But my body was still sore as if I had swollen joints and muscles. My body felt as if I was walking through taffy. It had been days since I was last at home. When Noah got off, he stopped by Mama's to check on the kids and me before he went home. By the time Noah had come, Mama was just getting up after drinking the night before.

Time she woke up, she started her stuff, "Shawnie! You need to clean up!" she yelled. Telling me to do this and that and the other while railing insults at me. I tried to defend myself. Everything that I told Noah a few days before he saw and heard for himself.

Noah was resting upon my bed when he heard Mama talking down on me. I wasn't even at home over the last few days, and she was treating me as if I was the one responsible for everything being messed up. Lizzy was the next oldest girl, but she was lazy as fuck! Still, Mama went in on me.

Finally, Noah, not being able to take it anymore, got up and said, "Hold the fuck on! You don't have to take this shit! Lizzy, y'all go downstairs and get some plastic bags, please?!"

"Noah, I can't! Please!" I cried.

"Ah-ah-ah," he shushed me, "Girls! Get me some bags!" he yelled.

The girls ran downstairs and got a few garbage bags. Noah started packing me and the babies' things. I wanted to stop him. I tried to stop him, but I couldn't. He took bag after bag to the car. Then he put the babies in the backseat. He took me by the hand and walked me out the door. My mom saw and said, "If she leaves, she can't come back!" "No problem!" Noah said, "She won't be back!"

Noah wasn't Quint. He said that all he needed was what he came into the world with, and that was God himself. I never had my own place before. I never had my name on a lease. I never had much of nothing in my life. Everything had changed right before my eyes. When I lived at home, Quint called me every morning to rub in my face about his new girlfriend. But, little did he know, my heart belonged to Noah the whole time. Still, I wouldn't brag about Noah to him. His jealousy, his hatred, his lack of being a man could have put Noah in a position to where he could take Quint's life--which was something he might have thought about a year and a half ago or Quint could take his. I didn't want to be like Shane's ex, Tammy, by getting someone's life taken away in any way, shape, or form because of me. So I moved on in silence on Quint's brainless ass.

When I was still living with Mama, Quint had been making his presence known--dropping by or just calling. When he came by, he would come to my room and just antagonize me. What I thought to myself was, 'Since you found someone else, move the fuck on! Why the hell are you still hanging around at your ex-girlfriend's house around her and her family? Bitch ass nigga! Get ghost!'

But naw. nobody told him not to come around anymore except Drew. He was the only one to tell Mama, "How you still let that nigga come around after he had been beating your daughter? I will never understand."

Mom, my brothers, nor anybody said nothing. He just came and went as he pleased. Then one day, he dropped in and went to my brother's room straight, capping, bragging on what all he got, and so on. The door to my old room was closed. He opened the door and walked in to find that my sisters had moved into my room, "Hey, where Shawnie at?" he asked my brothers,

"Oh, Shawnie moved in with her boyfriend. They have a townhouse in Decatur." They told me everything. I would have paid a fly on the wall just to see his reaction because he was still living with his grandmother.

Whenever I came to visit my mom's house, I would hear, "She thinks she's better than everybody," and "oh, she's on her high horse, and God is gonna bring her down," or, "She act like she don't know us. She wants to be white!" I heard it all. And all of this was said about me because I was no longer available to be misused and mistreated.

I felt free. I wanted to decorate our apartment, so Noah gave me some money to get a couch set from Mama's flea market. The couch was not new, but I knew I could clean it up and add pillows and plastic and make it look nice. I paid for the couch, and I wanted it delivered just like they delivered everybody else's stuff. But no. I had to call for days. Then Zay and some other guys put the sofa set on top of a truck filled with oil and tar. I said to myself, 'Why would you put a cream-colored leather sofa--that's already not in good condition--on a truck filled with tar and oil. That was downright low down.

Of all of my brothers that picked up my Mama's ways, Zay had taken on her opinion of me, and he could sometimes be as harsh or as cruel and she. Before, Mama helped Zay to buy a whole asphalt company. He had dump trucks and everything before he was 17 years old. He knew that Mama did more for him. He even admitted it in an argument we had. I remember every word. He said, "You just mad because Mom do more for me than she does for you!"

Mama overheard him say it, and all she could do was stare at Zay. I literally had to beg him to bring the sofa set. After he put the sofa on top of all the rubble, he decided that he didn't feel like bringing it after all. So he took it off the truck and left it in the rain and mud.

Samuel had a truck, so Noah borrowed it to get the sofa himself. Noah was so damn pissed that he wanted me to just get the money back. But I knew he didn't have the money to buy a brand new set. And I couldn't let them win. So we loaded the sofa up and brought it home ourselves. I used oil remover, bleach, and everything to get the sofa to look decent. Then I went and bought some cream and black pillows and some plastic covering.

Noah had a small beige table. I spray-painted it black and placed a floral arrangement on it as a centerpiece. I hung pictures on the wall and bought a table from Mama that originally had four tables to go with it; two of them were broken. We made it work. It really was a nice table set, so I wanted to restore it. Mama also had a radio on her bathroom shelf that the roaches had made a home in. I took it home with me, and Noah fixed it. Before we knew it, the apartment was beautiful. Then, we bought twin toddler beds; for Que, we got him a Scooby-Doo comforter and for Angelica, a Tweety comforter.

Noah gave them the television that he had bought for himself when he rented his room. They had cable and toys that Noah bought them. They were happy.

Though I had moved out of Mom's house, my food stamps were still being mailed there, so I went by there and got them and went grocery shopping. I filled the cabinets and refrigerators up like they had never been before. Every day that Noah came home from work, I had dinner cooked, the house was cleaned, and the kids couldn't wait to see him. Like clockwork, the babies waited at the front door. One was walking and the other was crawling. When Noah opened the door, all I heard was, "Daddy! Daddy!" I no longer had to worry about pampers, wipes, and formula. Noah paid for that. He caught me by surprise before when we were at the store, and I got a pack of pampers for Que and another for Angelica. The cashier said the total was twenty-seven dollars. I was looking down in my purse to get the money out. The next thing I knew, the cashier was saying, "Thank you, y'all have a nice day." 'What the hell?' I thought to myself. I looked up and she was handing me a receipt. Noah had paid for the babies' pampers. Then he said to me, "I'm their father. I'm supposed to take care of my kids." I didn't say anything. I just followed his lead. I started to notice his dominant persona over me. When he was at work, I told him I had to get up and make the kids some food. He told me to take care of the babies, bathe, and then get back in bed. He said he wanted me in bed by the time he came home.

Also, Noah didn't just have sex with me. He handled me like a porcelain doll. And he took me damn near everywhere he went except for work. One day, I told him that I needed to fix my hair. Since I didn't drive, I told him that the beauty supply store might have been closed by the time he got off. When he came home that same day, he had a black bag in his hands. He turned it upside down and dumped everything on the bed. There was a bundle of hair, glue, spritz, gel, eyeliner, lip gloss, earrings, and other stuff. 'How the hell did he know what I needed?' I wondered. He also didn't want my hair short. He wanted it long.

After I finished my hair, he took me into the living room and turned on some music and turned the lights off. He got a chair and sat in it. He told me to take off my clothes, "Dance for me." he said.

I remembered telling Noah that I wanted to be a stripper once. He knew that I had friends who did it. Noah also knew that I could dance. He said that he didn't want me to strip when I first told him. But he never said that he didn't want me to strip for him. I felt weird. Then he said, "Stop holding back." Then I thought to myself, 'Noah? This nerdy, quiet, shy person is asking me to do this?' "Come here up to me and stick your tongue out," he says. "Are you asking me to stick my tongue out like *na na na boo boo* and put my hands behind my ears like a kid kind of stick their tongue out? What are you asking me?" "Come here, baby. Stick your tongue out slowly, let your tongue curl your big, juicy ass lips slowly. Think about tasting me," he said. I did as he instructed, "Yeah, just like that," he whispered.

Then he lifted me from the floor, and I straddled my legs across the chair that he was sitting in. Then we went to the bedroom. Noah was getting up late for work almost every day.

When Samuel came over for a visit, I heard him say, "Everybody at work is asking me if you are ok. They said you fell asleep in the mail truck. Are you alright? That girl got your mind gone!" Little did Samuel know, it was the other way around. There was so much talk in the wind about Noah's girlfriend. So much that different friends and neighbors came by, knowing that Noah was not off of work at 2pm. One of Noah's homies named Mike worked in the same apartment complex we lived. He and Noah had been knowing each other for a couple of years. He had come to talk to Noah about something. That's how I met him.

During that time, I was making sure that Jamal was settled after being hospitalized. After about a month or so, Jamal, Que, Angelica, and I were walking to the bus stop. Mike was on a golf cart, and he pulled over to talk to Jamal. When I caught his eye, I saw what I thought to be a wink. But I didn't put any energy into it.

Then about a few days later, Mike came by with what looked like a notice from the rent office. I looked through the peephole in the door and saw him holding it in his hands. I asked, "Who is it?"

"Mike! This is maintenance," he replied. I opened the door to see what he had to give Noah, "Is Noah in?"

"No, he's at work." Then he did that look from side to side shit that Ron used to do before he put his hands on me. "Hey," he said, "You know, my boy said that he saw something on you that he didn't like."

"What did he see? Was it blood or something? I mean what?" I asked. "Naw, he saw…" then he rubbed my vagina and then said, "Damn, you shave too!" I slammed the door on him. I had to really gather my thoughts like, 'Did this shit just happen?' I wanted to kill him! He had no idea what the fuck I had gone through! If I had a gun, I would have blown his ass away!

I didn't know if I should have called the police or called Noah. The bottom line was that I didn't want to start anything between Noah and his homie. I was all over the place. Then Jamal walked into the living room, "What's wrong Shawnie?" he asked. I started crying and I told him what Mike had done. Then Jamal said, "Call Noah."

When I called, Jamal took the phone from me and told Noah everything that I told him. Then Noah asked for me, "What happened?" he yelled. I said, "Mike came to the door as the maintenance man. I saw where he had some papers in his hands. When he asked for you, I told him that you were at work and that I'd take the papers for you. Then, he put his hands in between my legs on my vagina" When I told him that, something inside of me snapped. I told him that I had been sexually assaulted my whole life and that I didn't move in with him for it to continue. Noah told Jamal to keep me calm.

I knew when Noah got off of work. When I knew it was time for him to come home, I didn't see him. I didn't even know that he was already home. He had gone over to talk to one of his neighbors, who knew Mike. He found out from them that Mike had already told "the boys" that Noah's girl was easy. The next thing I knew, Noah was walking through the front door with Mike held up by the back of his shirt, "Apologize!" Noah yelled.

"I'm sorry, ma'am," Mike said.

"Now, get the fuck out of my house before I kill you!" Noah yelled.

I didn't know that he could get that mad. I thought to myself then that I needed to be careful of what I told him because that was a side that I didn't know existed.

Noah and I had been together a few months after that incident. Jamal, Samuel, and Angeline were the only other family of Noah's that I had really seen. He didn't talk about his family much. But out of the blue, Samuel and Angeline came over to visit. While they were there, I overheard tidbits of their conversation that was about their mom and dad. Apparently, from what I heard, their father was extremely abusive and controlling. When Noah did speak of his family, he mainly spoke good things about his mother and how good of a woman she was. Then I asked Noah, "How come you don't go and visit your sisters? They're only ten minutes away." "Just," he said while shaking his head, "Don't open that can of worms."

Noah always told us he wanted to have the same thing, which was a good life. But due to his income, it wasn't easy. Not long after that, I received a letter from the welfare department to go to an emergency appointment or else we wouldn't get a check the following month.

Going into that office made me feel hopeless. It made me feel as if I was carrying on a family tradition of receiving handouts from the government. It was very discouraging looking at my own daughter like mine used to do me; maybe Grandma looked at her with that look of hopelessness in their eyes. I didn't want that for my kids. But I didn't know how I could change it. As I was sitting in that appointment wondering what the next step was, I saw a room filled with women. The office's employees broke the women up into groups.

In my group, there were two ladies with a box. The box had wrapping of fake money with a hole in the middle of the box. One of the ladies held the box and said, "This money box represents each of you, and there is only four years' worth of money inside. After the fourth year is gone," she held the box upside down, "there will be no money left. So, you all have a choice to either work or go back to school." Since Noah was the only one bringing in income, I chose to work. When Noah came home that evening, he asked me how the appointment went. I told him what they said. Then he told me to call the office back in the morning and tell them to cut it off. I looked at him like he was crazy. He looked back at me like I was even crazier.

Then he said, "Tell them your fiancé said to cut it off. Shawnie, I am a black man with a good job and education. A lot of times, those people can make your life harder than what it is." So, the next day, I called and told them to cut it off. My welfare worker told me to first send them Noah's name, date of birth, SSN, and his pay stubs. I told

Noah what they told me to do and he told me to tell them that he refused to comply. 'Whatever the hell that meant' I thought with my teenage brain.

I called the worker back and she asked me if I was sure. I told her that I was. I got one last check after that phone call. Then my check was completely cut off. I got a job at the department of revenue as a temp. I struggled every day trying to keep up. Then I had to keep going to the restroom. My body was hurting and so was my head.

At the house, dinner was not being made, the house was not clean, and the kids' dirty pampers were scattered throughout the house. Noah was pissed and I was exhausted. I thought at any time he was going to call it quits. After everything I was going through at work, I wanted to make sure that I wasn't pregnant. So I bought a pregnancy test to make sure that I wasn't pregnant. When the test showed negative, Noah threw it up against the wall because he said it was a waste of his money.

About two weeks later, I continued to get tired and hurt all over. Noah took me to the emergency room. I took another pregnancy test and that one came back positive. After that, I couldn't go back to work anymore. My body wouldn't cooperate. Feeling like I had no other choice, I turned to Mama for financial help. Like always, that door was shut to me. It got to the point where Noah and I decided to move to Bolton place apartments--the same apartments where we first met. They were nice apartments, and they were on the outskirts of Buckhead. Mama had gotten another apartment over that way. Since we were in the area, we stopped by her place. When we got there, I saw a guy who we knew named Tiger. He was on drugs. I saw him ironing a pair of pants and asked him how much he would sell them for. I needed a pair of pants because the ones I was wearing had a string holding them up; one end was through the buttonhole, and the other end was where a button should have been. He said, "Yeah, give me ten dollars."

I didn't have ten dollars on me, so I asked Mom for it. She told me to bring the pants to her and I did, "Those are some nice pants. One of the girls can wear this to school tomorrow." "Mama," I said, "the girls already have clothes. They have Tommy Hilfiger, Polo, and everything else." She told Tiger to get the pants and put them on a hanger for one of the girls for school tomorrow. I gathered my kids and told them that we were leaving. Noah and Jamal picked up the babies, and we walked out the door.

Mama jumped up and opened the door back and yelled, "And don't you ever come back you out-of-shape bitch!"

"Damn!" Jamal said.

"Y'all come on," Noah said while shaking his head.

I got in the car and couldn't hold back any more tears. By this time, Que and Angelica started to recognize what emotions were.

Back at Bolton, the rent was cheaper, Noah was closer to his job, and I was nearer to places where I could get things. Noah didn't like for me to ride the bus, but I told him that I would be fine.

Chapter Eighteen
A Queen In The Making

We were months into our apartments, and my stomach was getting bigger. Whenever I had something to do, I dressed the kids up, and we all got on the bus. Sometimes the bus took forever. On many occasions, I would see my brothers coming, driving through the apartments to pick up their friends. They would see us walking by, blow the horn, and keep on driving, passing us by.

Noah would get off of work and go to the Volkswagen shop in Decatur almost every day. By the time he got off, it would be late.

One day, I had to go to the dentist because one of my teeth started to decay really badly due to me putting that gold tooth in my mouth with super glue. I also bit down on my teeth a lot because of the pain that I was in.

The kids were at Mama's house because she said she wanted to spend some time with them. Plus, I knew they were bored at home. I went to the dentist by myself. They fixed my tooth and told me I needed to bring thirty-five dollars. It took everything in me to ask Mom for that thirty-five dollars.

When I asked her for it, she told me to come and get it. When I got to her house, my babies ran up to me and hugged me. When I went inside, I found that Mama was gone, and the house was a mess.

Lizzy and her sisters were there, so I got them to help me clean up. When Mama got back, it was dark out. I had to use her bathroom before she got home. When I used it, I had an odor on me, and it felt like I could have had a urinary tract infection. When I heard her come into her room, I finished up and came out. I waved at her when I saw her, "Hey, Mom."

Her response was a middle finger. 'What?' I said to myself. 'Oh well. Guess I'm going to have to figure out where to get thirty-five dollars from.' I called Noah to come to pick us up. The phone just rang every time I called.

It got to be 1 a.m., then 2 a.m.; 5 a.m.; 7 a.m. Still, there was no pickup. I started to worry about him. I knew he would sometimes fall asleep behind the wheel. I was scared, worried, and all of my emotions were all over the place. I fell asleep on Mom's couch.

I woke up to Drew's parents knocking on the door. When Mom answered the door, I saw her give Drew's mom a ton of money to throw Drew and Zay a birthday party. Then she sent money to one of our longtime neighbors who lost his mother.

I asked her again. "Where's Noah," she asked.

"He's out in Decatur at his shop, fixing his car."

"Yeah, he's fixing his car alright," she laughed a little, "He's under the car with one of his co-workers."

I was already emotionally discouraged. Then she added that. I didn't know what to think. He didn't call, come over, or answer the phone. Maybe she was right, I thought.

Suddenly, I felt a contraction in my stomach. A little bit of urine came out. I thought it was water. I was holding my stomach when my brothers came downstairs and saw me bent over.

"Somebody call the ambulance! I think Shawnie's in labor," they said.

I wasn't in labor, though. It was a little urine that was left when I used the bathroom before. Even that didn't strike up concern for Mama. Instead of being concerned, she said, "Don't call the ambulance to her in the house!" Mama argued, "Take her outside and then call the ambulance!"

My feet were swollen, and I couldn't move. I didn't want to go to the hospital; I just wanted to go home. But I didn't have a way home. When I found out that Zay was going to the flea market, I asked him if he could give me a ride back home because it was on the way there.

"Naw, I'm not giving you a ride!" he yelled.

I didn't know how I was gonna get home. I was thinking about letting them call the ambulance just so I could get the babies and me home. When I showed that I wasn't going into labor, everyone went back to what they were doing.

I sat down and watched everybody who was there coming in and out and going to and fro. A little while later, the mailman came and delivered the mail. I was surprised to know that something had come for me. It was my food stamps. I thought that they had already been cut off, but my worker kept them on for a little while but stopped the money.

After that, I asked Eddy, a man who worked with Zay, if he could stop by the food stamps office and then take me home. Knowing that he was on drugs, I offered to give him twenty dollars in stamps. He agreed without hesitation.

I got the babies, and we all got in Eddy's truck. Zay was riding with us. He kept saying over and over again, "Darn, you make me sick! Oo, you make me sick!" he was pissed. I didn't see why. He was going right by my apartment.

The babies and I were starving. We hadn't eaten at Mama's house because all she had was pork. We didn't eat pork. When we got home, the day was almost over. I went straight to the kitchen and made all of us some turkey bacon sandwiches and drank juice with it.

Afterward, I started taking Angelica's hair down so I could fix it up. When I parted her hair, I saw where she had ringworms in her head. Then I looked at Que's head, and he also had ringworms. They said that the boys that Mama adopted put dirt in their hair. Que not only had ringworms, but he also had pinworms.

I promised them that they would never go back again. Soon, it got dark out again, and I still hadn't heard from Noah the whole day. When it got dark outside, we all got in bed and slept until Noah got home.

I didn't have anything to say to him. Noah fell fast asleep as soon as he walked in the door. When he woke up the next day, his eyes were bloodshot red. When I knew he was up, I laid into him, "I guess you been out all night, laying up with your co-worker." From there, I called him every name in the book.

He let me lash out until I said everything I needed to say. He sat upright and spoke calmly, "When I got off work, I went straight to the shop. I've been working on you a car because I'm tired of seeing you and the babies get out there on the bus, and your family won't help us. You're pregnant, and I will never forgive myself if something happened to y'all.

When I got to work, my supervisor asked me, 'Have you been working on that car again?' I said, 'Yep.' He said, 'Is it for that girl?' and I said 'Yep.' Then he said, 'You love her, don't you?' Noah explained as tears rolled down his eyes.

Noah worked in the vault at the bank. He was supposed to have been wearing a dress shirt and tie. But due to our struggle, he wore shirts with holes in them, and he put on his long bank smock to hide them.

My mother, who didn't have nor show appreciation for my father, was trying to poison me against my family. No way was I going to allow her to destroy my own family because they didn't understand.

So from that day on, I kept their asses out of our business. I apologized to Noah, and I told him everything that happened and where that assumption came from. I told him that it would never happen again.

About a month or so later, Noah and Jamal drove my car home. What a blessing it was that me and my babies didn't have to ride the bus anymore.

Noah started to make overtime pay, and I told him that I wanted to help him make extra money. He told me, "Let's make a deal. You take care of the home front, and I'll take care of us financially. I'd rather for you to take care of our home."

I was a bit relieved. However, I was concerned about him having to do it all. Secondly, I didn't know how to take care of a home and a family. I was partly raised by my grandmother. I would see her doing things, but I didn't know how to do it on my own. There were no examples for me to follow. No blueprint to go off of. There was no direction to follow.

Here I was, not even old enough to get into a club or have my first drink, and I was expected to be a homemaker? Every day, I did what should have been done. For him, he wanted more even though I was pregnant.

He wanted a clean home and smart children. I taught them how to say grace and to pray at night. I also started them to learn how to read, write, and spell even though I could barely spell anything. I bought books and as much educational material as I possibly could.

Aside from the house and the kids, Noah also wanted me to keep my hair done long. He didn't like short hair. He didn't even mind weave or extensions as long as it was past my shoulders. I, however, wanted braids with a couple of blonde streaks in my head. When Noah took me to the hair place, I paid for it, and I liked it.

On the way home, he was quiet the whole time, "Noah, is everything okay?" I asked.

"I'm fine!" he yelled.

"What the hell is wrong with you?!"

"Why the fuck did you get braids? And blonde motherfuckin' hair put in your head?"

"Because it's my motherfuckin' head, that's why!" I yelled back, "You're not my fucking daddy. You don't tell me what the fuck to do with my head!"

"Yeah! That's your damn problem! Nobody tells you shit!"

"What the fuck do you care about my hair anyway? All you want is some pussy! You don't care about the kids or me!"

The next thing I knew, he pulled the car over recklessly, "Let me tell you something! Don't you ever in you motherfuckin' life tell me I don't give a fuck about my children. I will take them away from your ass, and you will NEVER see them again! Do you understand me? Get the fuck out of my car!"

I got out and slammed the door. I started walking up Marietta Blvd. It was almost 11 p.m. I saw a bus and thought about getting on, but I had no money, so I walked to Mom's apartment in Bolton. I didn't tell anyone that Noah and I had an argument. They already wanted to see us fail.

Before long, he pulled up to Mama's place. I was already outside. "Get in the car," he said.

"Fuck you, nigga! I wish you would put me out of the car again late at night again. I wish you would!" I yelled.

Noah got out of the car. He was in tears, "I thought something happened to you," he sobbed, "I jumped on the Marta bus to see if you were on there. I almost lost my mind!" he yelled.

"If something *would* have happened to me, that would have been on you!" I shouted.

"Shawnie. When it comes to my kids, don't play with me when it comes to my kids. You don't know what I've gone through as a child. Leave our children out of arguments," he cried.

I learned that Noah would go into beast mode when it came to our children. It was as if he was trying to protect them from somebody. He was not a father who would not treat our children's lives as a revolving door that he could go in and out of. He really loved his children. But the arguments didn't stop.

After a while, Jamal's health was better, but he still continued to stay in the streets. Once he was on his feet again, he told Noah and I that he wanted to treat us to Steak and Ale in downtown Atlanta. We really didn't go anywhere without our own money, but Jamal said that he would pay for everything.

Jamal had gotten thousands of dollars back from his SSI settlement. When we sat down at the restaurant ready to order, I could tell that Noah was very uncomfortable. Everything we wanted to order, Jamal would tell us to choose something cheaper. If we had gone any cheaper, we would have been ordering bread and water. Noah didn't like that at all. I started to get frustrated, and I just ordered some sort of dish. Noah did the same. Noah knew I had an attitude, but it wasn't towards him.

When the waitress brought the food out, Noah said, "Hold on, ma'am, take the food back." he yelled.

The waitress looked stunned. He got up and walked out. I went behind him. On the outside, I asked, "What are you mad at?" I yelled.

He really didn't know what he was mad about.

"You sitting your ass in there with an attitude!"

"Noah! You're fucking frustrated because we don't have any money!"

"If somebody offered to buy us food, what the fuck are you mad about?!" he shouted.

The next thing I knew, we were in the middle of the street in downtown Atlanta yelling at each other. While we were arguing, I saw a taxicab coming towards us, "Taxi!" I flagged it down.

"So you just gon' leave me?" he asked as I got in the car.

I didn't say anything. I closed the door, and the cab started to drive me away. I looked through the back window as the car went forward and saw Noah still standing in the middle of the street as if he didn't give a damn anymore. At that point, a car would have hit him, and he wouldn't have cared.

"Hold on, sir! Stop the car!" The driver did as I said, and I got out. I walked back to Noah, who was still standing in the same spot, "Why are you standing in the middle of the street like that, Noah?"

I was crying and he was crying. We both walked back to the restaurant where we were parked and got in the car. Jamal sat his ass in the back seat, talking about, "I'm not obligated to do anything for y'all or anybody!"

I looked at him and said, "After your brother has given up college and everything to help y'all, you're living with us because nobody else wanted to tell you in because you're HIV positive, and yet we allow our little babies to be around you when your own sister won't allow you around her bigger kids!"

Noah and I didn't say anything until we got home, "I'm done looking out for my extended family, Shawnie! I let this man drive my damn car with no driver's license just so he can get back and forth to his appointments! I have run from Techwood to Bolton, putting my life on the line just to make sure he's good, and this is what he tells me?! Even though he's *not* obligated, don't tell nobody that's been there for you no bullshit like that!"

The thing was, I knew how Jamal was. He lived with my family for years, and he jumped on whoever's side he thought was the bigger bully but bullied the ones who cared about him. Jamal had some fucked-up ways, but according to Angeline, a lot of it came from his childhood.

A lot of their childhood had started to unfold, especially about their dad, Edward, who was cruel to their mother. The night that I overheard them talking about Edward, they were talking about Edward and Martha's wedding night and how he hit her in the ear with a shoe and telling her that he was in charge. Noah disliked Edward so much that he doubted he could ever be anything like him.

As I got deeper into my pregnancy, I thought that Noah's sexual desire for me would change. But it didn't. My stomach was getting bigger, and my feet were swollen. To me, I felt unattractive. Noah walked into the kitchen where I was. I was wearing a t-shirt and panties. He poured himself a cup of juice and watched me as I cooked.

Then he walked up behind me and started kissing me all over my neck. "Noah, I feel unattractive," I said.

He put his lips close to my ear and said softly, "Why? I did this to you." He kept his lips on my ear as he sat the juice down on the counter, and with the same hand, he slid it into my panties, "What I tell you about wearing panties?" he whispered.

"Noah, please, baby. I'm a turnoff."

"You feel that?" he whispered, "This is where I put my babies. I love to see you pregnant. It makes me feel damn good that I can see what I do to you." He pulled my panties down in the kitchen. He stooped down on the floor and picked one of my legs up and put it over his back. I had to hold on to the stove and the counter to keep my balance.

He stuck his tongue so far up my vagina and licked the orgasm out of me. Noah had blown my mind with the shit he had in his head. I tried to walk out of the kitchen, "Where are you going?" he asked.

"I gotta sit down, baby."

"Not yet. Bring your pretty ass over here."

He turned me around and put me on the living room coffee table, pregnant, swollen feet and all, and fucked me from behind. When it was time for me to give birth, it was no problem because he had opened me up good enough.

After I gave birth to our son, Gabriel, two weeks had barely gone by, and he asked, "How long do I have to wait?"

"Long enough for me to heal," I answered.

After the blood stopped, Noah started. I had to rush and get the depo shot. Almost every night, he was turning me over. I couldn't breathe. He wouldn't let me stop to catch my breath at times. I had to beg him, "Please, please just let me breathe." All I would get in response was, "I own you. You understand me?" he whispered.

"I understand," I replied.

We fought, we fucked, we fought, we fucked, we fussed, we fucked, and fucked until I got pregnant with our fourth child. While I was pregnant, he slept under my stomach and treated me so fragile. I listened to music while I was pregnant and danced with the baby inside me. He would see me dancing in the living room and would dance with me.

This day when he danced with me, he put his forehead up against mine and said, "Marry me. Marry me, Shawnie. Will you? Say you're going to marry me."

I thought I was in the twilight zone. I remembered him telling me years before that if I was his wife, I would never have to worry about anything. No one ever thought of me as a wife before. I didn't know how to answer him. I slipped out of his arms like a deer caught in headlights and ran to the room and shut the door.

"Shawnie! I don't even have a ring yet!" he yelled so I could hear him through the door.

It didn't matter whether he had a ring or not. It was the fact that he asked. Days had gone by, and we didn't talk about the marriage thing. Then weeks turned to months. I thought he had forgotten all about what he asked.

We were out at Chastain Park one evening, walking the entire park. We came home exhausted afterward. As tired as we were, he told me that he had to run to the store to get something. While he was out, I went ahead and got in the tub. While I was bathing, I heard a knock on the door.

"Who is it?" I asked.

"It's me, baby. I gotta get something. I left my keys in the car."

I got out of the tub and wrapped myself with a towel before I opened the door. "Come here," he said. I walked up to him. "I got you!" he yelled.

"What? What's wrong?"

"Shawnie, I've been with you for almost two years. You're a great mother to our children, you're a great girl to me, and I know one day you're going to be a wonderful woman."

I was looking at him, wondering if he was okay. Then he dropped to one knee. I had nothing on but my towel, but he took it so I couldn't run. I covered my face, "Shawnie, on this day, March 7th, 1997, will you be my queen?"

"Yes!" I answered from behind my hands. Then I moved my hands from my face and asked, "You're gonna marry me?"

"Hell, yeah!" he shouted, "You belong to me!"

I was so excited, I told Mama and Grandma. Their reaction was less than enthused, but I was happy. I started planning immediately. We both agreed to July 12th as our wedding date. Before then, I was blessed to meet Lisa, a young lady with an up-and-coming boutique. She and I had become really good friends.

She made my wedding dress, did my invitations, and went above and beyond to help to make my wedding day special. Noah and I didn't have a lot of money, so we planned for a small gathering. I didn't ask

Mama or nobody for help. 'I know I'm not going to get it, so why ask?' I thought to myself.

Little by little, we paid for the cake, invitations and put money on the venue where the wedding would take place. I took some invitations to Mom's house and put them in her mailbox. I don't recall if we were speaking or not at that time because we had constant fallouts.

After weeks and months of getting our wedding together, I took a bit of a break and went to Mom's house. I had to get my sisters ready to be in my wedding. Lisa called and said that she needed to do a final fitting.

Days before, word had gotten back to me that Mom said, "That boy is not gonna marry her." Well, that evening, Lisa came over to do the final fitting. Mama was in the kitchen when she came.

Lisa took the cover from over the dress. "WOW!" all my sisters said.

"Let me see!" Mama said as she held up a mixing spoon in one hand. Her other hand was on her hip in disbelief. Mama called Grandma and said, "It's for real! She's getting married!"

"Well, you are the mother of the bride Patricia. You have to pay for everything. Patricia, if you don't pay for the wedding, everybody is going to look at you, and you'll look bad if you don't," Grandma explained.

Our wedding went from a small gathering to a huge event. Mama didn't hold back. She had so much food and Cristal coming out of fountains. Then she had people to layout the venue out.

On the day of the wedding, I was getting dressed, and Mama was doing my makeup, "Shawnie, turn around and stop moving!" she yelled. Then she took in a deep breath and blew it out. Then she looked at me. OMG! There she was! It was her! I hadn't seen her since my 7th grade prom.

'Hello Mama,' I thought to myself, 'I knew you were in there. Allow Patricia to let you out.' I felt like Patricia was Mama's alter ego that kept her suppressed. After seeing her, I didn't want to get married anymore. I wanted *that* mom right there.

I didn't want anything but to shut it all down and close the door and just hold my Mama. By the time I got to the venue, I had cried most of my makeup off. Nobody knew why I was crying. For the first time, I felt like the little girl that I was. I wanted my Mama. I wanted to go home.

Then, it was time for me to walk down the aisle. I saw Noah waiting for me. I knew that God was placing me in good hands. He was who I prayed for. Then, the music began to play as Noah's friend, Meliv, serenaded us, singing, "One...look in your eyes there I see..." He was singing "Here and Now" by Luther Vandross.

Our wedding was blessed by God to be on such a beautiful Sunday morning, with me marrying the love of my life. The wedding was gorgeous.

Mama called days after the wedding, telling me that I owed her nearly forty-thousand dollars. I didn't ask her to pay for anything. She wanted to look good to everybody, although I appreciated everything. We had paid for everything we could afford to pay for, and at that moment, I snapped.

"Everybody sitting around living good off of the sacrifices I made! But God is gonna punish all of you!" I yelled.

Noah and I had a hard enough time and to get hit with that was unexpected. I later got a job at a recreational center where I taught dance classes to help pay for whatever expenses were left over after the wedding. The end of the summer was coming along with the end of my job.

In the final two weeks of my job, I went to the doctor and was diagnosed with Fibromyalgia, arthritis, chronic fatigue syndrome, and depression. I had just gotten married. That news was the last thing I needed.

When I went to work to finish out the end of my job, my supervisor instructed me to go to the pool with the other kids. I was confused because that was not my job, my duties, nor did I know how to swim.

One of the employees got disgruntled about something and decided to take it out on me. A grown man challenged me to a fight. He was in my face yelling, "I will kick your ass! Your husband, your brothers, and anybody in your family's ass!"

I was a married woman with children and to drop down to the level of a child was not my style. I went back to my supervisor and explained what had happened. Mario admitted to it all. The supervisor told me if it ever happened again, me and the guy would be fired. 'What the FUCK?!' I thought. I went home pissed.

Noah laid on the floor as I told him what happened. He just laid there and said nothing. A part of me felt like he didn't care. I only had one week left, so I went to work.

Around late noon, one of the kids ran to me screaming, "Mrs. Sharrif, Mrs. Sharrif! Your husband and Mario are upstairs fighting!"

"Look, lil boy," I said, "I don't feel like playing today."

The children were aware of what had happened the day before, and they liked to make jokes about it. But what they were telling me was no joking matter. "Mrs. Sharrif, I swear to God!" he yelled.

The boy convinced me enough, so I started walking up the stairs to see for myself. I got up halfway to hear a lot of commotion. I was shocked to see Noah there. He had come to my job on his lunch break.

Noah knew that Mario was the janitor and didn't have any business going to the pool area. I was going to let it all go, but Noah showed up and used the mop that Mario was mopping with and broke the stick on his neck and started choking him.

Noah was about 280 pounds to his 140 pounds if that. I was pissed at Noah because the police came and locked him up. I reluctantly called Mama, and she said, "What the hell you get that man locked up for? You're a no-good bitch! You got that man going to jail for you!"

'First of all,' I thought, 'I didn't know he was coming! And secondly, I didn't even think he was listening when I first told him! Hell, he shocked the shit out of me!'

Mom called one of her connections; A lady named Renee. I don't know how much Mom paid, but he was out in no time, and that case was dead and buried.

After that day, I learned that Noah's possessive attitude ran deeper than I thought. I tried to tell Mom time and time again, and she didn't believe me until one day when she got a visit from one of her old friends, Don. I hadn't seen Don in years. He had spent time in prison for murder and was just released.

I was so happy to see him. He put his arms around my neck to give me a hug, and Noah caught his arm and said, "Keep your hands off my motherfuckin' wife!"

I looked at Mom, and she looked at me. Noah stormed out the door. I apologized to both of them. Mama's mouth was wide open. When I got home, I called her, and she said, "Shawnie, I am so sorry. I apologize for what I said when he got locked up."

"I told you, Mama. I've been trying to tell you."

"Damn! I had no idea he was like that!"

Another time, Noah and I went down to one of Mama's nightclubs. While we were there, one of the security guards tried to talk to me, and Noah snapped on him. Mama told me to just stay away.

Then, our arguments got worse. "I take care of you!" Noah would yell, "You don't work, you fucking drop out! I take care of you!"

"Didn't nobody tell you to get on your rusty ass knees to ask me to be your wife!" I yelled back.

Everything I heard Mom say to my dad, I could now hear it coming out of my mouth. Everything Edward said to Martha, Noah could hear come out of his.

"You know what your problem is, lil girl? You don't know how to respect a man, but you gon' respect me!"

"And you know what your problem is, Noah? You don't know how to respect or talk to your wife!"

"You're not a wife! You're a freeloader! Just like the rest of your family! Always looking for somebody to use!"

"Then why the fuck you bring your ass around my family and marry a member of my family?!"

The arguments were nearly the same every time, and it went on and on and on and on. On top of that, he bought me my first house built from the ground up. I was in my early twenties, not only with a brand-new house but now pregnant with baby number four.

The house that we bought was everything that I wanted it to be, except I didn't like Dekalb County. It was too far away from everything I knew. Noah wanted to move out there because he felt that we had no help.

The shop where he was learning to become an automobile tech was also in Dekalb. And if he needed help, he had friends he could call on. I kept my feelings about that place to myself, though.

Besides, there was a great theme school nearby for the kids. And like Noah said, I wasn't paying for it. I wanted to be submissive to Noah, but everything I had gone through with Quint, I was about to go down that road again.

I instantly recalled myself being on my knees in the pouring rain while I was pregnant, begging Quint not to leave me. I promised myself that that would be the last time I begged anybody to be with me.

I wanted to be everything Noah wanted. He sat me up on this pedestal. He told me that he was going to spoil me by giving me everything I wanted. He said, "I'm going to make sure I make it hard for the next man to get you."

He wasn't lying. Noah even paid for me to have a lifetime membership at Jenny Craig. He also told me that he was going to put as many babies in me as he could, so the program was going to be needed.

After I lost the weight from carrying Manny, I was able to wear clothes that I hadn't before. Noah hovered over me. Then it became a game of some sort. He started buying me sexy clothes to see how many men would look. Then he took me to a strip club and asked the manager there how I could become a stripper just to see if they would allow me to apply.

Then he took me in front of his friends. The next thing I knew, his friends started trading in their wives to try to keep up with him. So when I got pregnant the fourth time, I was happy. I needed a break.

Every day when Noah came home, he massaged my feet and rubbed my back. On some days, I would sit in the tub, and he would take a pitcher of warm water and wash my hair. Although I didn't like Decatur, the new house was comfortable.

Then, about a month after we moved in, Jamal lost his battle with HIV. Mama paid for his service to make sure he had a good burial. So much loss had hit our families. Uncle Derrick had died the year before. I wished they would have been able to meet their niece, Queenie. A beautiful baby girl that God blessed us with.

Chapter Nineteen

Sink Or Swim

After I gave birth that November, my body needed a break. Noah had no choice but to give me a break because he was stressed the hell out. He had been with Trust Company, now SunTrust Bank, for years. His co-workers got jealous when he bought a brand new house. They went and told their supervisor about his new place behind Noah's back, and he was quickly demoted from head vault teller to just a teller.

He went from making $1,100 every two weeks to making $525 every two weeks. The mortgage was $689.86, not including lights, gas, phone, water, food, cable, and other household utilities. Noah was working on cars as a hobby, but he applied to and got hired by U-Haul to be a tech. It was a huge change for him, but he kept pushing.

At the same time, I decided to pursue my music career. So, Noah took me to Peter Troy's house. Noah met Peter at the bank. He had a house around the corner from us with a studio in the basement.

I recorded songs that I wanted to sell, but P.T. wanted me to sign as an artist. Noah and I discussed it. Then I agreed to sign an artist development deal. Soon, I started doing music all over the city. Then, I was asked by P.T. to join two other guys on his label. He promised me that if I grouped with them, he would push me as a solo artist.

After performing at Hot 107.9 Birthday Bash, Def Jam South approached P.T. about signing me. He told them it was no deal if it was going to be without the two boys. I found out about it from P.J, a woman who was also signed to P.T., who was secretly mad at P.T. because he tried to sleep with her while she didn't want him.

Due to P.T. not honoring his contract, it was now null and void. Noah, being a DJ, knew exactly how to set up a studio, and he did just that. He borrowed $1,800 from his brother, gutted out the garage, and started Nustyle Entertainment. I signed with Noah, and so did the other two artists from P.T.

Noah then brought on his childhood best friend, Calvin. Calvin was good at being a manager, but his bulldog mentality was too much to deal with at times. Soon, Noah and I started to bump heads, and the fighting got worse.

Still, we tried to make it work because we were in debt and money was tight. But the life that we had made for ourselves began to unravel. I was so hurt about my first record deal not going through. All I wanted to do was forget about the music altogether and go back to how we used to be. But Noah seemed possessed by it.

The idea of having enough money to take care of my family, his family, and our own family was so desirable that he didn't realize that our family was being compromised. In our home, we didn't drink or smoke or allow people into our home who did. But those rules subsequently change without us realizing it. We made friends with other artists, and they started to spend the night at our home. Then one artist told us that his girlfriend was a prostitute and sang such sympathetic tunes about how horrible his life was. Noah and I, being gullible, wanted to help fix things for him while we were falling apart.

Come to find out, his girlfriend was a well-known groupie that he was fully aware of, comfortable with, and made the decision to be with her anyway because he was too lazy to work a job, so he depended on her to take care of him. That was my first introduction to a narcissist. The first thing they do is give off the impression that they are this stand-up person.

This same guy met one of my childhood friends and dated her. After about a week, he moved in with her. She was in a wheelchair with two boys and, like us in the beginning, she thought that he was this stand-up guy. He stole her food stamps, her CD and DVD players, and left her pregnant with her third child.

I felt so damn guilty because there we were, thinking we could help him get settled so that we could move forward with the music. Everything we did was in the name of music, music, music. Noah and I were two people in a marriage because the law had papers that said we were married.

The fire that once burned in his eyes for me had burnt out. The man that I wanted to hold me and love on me had become a memory. Every day we woke up, we just went through the motions. We only got up to see another day simply because another day had come.

While dealing with the stress in my marriage, I was also tackling the stress of DeKalb county--or should I say "De-Crab" county?" Throughout River Road and Panola Road, there were competitions on who had the biggest house, which subdivision you lived in, what school the kids went to, and which church you studied with.

I even had blood relatives who lived out that way. When they found out that we lived on rover road, they copped a fucking attitude! Their body language, actions, and even their facial expression were like, 'How could y'all afford to get out here?'

It was a true and living inkwell. A lot of our people had lost their way, including myself. I was caught in the middle of all of that. I would even bounce checks just to keep up. I lied on our children's lunch forms, putting down that we made so much money so that our kids had to pay for lunch.

I didn't want them to have to experience what Zay and I had gone through in school. I didn't want the school to know our financial situation because I didn't want them to feel that they had the green light to bring harm to our kids.

I played the part like anybody else. But that shit got exhausting! Plus, I learned that pleasing motherfuckers could break a person and their bank account. I had to learn that it cost to make more than what I could give.

I felt trapped in Dekalb. I didn't feel freedom. The freedom that I used to feel when Joey was alive. Ironically, the structure of Dekalb was made the same way I was feeling. That there was only one way in and one way out of that son of a bitch, and I wanted out!

All of the stress that I was enduring was triggering so many episodes of pain. I constantly had to go to the doctor. During my many visits back and forth to the hospital because of the amount of pain I was enduring, doctors had put me on many different medications like Soma, Elavil, Zoloft, and Ambien.

I needed Soma to get up, I needed Soma to cope, I needed Soma to numb me, I needed Soma to put me to sleep, I needed Soma, Soma, Soma. I needed it so much that I had become addicted. My prescription was ninety tablets to be taken over a thirty-day span.

I had three different doctors at three different pharmacies, and each of them wrote me a ninety-day supply. I was taking about three hundred pills in a ninety-day time span. Then I learned how to order pills from Canada. I get sick every time I realize how much money I spent knowing we didn't have anything.

Now, around this same time, Mama's house was in disarray. Kizzy had given birth to three children, Taylor, Bianca, and Deontay. For three years, Mama asked Lizzy who the father of her children was. Lizzy said over and over again that a boy named Dee was the father.

So Mama and Drew rode around the city, looking for the guy, but they never did find him. As Taylor got older, Mama started to notice some features that looked familiar. Then one day, Mama told Lizzy that Drew told her that Taylor was his child. Oh, but Drew never said anything to Mama about Taylor. Mama just wanted to see what Lizzy was going to say. And Lizzy said, "Yes, she's his child."

When everything unfolded, it turned out that Drew and Lizzy had a relationship behind Mama's back. Her own blood niece, and now adopted daughter, was sleeping with this man behind Mama's back.

Everything that Drew bought for Mama, Lizzy either cut it up or broke it out of hatred for Mama. All the while Mama was up this girl's ass, Lizzy couldn't stand her, and I saw it first hand.

I used to hide Mama's cigarettes and alcohol from her out of fear that she would get cancer. My childhood best friend's mother had died from throat cancer, so I did what I thought was right to keep Mama from having the same fate.

When I first moved out, I begged Lizzy to continue to do the same. But her little, low down dirty ass gave her exactly what I told her not to because she could have cared less. After Mom found out, Lizzy told everyone else in the family, "Well, she knows now. Me and him might as well just go on ahead and be together."

But Lizzy wasn't the only girl in the neighborhood who went behind another woman's back with her man. Some other girls in the neighborhood were doing the same thing. They gave themselves the tile, "The Home-Wrecking Whores". They prided their little dingy asses on fucking other women's men.

Then they found themselves as being someone's beat-up whores because easy women are not going to have that same kind of respect as women who do go whoring around.

I truly felt sorry for Mama, but she still chose to stand by Lizzy even after she and Drew had broken up. Deep down, Mama was still hurting. So bad that she went through a mental depression. Even before that, I knew Mama's mentality was disturbed. I knew from when she told me one day that she knew God was going to bless her to carry another child again.

Mama had a hysterectomy about five years prior to Drew and Lizzy having a baby. Drew's excuse for messing around with Lizzy was that he knew how badly she wanted another baby, so he and Lizzy used a turkey baster to get her pregnant.

To me, that was an assault on her intelligence. Not an insult, but an assault, and for that alone, his ass would have been the hell out of my life. But Mama made herself believe it. So much so, she had Taylor calling her Mama. I couldn't just stand by and watch that misery.

Drew had done a lot of shit behind Mama's back. He even got a high-priced life insurance policy on one of my brothers and tried to have the break tampered with. Then, the police showed up at Mama's place, burst the door down, and took her to jail.

She managed to get out on probation. When she got out, her money and businesses were gone, along with Drew and all of her "friends." She was down to nothing. She had no choice but to live with one of her kids.

One of my brothers bought a house in Douglasville. My brothers, the ones that Mama had done so much for, told her not to come out of the room when their girlfriends were over because they didn't want anyone to know that their mother was living there with them.

As for Lizzy, well, she had gone to apply for assistance at the Douglasville DFCS office. She brought Taylor with her. When she was seen, the service workers there saw how poorly a wound on Taylor's arm was treated, so they opened a case on Lizzy.

Eventually, she ended up losing all of her children to the system.

Mama tried to get the kids herself. Since she had a felony on her record, they denied her access to the children. So she called me. She told me that the kids were taken and then went on to tell me, "You know, your kids can get took too."

"Where in the hell is that coming from?" I asked.

"I'm just saying though," Mama continued, "Don't act like something can't happen to you and your kids."

"What the hell I got to do with that?!" I yelled back, "And why are you bringing me into it?"

Mama told me that she was denied custody because of her record. She told me that if I got them, the family would pitch in and help out. So there I was, feeling guilty. Thinking that if I didn't, that same kind of cosmic curse was going to get me by way of me losing my children. So, I took them in.

Honestly, I wasn't in any kind of shape to take those babies in, but I did it anyway.

DFCS had initially run out of homes to send the kids because of unseen medical and mental conditions. So, they dropped the kids off with us. They had with them a few clothes and a bag that was contaminated with roaches from their previous foster parent's house.

Now, I was twenty-five years old with seven children under one roof, a progressing disease, a home about to go into foreclosure, a marriage that was falling apart, and an addiction to pain killers.

Then Lizzy would call the house every now and again after she had laid up with other men--making more children--asking me, "Where those kids at?"

That shit pissed me the fuck off! Then one Easter, the family came over to my house unin-fucking-vited. All of Mama's money had run out, so I inverted her and her alone. She took it upon herself to call the barrel of freeloaders that ate off of her for free for years! They were known to get plates and stack them in the car. Not buying a damn thing!

The next thing I knew, cars started pulling up at our house. Our light grey carpet turned to the color of red clay. Boxes of beer were being shoveled in my refrigerator. Mama had told people that I was cooking for everybody! Fifty-plus people had to have come to our three-bedroom starter home!

I only had two bags of leg quarters, rice, and a few vegetables. Noah and I were broke! Then Lizzy walked into the kitchen and saw me struggling to make seven plates. She fixed herself a plate and didn't even ask if she could help with her kids!

She looked at them as if they were pets or something. Soon, I realized how little respect my family had for me. After they got themselves a plate, nobody helped to clean anything. They just left. They did to me what they had done to Mom for years which was 'take.' I was not about to go down that path!

I'd be damned if I was going to cook and cater and deplete my own family for them! I couldn't believe that I had fallen prey to my mother. Thinking that she loved me because I took in Lizzy's kids, all the while putting myself further down harm's way. With all of that going on, I felt as if I was going through a fog just trying to keep it together.

And I remember I reached out to B98.5 FM and got in contact with radio personality Jordan Graye. I remember being so down, and I told her a bit about what was going on. So she sent us $350 of her own money.

I get embarrassed thinking about it because of the successful woman I ultimately became. Although our situation was true, I couldn't believe that a complete stranger, someone I had never met before, trusted in my honesty about everything that was going on.

My family promised they would help me if I got them. But nobody, and I mean nobody, came to help me and my family.

With Mama, she was still going through the saga of Lizzy and her sisters. All of them except for little Jay. A man from Warrington, whom no one had ever seen before, had come to Mama's and told everyone that he was Jay's biological father. There was no DNA test to prove that he was, but Jay was sent to live with him anyway.

Not only was Jay taken to a place that she had never been, but she would also be surrounded by total strangers miles away from home. And what happened in Warrington? To this day, I don't even know.

Meanwhile, the rest of Jay's sisters got themselves an apartment. Mama asked if she could stay with them until she could get back on her feet. Well, it got back to me that the girls told Mama, "She had to go."

Soon after that, they went out and found their biological mother, Sandy, and moved her in. At that particular time, I was still distancing myself away from my family. Later on, I didn't have a choice but to go back because Joey had gotten sick.

I went to visit him when he was admitted to Grady Hospital. I didn't want to make the same mistake that I made with Shane, Derreck, and Teddy by not telling them that I loved them. I got to tell Joey just how much I loved him before he passed on.

After he died, I accompanied Grandma in the hospital as she was making arrangements for him. Then we ran into an old friend of the family, Glenda, who worked at the same hospital. She asked how everyone was doing. When she was about to talk to me, Mama cut her off by saying, "Oh, we gotta go!" I noticed that, but I said nothing.

A few days later, the family attended Joey's funeral. Avery went to their seats after standing in line and viewing his body. When I sat down next to Mama, I wanted some more room, so I asked her if she could move down some. But she kept saying, "Yes Lord! Praise God!" as loud as she could so she could pretend that she didn't hear me.

After the funeral, Grandma pulled me to the side and asked what had happened between Mom and me. I told her that I didn't know. When we went to the repass, all of our cousins were there, and I guess Mama was embarrassed because she no longer had what she used to have. But hey, I didn't do it.

I helped in the beginning, and everybody turned on me. I got nothing and still had to go home and face my reality with all the fussing and the fighting.

A while later, Nixon was released from prison. He got my number from my family and started calling me at night, telling me that he wished I would have married him instead and how much he loved me and how badly he still wanted to be with me.

I tried to pull away from him, but I was lonely and needed

somebody. Somebody to at least talk to. I needed a friend. Noah's attention was entirely on the music. While his attention was on the music, the medicines that I was taking took me from 135 pounds to 235 pounds in a matter of months. I was no longer attractive to Noah.

He started looking at me out of the corner of his eyes like he hated me. He even told me to stop telling him that I loved him. So, I did. Noah stayed in the living room talking to K.J., one of his artists, until the sun came up.

So, I moved the bedroom to the living room to be closer to him. Then he started going to the bedroom. Later, I found out that he had been going to strip clubs not only to promote but to get private dances from strippers to make him and Calvin look good as CEOs who had money to burn.

It might have looked good at the club, but at home, everything looked bad. Very bad!

Then, he came home at around 1 or 2 in the morning from the clubs trying to push his artists and took a shower. Then he walked on the side of me while I was sleeping and put his penis in my mouth.

'So let me get this straight! Not only did a bitch grinding all over you get your shit on hard, but you come to me to relive you after another bitch done took you there! Get the fuck out my face with that disrespectful bullshit!!'

I was angry and hurt. A few days later, I went to Nixon's sister's house because I knew he would be there. We met up, and we started talking. While we were talking, I was eating a plum. He took the plum that I was eating and bit off the same part where I had bitten it. I knew what was about to happen. So, I took some Soma so that it could numb me.

I didn't want to be whipped by my conscience due to me stepping out of my marriage. I laid down to what I thought would be one night of pleasure and prayed that a lifetime of pain wouldn't follow.

My mind was on the way Noah's hands felt, his body, his map that he followed that pleased me in every way possible. I had already prayed and asked God for forgiveness in advance. I even removed my wedding ring. The medication had set in. I was about to do the unthinkable and sin.

Then I heard the sound of chalk scraping fast and hard over a chalkboard like *Screeeeeeetttch*! 'What just happened?' I asked myself. 'What the fuck? What the hell was this?' I had buyer's remorse, and I wanted a refund. I didn't feel anything. There was nothing.

'You mean to tell me that my once in a lifetime one free night pass to step out on my marriage amounted to watching paint dry?'

That grown man still had everything of a little boy. I wanted to grab him by the shirt and say, 'Motherfucka, did you grow? You must have been in jail when your manhood was waiting on you! Nigga, you just a pretty motherfucka! You should have been kept at the bottom of the bathroom cabinet like an old perm box! Really, my nigga? Really?'

I wanted to cry. Not only did he have nothing to work with, but he came before he went. I didn't even want to admit what happened to Noah out of just sheer embarrassment. I went home horny, lonely, and wet because my period had just come on.

I didn't say anything to Noah at first, but it was on my conscience so badly that I had to tell him. When I told Noah, he patted me on top of my head and said, "Well, I'm glad I got the truth from you and nobody else."

Oh well. We went on back to fussing and fighting as usual. It was clear that we had grown apart. I didn't want the music anymore. What's more, I became sicker and weaker. Noah became distant.

In me, he saw poverty, lack, not wanting anything out of life, easy to give up, looks nice and dresses nice, but deep inside is a cold shell and a dead end. I had the gift and the ability to get us out of financial hardships, but I wouldn't do it. In me, he saw Edward.

In him, I saw a bully, a dog, evil as long as he got what he wanted, fuck me being sick or hurting as long as he wasn't broke no more; a user using me to make him rich so he could turn his back on me. In him, I saw Patricia.

Every day that we woke up, and every night when we went to sleep, we sparred with each other as if we were fighting the abusive parent. I had a point to prove. Noah had a point to prove. He hated me, and I hated him.

He wouldn't sleep with me so, fuck him! I could fuck myself! I didn't need him! He lied to me, and I lied to him back. Even so, we still had no money, and the kids needed us both. I needed for him to pick the kids up and take them to school and bring them home.

Other times, I had a hard time contacting Noah. Sometimes, I would call K.J.'s phone to look for him. Then K.J. started to talk to me any kind of way, and Noah would say nothing. Then K.J.'s cousin came over to the studio with him. The little jug-headed bastard tried to feel on my butt, and Noah said nothing.

Then we had a meeting at a radio station with a radio personality. This man looked at me as if he wanted to stick his tongue down my throat. Noah was standing in between us, then stepped back so the guy could get closer to me. His reason? It was all in the name of music! After that, the fighting got worse.

"You low-life bitch! That's why you're a fucking dropout! I hope you die!" Noah yelled.

I saw Angelica and Que put their hands over their eyes and ears while they were yelling, "Daddy, please don't say that to mommy! She's already sick!"

I really was. I even had to wear a wig because all of my hair had fallen out. All of the medications that I had were kept in a clear bag that once held a bed-in-a-bag suite. The bag was big enough for a king-size comforter and was filled with medication.

When I would be at home alone with the kids, Angelica would pull my wig back every day to see if my hair had started to grow. But it didn't. Not only did the pills make me gain weight and lose my hair, but they also made me crave sugary foods.

I once ate an entire box of Little Debbie cakes, five and ten dollars worth of chocolate chip cookies from Subway, whole Sara Lee cheesecakes, gallons of orange Sherbet ice cream, tons of Almond Joys, and cream cheese and Ritz Crackers. I was slowly killing myself.

I could barely keep up with Noah in an argument. But that still didn't make the insults any better, "You fucking Junky! You act like a crackhead!!" he would say.

"Fuck you, Noah! One day, this gutta' rat is gonna have to share her cheese with you while you're trying to put me down!"

Then, lo and behold, both of his brothers and sister, including Mavis's two children, had to come and live with us until Mavis's section 8 approved her home. So, now, it was not only the seven children in the house plus Mavis's two, me, Noah, Samuel, and Messiah were all in a three-bedroom house that was headed into foreclosure.

To add, the lights got cut off, the food dwindled, and I broke. I had nobody or nothing. I had no win. Then the pills I was taking led from one side effect to another. All kinds of thoughts ran through my head. Bells and whistles ringing in my ears, "You're gonna die and lose your own kids by trying to hold onto someone else's."

Regardless, I continued to try, even with the attempt to try to permanently adopt the kids. One day, Douglasville DFCS came to visit the kids, but I wasn't at home at the time. I was at the doctor's office with Lizzy's kids.

Before the worker arrived, she begged me to allow her to come and visit the kids in the early part of the day so that she could pick her daughter up from school later on. I had no problem with it at all. However, my doctor's appointment was longer than what I had hoped for.

By then, my own kids had gotten out of school and took the bus home. By the time I got home, the same worker that I had whose favor I had granted called Dekalb County DFCS on me because our key latched kids came home from school, and she was pissed because she was late to pick up her own daughter.

Now, we had always instructed our children to go to our next-door neighbor's house if Noah and I weren't at home. Now my kids were at risk of being taken into custody.

A few nights later, I remember laying on the living room floor next to the fireplace, where there was a plug-in faux fire log. I recalled a passage from the Bible that said, "When your mother and father forsake you, I will take you up."

The glare between the couch and the fireplace was a collective image that made out an image of God himself standing before me with both arms wide open. And something inside of me said, "Don't walk, child. Run! Run as fast as you can into the arms of God!"

I remember falling to the two bronze feet of the image that stood before me, and I cried, "I'm sorry, God! I'm sorry! I put everything before you, and I'm so very, very, very sorry, God! Please forgive me, Father! Can you please forgive me?"

I wept, and I wept, and I wept. The very next day, I asked Noah to pray with me. He cursed me out. Day after day, I asked Noah to pray, and he would curse me out down to a living dog. So I prayed. I gathered all seven of the children and formed a prayer circle. Then little by little, my husband's siblings moved out.

And then, because the Douglasville DFCS worker contacted Dekalb County, they ended up finding out that Douglas County had not informed them that their foster children were in their jurisdiction.

You see, Douglas County was receiving government funding when the whole time it should have been Dekalb. When Dekalb contacted Douglas and got answers from them, social workers from Dekalb showed up at our house.

After three years of raising Lizzy's children, they were taken away from me so fast. I cried so hard for those kids. Lizzy made it clear that she didn't want her kids. She was given chance after chance to retrieve them from DFCS many times before and told me in plain words that I could have them. I didn't know what was going to happen to them, and I missed them so much.

Before I knew it, it was back to being just the six of us in the house; Me, Noah, Que, Angelica, Manny, and Queenie. Then, strange things started happening in that house. The stove had caught on fire all by itself without anyone cooking. Then I started having bad dreams about slaves being killed on that property.

One night, and I can remember it like it was yesterday, Noah and I laid in the bed and the bedroom door flew open! I know I heard someone, or something, say, "Get Out!" I thought it was just me. When I asked Noah if he heard anything, he repeated the same thing that I thought I heard. So, we both heard it.

Not even long after that, our bathroom caught fire. The blessing was that it didn't spread to the other parts of the house. And then it happened a second time.

After that, Noah and I tried to put the house up for sale. Come to find out, the houses were built across the street from a landfill, so it was hard to sell. So, we were left with no choice but to walk away after seven years of living there.

Between not having any money, bill collectors and lawyers sending letters about foreclosure on the only home that our kids had ever known, DFCS in and out of our lives, and having nobody to help or to talk to, sent me into a very deep depression. I lost my way.

The kids, Noah and I packed our things into a small U-Haul truck and took one last look at the house that we saw get built from the ground up.

Chapter Twenty

Learning How To Fight Back

It had been so long since Noah and I lived in an apartment, but we had to move into one. The last time we were in an apartment, the kids were still small, and Queenie wasn't even born yet. Now it was six people in a three-bedroom apartment. However, the bedrooms in the apartment were bigger than the ones at the house.

I might not have liked the house at first, but to move back into apartments was what I considered below the level in life that we had in mind. I felt like a loser. Especially when the kids had to leave their private school to go to a public school.

We hadn't moved into the apartment for a good month when a lawyer contacted me regarding Lizzy's kids. Lizzy was on the phone also. The lawyer asked me if I could get the kids if they were able to get them back from DFCS. I would have, but I was too ill. Then he asked Lizzy if she wanted to try to get her kids. She said nothing. After that, we never saw nor heard from them again.

Meanwhile, with our kids, Angelica and Que felt out of place. Que was now in middle school and started to hang out with the wrong crowd and use profanity. Angelica came home exhausted daily because the public school system was so overrun with the lack of funding, teachers, parental involvement, and so much more.

I found out that Angelica couldn't do her homework because the teachers needed her to help other kids who were falling behind. So they basically had our daughter helping the teachers to teach.

Angelica would come home crying because of the school assignments that her class was doing. She had already done them two years prior. Although I was young without much education myself, I knew that I didn't want our children going backward.

Then when Queenie was old enough to attend, she came home with her hair bows pulled from her scalp all the way down to the bottom of her long ponytails. And Manny was constantly getting into fights. Enough was enough. I tried to get vouchers to send them to an all-girl and all-boy school, but that was wishful thinking. Then my Godmother told me about homeschooling. I called the Dekalb County Board of Education and asked them what I needed to do.

I was told to withdraw them from school and submit a declaration with an intent to homeschool along with an attendance form that I had to submit every month. Then I asked about books and other education material they would need. The lady who I was speaking to about this said, "Those are your children. You find them a curriculum." 'Ok, I will,' I thought to myself. The next day, I went to the elementary school and withdrew the youngest three. Then I had to get ready to go to Que's middle school.

I had it made up in my mind that I didn't want to ask Noah for shit! Even though we lived together and slept in the same bed, things were still the same. When he found out that I was going to homeschool the kids, he got nervous. I was as well, but it was too late to turn back. So the next day, Que and I were walking to his school. Then I saw a U-Haul truck come towards us and pull over. It was Noah driving one of the trucks he was working on. He picked us up and gave us a ride to the school. When we got there, he came inside with us and helped to get Que withdrawn from school.

On the way home, we didn't say nothing to each other. That was what he and I had come to. We hardly spoke. Just asking each other the questions that needed to be asked, responding to what we needed to respond to. Basically, we just stayed out of each other's way.

The only reason why we were still living together was because we didn't have enough money to separate. Plus, I had no place else to go. And if I did leave, what about the children? Now that they were homeschooled, they not only witnessed more fussing and fighting, but they also witnessed the amount of pills I was taking.

I was taking so many pills that when I was flatulent or belched, I could smell the medication, and so could everybody else. Noah had given up on me at that point. He even told me he did. He said that I had the opportunity to get us out of financial hardships by using my

God-given talents. I wouldn't try to take it, and he would be stuck in a dead-end job forever because of it. He looked at me as if I had given up and even lost respect for me. I guess he felt like I was Edward by having what it took to keep my family from suffering and from going into poverty, but I refused to do it. But that wasn't the case.

Noah didn't understand what my body felt like. On top of all that, he and Calvin were telling me to lose weight that I gained so that I could go back to do the music. But how? All I could do day-in and day-out was lie in bed. I didn't even know where God was. I prayed, but I didn't feel him the same way. I didn't feel me. One day, I had slept so long. I woke up to Noah vacuuming the apartment. Then Angelica brought me some grilled cheese and a bowl of soup while I was still in bed. Then I looked up to see Noah standing over me.

"You did this for me?" I asked. "Yes, I did," he replied, "I wish my father had done this for my mother. I took a good look and noticed that the kids were happy to see us talking to each other. Then I looked around the bed for my pills.

"I hid them," Noah said.

"Noah! Please!" I yelled.

"Shawnie! You're gonna die and leave these babies! Please, Shawnie! Please stop taking them for our children's sake!" he cried hard wet tears, begging me to stop taking the pills. The kids saw him on his knees, begging me to get better. But I couldn't shake them. The medication had such a stronghold over me. So strong that it wouldn't let me go. I couldn't cook, I couldn't homeschool, I couldn't function. I escaped from everything by taking the pills.

Then Noah's attention focused on the children, and he started to let me go. After that, days went on as normal as we knew it. Then Noah came home one day to tell me that he was laid off from work. 'Here we go again,' I thought to myself.

The economy was in a downturn, and there were really no jobs that were hiring. So Noah turned to a friend who taught him how to do auto repair. He worked for him to keep the rent paid. Due to my illness, I started receiving SSI. Once again, I had to ask for food stamps. Noah had a problem with that. But how were we going to tell our children that they couldn't eat because we were too prideful to ask for food stamps? The blessing was we were able to make the rent.

In time, Noah bought a green 2000 Pontiac Plymouth and started up his own roadside service business. He tried once before while we were still living at our house and tried to network with people to build up a customer base. But we didn't realize how clique-ish people in Dekalb county were. When he told people that he was a mechanic and could fix their cars, they would ask him if he was a Jehovah's Witness, a seven-day Adventist, or what church he went to. If he wasn't affiliated with their denomination, they wouldn't allow him to work on their cars. Even while he was working at U-Haul, he begged the men he worked with to teach him how to fix cars so that he could make more money. But the crab-in-the-barrel syndrome was so strong in Decatur that older black men wouldn't show a young black man how to help him make a living for his family. Them helping another person meant taking something away from themselves. They didn't help one another because they didn't want anyone to have more than what they had. Unfortunately for us, we had fallen into that barrel.

Noah got out every day to hustle. That year, while living in the apartments, the summer was extremely hot. Noah wasn't only hustling for the family, he was also the only one driving. So he would have to take me to the store to buy groceries. He was tired, and his eyes stayed bloodshot red, and he kept stomach aches. The most I could do was give him some baking soda and Coca-Cola to make him belch.

Then one day, he got a call from Samuel, asking him to come to Buckhead to fix one of his co-worker's cars. I was at home with the kids. Later that same day, Samuel called and said, "Uh, Shawnie. Noah's gonna have to go to the hospital."

"Why? What's going on?"

"He said his stomach is hurting and he started vomiting. The ambulance already came and got him."

I got up and put the kids on some clothes. Samuel came and picked us up in his little silver Toyota Camry. Noah was in triage when we got to the hospital, lying on the hospital bed still in his uniform, barely awake.

I walked over to him and said, "Noah?" He heard me and tried to open his eyes. When he did, tears came from both sides, "Baby, please," he said, "It hurts." I was numb. I really didn't know what to feel. Then I saw Angelina lay on his chest. With every tear she cried, she would make a cross on his forehead with her tears. I knew then that I had to put my hurt aside and fight for their father, for them, for my family, and, yes, for my husband. He laid there completely helpless. Finally, when one of the nurses came in, I asked her what was wrong.

She said, "He has Pancreatitis and we've just diagnosed him with Diabetes," she explained.

I didn't know the severity of what was going on with Noah. I didn't know what Pancreatitis was or what it was supposed to do. Then the doctor came in the room while Noah's siblings were there. He asked me if he could speak with me alone.

I said, "These are Noah's siblings. Whatever you need to say to me, they need to hear it as well. "Well, Mrs. Smith, your husband is a very sick man. He has to have surgery to have his Gallbladder removed. He has Diabetes…," the doctor went on and on.

I broke down. Begging God, negotiating with God, and bargaining with God. I just wanted my husband alive. Noah was incoherent. Going in and out of consciousness. The doctors put him on a Morphine drip. I was scared as hell. I'd never been so scared in my entire life.

Noah was about 5'8" to 5'9," and he weighed over 360 pounds. I knew something wasn't right about his health because his fingers started to swell, and puss would come from beneath his fingernails. He was barely able to breathe. Noah and his siblings suffered severe hunger when they were children. So when they were able to sustain themselves, they would eat out of stress, comfort, worry, boredom, and no matter what, they ate a lot. Noah, Mavis, Angeline, and Messiah were all obese. Noah's obesity has taken a toll on him.

While my weight gain was due to the pills, I still cooked healthy food at home. What I didn't know was that Noah was out eating Chinese food at work as well as at other fast-food places after eating his lunch that I sent with him and then coming back home for dinner with the family. He didn't tell me this until later. Noah had kept so much from me out of pure shame or stupidity. Then I got pissed because everybody on both sides of our family started to blame me! I told everybody that Noah was a grown-ass man. Whenever I got in the car with him, I would find honeybun wrappings, Dunkin' Donuts pastries from gas stations, cans of Sodas and energy drinks, candy bar wrappings, chips, and various miniature cakes and pies. The same kind of shit that I didn't even eat!

After Noah was given a hospital room, I took the kids down to the hospital cafeteria and bought them some food. They were all worried about their daddy. After bringing the kids back to his room, we stayed there and watched over Noah until it was late. By the time it was dark outside, a nurse had come in the room and saw all of us crowded in the corner of the hospital room where there was only one green armchair. The nurse told us that all of us could not stay there. When I heard her say that, I didn't know what I was going to do. First, I knew that my family wasn't responsible. I didn't want to send my kids with them. Then there was Noah's family. I knew they didn't like me, so I didn't know how they would treat my children.

Secondly, I didn't want to leave the hospital. I wanted to make sure that Noah was very well taken care of. I was in between a rock and a hard place. Whether I leave the hospital and Noah perishes from lack of care, or I leave the children and risk their safety. Truthfully, I didn't trust anyone with my children. They were always with me. So much to the point that they were attached to me.

I begged Mavis to please take care of our children. I knew she didn't care for me, but that was not the time. I begged them all just to please look after the kids. Samuel and Messiah hugged me so tight and said, "We got the kids."

As tired as Noah was, I had to tell him where I was sending the children. I said, "Noah? I'm going to have to send the kids to your family." As tired and semiconscious as Noah was, he said through a tired and weak voice, "no, no!" He shook his head.

"But Noah, the nurses said that we all can't stay here,"

"No, stay together. Stay together," he shook his head again. I could feel the determination he had of wanting to keep up together.

I was crying, hurting, and unsure. I thought about where to send our children long and hard. That was one of the hardest decisions I had ever had to make in my entire life.

Late that night, around 1am in the Morning, Samuel took the kids to Mavis's house. I stayed at the hospital with Noah. I called my mother and told her that Noah was fighting for his life. She told me that my brother's girlfriend's mother was sick and dying from cancer, so she had to see about her. Meanwhile, Noah was fighting for his life. I had to fight for my family.

All the money that I had on me was to pay the rent. I had to choose between the rent, the car note, and insurance on the only vehicle we had or food for myself at the hospital. But I knew I had to keep the vehicle straight because Noah had just started to do the roadside service business and all of his tools were in there. So, I paid the insurance. I paid it with a check that I knew was not going to clear just to buy time. Then, I called the car loan people to tell them that Noah was sick. So they deferred the payment. I had to spread that money thin.

Every day I washed Noah's body and lotioned him down. He was hooked up to so many devices. He had antibiotics running through him, a tube going through the hole of his penis, and all kinds of things on each of his arms. On top of all that, they had a sign on the door that said NPO which meant no food, no water, nor anything else that was ingested by mouth because they were cleaning his system. He hadn't had any water. Then one day, he looked at me and whispered, "Water. Water. Shawnie, please. Water."

"But the doctors said I can't" "Shawnie?" he put his hands together in a prayer position as if he was saying, 'Please. I'm begging you."

That broke my heart. I went and got a clean rag and put ice in it. I ran the rag under cold water until it was soaked. I went back to Noah's bedside and said, "Honey, I'm going to wash your face with this rag," I said aloud. To make sure no one heard me, I brought my lips to his ear and whispered, "I'm going to run this over your mouth and I want you to suck the water out of it. Do you hear me?"

He nodded 'yes'. I did that countless times.

Then I would hear, "Shawnie? Shawnie?" Noah whispered as he could barely speak, "Bathroom." I jumped up and moved all of the wires as fast as I could. I helped him up. He took two steps and then stopped. He looked at me, and then bowels went everywhere. It wasn't the normal color as a regular stool, but it had the rock-like substance in the stool. He was looking at me deep in the eyes, and tears started to run from his. I said, "Hold on, stop! And I damn well mean it! You have taken care of our babies for years! You better not cry or feel bad! Do you understand me? I wish you would cry!"

I took him on to the bathroom and washed him down. I asked the nurses for towels, rags, soap, and gloves. I cleaned him and the room. The nurses came in and said to me, "I've never seen a woman love her husband as much as you do. Most people would call us or a custodian to clean up waste. My hats off to you ma'am."

Noah was my husband and my responsibility. I didn't know how we lost touch with each other, but we did. Some people thought that just because you're married you can't be lonely or struggle. I heard people say all the time, "You got somebody. I'm doing it by myself," or, "At least you're not alone." Well, that wasn't true. A person could be lonely, single, and struggle in all aspects inside a marriage. Just because some people are married doesn't make anyone exempt from the same struggles and loneliness that a single person goes through. Although Noah and I were going through the motions in our marriage, his life was more important to me than how angry we were with each other. I made sure he was taken care of. We were there for days, and not one visitor came until one of his friends, Garland, showed up with his girlfriend, who just so happened to be a doctor. She had the nerve to come to my husband and ask him in her Jamaican accent, "You're not eating healthy at home. Do you want me to come cook for you?" It took everything in my power to keep me from knocking that disrespectful ass bitch out! Since Garland and Noah were friends and Noah was an apprentice under him, I didn't want to wreck their relationship by going off on his girlfriend. But I was so very hurt.

I looked at Noah lying in bed, fighting for his life; our children were at Mavis's house going through God knows what. I was the only one who was able to fight for all of us. I had depended on Noah for so long that all I could do was pray and ask God for guidance.

I was lost, confused, worried, and damn near hopeless. But I had to go on. I couldn't take the pills and become numb. I had to take them to cope, and unfortunately, I needed them more than ever. I was sleeping on what was supposed to have been a bed in the patient's room, but it was small and very hard. It was so uncomfortable that it triggered my illness, causing more pain. Still, I had to fight through. Two weeks later, Samuel came by the hospital to give me the eviction papers that were on the door of our apartment. Noah had been laid off from his job. With that happening, it ended our medical insurance. We had no money.

Every day it was a battle and mine to lose. However, losing was not an option. I had to deal with the reality that we were about to be homeless. I had no idea where we were going to go or who could help us. Then, I called Mom to tell her that we were about to get evicted from our apartment and if we could stay with her for a few weeks until we could find our own place to stay. I didn't know how or with what money we couldn't find anywhere, but the clock was ticking. I said, "Mom, we were served with an eviction saying we have to come to court. But I know we're not going to be able to meet the rent because we have no money. Is it okay with you that we stay until we can get back on our feet?" "Well," she said, "Quint's Grandma's house burned down and they needed somewhere to stay. SO I told them that they could move in with me, so no." she replied.

"So, do you know anybody who got a place for rent?" "Yeah. The man renting me this house name is Manuel Hutchison. He's African. Tell him that you're my daughter and you need a place to stay as soon as possible. And tell him I need a new stove." I wanted to yell at her and tell her to tell the guy herself. I sat there and thought to myself, 'This motherfucker that beat and dogged me out, you're willing to help them?! But the man who got out and took care of your daughter and grandchildren is fighting for his life, and this is the shit you say to me?'

I then had to put on the biggest shoes of my life to make the hospital believe that money wasn't an issue for us. Just as long as they took care of my husband. Later on, I reached out to the medical financial department and applied for emergency Medicaid.

Nobody, and I mean nobody in my family, lifted a finger to help me. Nobody came to the hospital to see Noah. Not only was it hurtful, but it was also embarrassing. I thought that my family would be there for me in a life-or-death situation. I thought that since it was serious, they would have shown some kind of support.

I mean, I've seen these people break their backs and go out of their way for other people. But not me. They abandoned me. They left me. They really left my family and me out to dry. I was actually shocked. I knew that they had always let me down, but for one second, with all the sadness and the life-threatening things going on in my life, I thought they would set aside everything and be there…. they didn't come.

Derreck, Teddy, Shane, and Joey were all dead. With all of our loved ones dying like that, I thought that their hearts might have softened. Apparently not. Beforehand, I never thought that I would be able to cast my family off, especially after what happened with my mom and Teddy. I never wanted to be at odds with my family in case something ever happened. If Noah's siblings hadn't pulled together, I didn't know what we would have done. I was so hurt and broken that I grew a hatred and numbness that I never thought I could have.

After about 2 weeks of staying in the hospital, Noah was finally getting discharged. He had lost so much weight. It was bad enough that no one was willing to help us. Then, to add insult to injury, Mavis called me and said that my mother had picked up the kids and took them with her. I couldn't even get mad. Although we had gotten an eviction letter, we still had a few days before it was in effect, so Noah and I went back to the apartment to spend the rest of the days there. Then, Mom dropped the kids back off at Mavis's and Samuel brought them back to us. When they got home, Angeline and Que looked at me and asked, "Ma? Who's Quint?" I almost fainted when they said his name, "Where did you hear that name?" I asked.

"Grandma said that you treat her like she is Quint or somebody. She said that you didn't want her to see us," they explained. I was pissed! So now, they've told my kids about Quint, which I asked them not to do! If ever they were to hear about Quint, Noah and I were going to do it our way. I was already filled with rage and so many other emotions.

I picked up the phone and dialed my Mama's number, "Mama?" I said, "Why did you tell my children about Quint?!"

"What you mean, lil girl?..."

"Stay the FUCK away from my family!" I yelled after cutting her off.

Then Mama called Grandma and lied about what I said as usual. She told Grandma that I told her that she almost made me lose my husband. As colorful as Mama was, she didn't possess that kind of power. Only God himself had that power, so I know I didn't say that.

I knew what I said. But it got around the family that I called and cursed her out. But I was already at a point where I didn't care about what they thought.

I went ahead and called Manuel Hutchison about the house he had for rent. He told us to give him eight hundred dollars down and we could move in. I called and asked Messiah if he had any money that he could spare. He gave us his entire check. Along with the check I had from SSI, I was blessed to make the payment.

The house was a royal blue and white color with a screened porch. It looked small on the outside, but the rooms were huge! It had three bedrooms and 2 ½ bathrooms, a pecan tree in the backyard, and a separate garage from the house on the side. The house was nearly one-hundred years old, and it was in Atlanta, which meant that we were moving right back to the city.

For a vehicle, Noah and I used a van that his friend let him borrow. But Noah was so weak and sick that he couldn't do anything. So, Messiah, Mavis's son, and I had to move everything out from the apartment to the house. After about a week of resting in early

September, Noah got up and said, "I gotta go back to work."

"Noah, you gotta heal," I told him, "You still haven't had that surgery." Noah got up anyways and went to put in an application at Advance Auto Parts. The next day, he went to Buckhead looking for a job. While he was out, driving around looking for places to apply, he had to pull over to the side of the road sometimes and throw up. But he continued to push. Eventually, he ran into an auto shop called Atlanta Tire & Auto, where black men ran the shop. The men who ran it were all republicans, and they believed in helping each other and upholding family values.

When Noah went inside, he was quizzed by one of the guys to see what he knew about cars. Noah was able to answer the questions correctly. Then Charles, the supervisor, asked Noah if he could pass a drug test and background check. Noah told them that he could.

When they asked Noah how much he made at his last auto repair job, he told them he was making $11.75 an hour. All the guys looked at each other and burst out laughing. Then they said, "Come on man! With all of that knowledge you have, there is no way you only made $11.75 and hour! If you could pass a drug and background check, something had to be wrong!" So they gave Noah an address to go to get tested as well as do a background check. Everything came back clear. Noah didn't understand what was happening, but there really was something wrong. He didn't know his self-worth. He didn't know that jobs made offers to people who were knowledgeable and experienced. He thought that jobs only hired on the going rate. But this job offered him a salary. Something he never had. He was barely making $20,000 a year to take care of a family of six, including himself.

He came home after he was hired and sat down on the bed next to me and said, "Shawnie, Do you know that people earn tons of money per year in this business?" He and I were both shocked. Unfortunately, his co-workers at U-Haul didn't tell him this nor help him. Those older black men knew that Noah had what it took to be a great technician. But, instead of telling him of his potential, they lied to him and held him back. Noah looked up to them. He admired them. But they wanted to be the only ones who others looked up to. But God is a good God. Anything and everything is possible through him.

Chapter Twenty-One
Realizing That God Loves Us Too

Now, Noah was able to get back to work, working two jobs while he was still sick. When the winter came in, it got really cold outside. Because the house that we were living in was so old, there was no proper insulation. The heater was broken and the back of the house got extremely cold. The toilet was leaning to one side, cold air seeped through the windows, and the roof had a leak. The master bedroom was the only room in the house that got heat. The kids couldn't stay in their rooms. They brought their blankets from their rooms and laid them on the floor around our bed every night.

Noah would come home, and we waited for him to bathe and then come to us and join our circle of prayer. Then, after we prayed, we all got under the covers and as a family and would watch Roots or The Nanny almost every night. Although we no longer lived in a brand-new house, we were still grateful for that one-bedroom in that very old house on the westside of Atlanta. We came to appreciate it because that was all we had. Even though the rooms had rain coming through the ceiling and the back was very cold, I felt a freedom that I hadn't felt in a very long time. We called that house, "The Blue House."

Even after a whole month of being out of the hospital, Noah was still not fully recovered. He still vomited from time to time. We knew that he needed to get that surgery. But he still got out there and worked. All I could do was pray for him. He went to his first job at Atlanta Tire & Auto and then to his second job at Advance. At Advance, customers came in and purchased brake pads, lights, starters, and other parts for their cars. So, Noah started asking customers if they had a mechanic to put the parts on for them. A lot of them replied that they didn't. Before long, Noah was getting one customer after another. The people on the west side didn't give a damn about anybody's personal life. They just wanted their cars fixed. They could have cared less about which denomination a person belonged to as long as their cars and themselves were good to go.

Noah gave me some money to buy the kids some shoes. They had worn flip-flops for so long that I hadn't realized that the weather was changing. I was given enough money to get them all a pair of K-Swiss. I also got Noah and myself some clothes and shoes. When it was time to pay the rent, I called the owner of the house, Manuel, so that I could pay what we owed for that month but I couldn't get a hold of him. Then, on an early weekday morning, a gentleman showed up on the porch stating that the house was going into foreclosure because

Manuel had not paid the mortgage. We found out that he pulled money out of the house before he fled back to Africa. At any time, the people could have put us out. For months, we were on borrowed time. We were practically homeless because the house didn't belong to us, and if we had been told to leave, where would we have gone?

Noah and I drove around the city almost every day until we found a house that was newly built. We got in contact with the owner and learned that he was also African. That made us uncomfortable, but we had no other options. The house was on University Avenue, right off the expressway. During that time, Atlanta was going through a regentrification. What was the hood was no longer the hood. We packed our things and moved in.

It was a two-story house and very comfortable and closer to Noah's job. After we moved in, Noah got sick almost immediately and had to go back to the hospital. This time when he went, they kept him to proceed with the surgery he needed. He had private insurance through his job as well as Medicaid. But that wasn't the greatest of my worry. I was worried about him going through the procedure and how it would affect our lives, wondering if it would start falling apart.

While Noah was getting his surgery done, I was shocked when his manager from Atlanta Tire & Auto called and asked, "How can we assist your family in your time of need?" I didn't even know how to respond. Even more, co-workers from both of his jobs came to visit him. After Noah got his gallbladder removed and his diabetes under control, he started to look healthier. Noah had gone from nearly four-hundred pounds to one-hundred eighty-five. The most that he picked up after he was released was fifteen pounds. After he finally started to heal, his whole demeanor had changed. He was very well employed, and his business was on the rise. He was no longer that gullible country boy anymore. He found himself so much that I was left behind. I had to come to realize that his change was so much that I hardly knew anything about him anymore. We hardly knew each other.

I also started to realize that we had done so little talking and so much struggling that we didn't even take a break to learn each other. We didn't even know ourselves. We were so busy fighting over our past and our parents that we saw through each other that we had never even introduced ourselves to each other. Things we both wanted to say to our parents but never had the balls to say came as an opportunity to say to each other because we knew we were both harmless to each other. The other wasn't going to leave, so we slung degrading insults as if we could give a damn about each other. The scars we caused were reopened every chance we got.

We were strangers. Maybe that sounds crazy, but it's not. We had both come from a rough childhood, then we got together and started having a hard time. It was like we couldn't catch a break. We had no therapy, no support, and no outlet, so we had to suppress our emotions.

As Noah's business started taking off, I started doing extra things around the house so that he could see me. I also tried to make it look like I had business about myself as well. For example, whenever customers came to get their cars fixed, I would go to the door and offer water or drinks to them. I tried to help as much as I could and hoped that he would notice. But he still looked at me as if I was nothing. I tried to overcompensate so that I wouldn't be viewed as a burden. It felt like he was tired of me. Then, he started treating me the same way Mama was treating me when she got back on her feet. That hurt me on the inside. I had no money of my own. Nothing. I was empty and burdensome, and I couldn't do anything about it. The situation was like being on the job and having no idea what to do to satisfy the boss. The boss knows he's going to get rid of you and you know that it's only a matter of time. So you go out of your way to please him. He jokes and smiles with everyone else, but when it comes to you, his mood changes. Then you try to make it look like whatever it is you're doing is important and try to make yourself important, but that doesn't work either. Noah had become so rude and disrespectful. He told me that I would be in the same boat as a person on welfare and in the projects if he ever died. Nonetheless, I still tried to be warm and welcoming to the customers who came by. Then he said, "Stop running out there! You don't have to run outside every time somebody comes!"

The chills that had come over me could have frozen water. All I could do was pop more pills and eat sherbet and gain more weight. I cried a whole lot. Then, he stopped taking me places, so I had to catch the bus. My body flared up all the time. I called the ambulance many times because I was hurting so badly. Not really, I was hurting because my body needed the medication. Finally, I got taken to the ER. When I was discharged, I called Noah to see if he would pick me up. "Noah? I called an ambulance and they brought me to Piedmont. Can you come get me please?"

"I'm at work," he said quickly.

"Well, I have no way home."

"Uh, I'm at work," he said very cold-heartedly.

I had to call Samuel instead. He brought me home. Then Noah got home, took a shower, and went to bed. A few days later, he finally gave me a ride to the store. One of Noah's customers had written him a check before. So he stopped by the bank on the way home. He left me in the car while he went inside. I waited in the car for what seemed like hours. I saw people who had just arrived at the bank walk in and right back out. Then Noah came out and started walking back to the car with a blue folder in his hand. He left me sitting in a hot car while he was opening up a new bank account. He told me nothing after he got back in the car. We hadn't had a bank account in years, so he opened one up without me. He was moving on with his life.

I cried the whole night. I even slept at the bottom of the bed. The following days that had come, we argued and argued. It was clear that he wanted out and I wasn't going to hold him hostage. Then he asked me, "If you had the money, would you move out?" Then I asked, "If I had the money, would you want me to move out?"

Noah and I were worlds apart. We were just there in the same house. Not even on roommate status. Then he didn't want me answering his phone out of fear of scaring his female customers away. I needed to figure out what to do in my life because I was too worried about him.

I started accusing him of cheating on me, and then he called me the worst thing that he could have ever called me, and that was a fucking mooch! He told me that I was mooching off of him. I knew then that something had to give. I mean, this man was looking at me out of the corner of his eyes as if he wanted me gone! I had to find "Shawnie". But all I really had at that time was God and my children. I was receiving SSI, but they cut my check to $80 per month. Then, they changed the doctor that I was seeing before to a doctor named Dr. Meadows. When I first walked into his office, I was hoping that he would write my prescription. When I was called to a room, this handsome, very kind gentleman walked in the room and looked at me eye to eye.

"Hello, I'm Dr. Meadows. Nice to meet you.

"Nice to meet you too," I replied.

"Now, I just have one question. Who in the hell put you on Soma?"

I went down the line of all the doctors and pharmacies I got the prescription from. Then he said, "This is a very heavy narcotic, and I'm going to help wean you off of this." I was happy but scared at the same time. Taking the medication was like holding on to a chair or a rail. I needed them to keep me up. I didn't know what would happen without them. Dr. Meadows told me that he knew I had a very real condition and Soma was not going to work. He didn't take them away from me right away. Instead, he started to go down on the quantity of pills. At first, it was ninety, then it was sixty, then thirty, and so on.

Then one day, it happened that Noah was taking some Tylenol three for a toothache that he had. I didn't have any of my medicine on me, so I took one of those. They didn't make me feel numb, intoxicated, nor high. It did take a bit of an edge off the pain, but not like the Soma and Demerol did. The Tylenol, along with Ibuprofen, helped to manage the pain. I told Dr. Meadows what I had done, and he immediately stopped the Soma. Tylenol was a very mild control medication. Anything else would have been too strong; he kept me there at Tylenol three.

That was the beginning of my journey to get off of Soma and everything else. For more progress, I attended an AA meeting. I was told that one must take one day at a time. And it was truly one day at a time. I was battling with myself. My mind would tell me, 'You need it. You're hurting. It's red pain. All you're doing is getting through.' The body aches, the chills, the withdrawals, and the shaking was worth enduring knowing what stood on the other side; that was freedom.

Although I started to work on my medication addiction, I was still dealing with depression. I was so depressed that I wanted the weather to be bad so that I could have a reason to hurt. I kept a thermometer near my bed, hoping to have a fever. I even lifted my weights at an angle to make my arms flair up with pain and swelling.

I wanted it to rain so the weather could match my feelings. I didn't want to hear good news and I wanted a reason to cry. I wanted pity, and I had to realize that Noah wasn't attending the pity party any longer. In fact, he revoked the invitations and decided to get himself and the kids out of harm's way while getting on with his life. He told me before that he had given up on me; he proved it every single day.

Then, I remember getting out of bed and going to the bathroom. I looked at myself in the mirror and said to myself, 'You're fat, dumb, and a high school dropout. Nobody loves you. Your own mother hates you. You have no money, no job, or nowhere to go. You can't even buy yourself a bag of chips and a drink! You're broke! You're broken! Everyone had given up on you! You accuse your husband of cheating on you with other women because you're worthless! Just look at you! And... what are *you* going to do about it?'

I looked at my hair. It was already falling out, so I took the scissors and cut the rest down to the size of a short fade on a boy. Then, I called my nephew, Kerry, to set up a computer in our house because I wanted to type a letter.

After he set it up, he told me to go online and download a program that would allow me to type the letter. I didn't know what he was talking about. So he moved the cursor to the top of the computer and started typing, *www.*

I asked, "What is the 'www'?"

"Auntie," he replied, "that's the world wide web, and you can do anything on a computer." My family and I had gone through so much hardship that I didn't realize that the world had moved forward. I was so messed up on those pills that I didn't realize that life was passing us by. I had no idea what the hell the internet was supposed to do. All I knew was that I was paying for it because it was a part of our cable package.

When I sobered up completely, I had no idea that I was already twenty-eight years old. I was knocking on thirty, and the world had changed so much. When Kerry got it all set up, he opened me up to the world. I will always be grateful to him for that. I surfed and surfed the web and learned the computer. Then I found out about homeschooling online. So, I started to homeschool the children and myself. I would get up early in the morning and stay on the computer until nightfall. There were so many connections and information that I wanted to eat it all up!

I later enrolled myself in an online accredited school. Noah gave me the money to attend. Through that curriculum, I learned GUM (grammar usage and mechanics), English, English as a second language, American lit, Math, and oh my God, everything that I had missed out on as a kid. I learned to speak better and taught my children. Noah saw me learning and he started making small conversations with me. Then I went and bought myself a pair of glasses and I was on a roll! Any money that I needed, Noah gave me. Then one day, he surprised me with a cell phone of my own. Even more surprising, he went out of his way to be nice to me. Though I appreciated Noah being kind to me, I could have used that a long time ago. But I needed to stay focused on myself. So every night, when the day of learning had come to an end, I made sure that I put my kids in my prayer circle with me. For sure, I stopped asking Noah to pray with us. I stopped putting Noah, the kids, and myself before God. I couldn't say that I loved God and truly mean it when I didn't even love myself. So all of the times that I said that I loved God before, I didn't really mean it. It was just something to say. It sounded good, but it was a lie. I had come to understand that in order to love God, I had to first love myself and know what "love" meant.

I knew that my children loved me and that Noah loved me. But how could I be sure? Love was a stranger to me. Again, like it was for many people, love was a luxury that I couldn't afford. I wasn't able to feel it, touch it, or even understand it. Every day, morning, noon, and night, I prayed. I changed my eating habits as well. Being a Jenny Craig lifetime member was beneficial because I was able to go back to it. But I wanted to learn how to eat regular food because Jenny's meals were so high that I couldn't afford them on my own. So, I joined Weight Watchers. I purchased pre-prepped meals from Walmart. One night, I was getting ready to purchase some of the meals with dessert when the cash register started having issues. The woman at the register called for her manager to come over.

Then this tall, beautiful girl came over to get things working again. She looked at my groceries and asked, "Do you like those Weight Watcher meals?"

"Yes, I do," I replied, "I'm trying the new ones. And I want to try to lose about twenty pounds."

"I'm on the program too."

"Oh wow! Did it help you lose weight?"

"Girl, yes! I lost about fifty pounds."

I smiled, "I'm trying my best to get there!"

"Maybe we can keep in touch. I'm Lucy, by the way," she said as she wrote down and gave me her number.

"I'm Shawnie, and here is my number." I was so happy to meet someone else who was on the same journey as me.

Lucy and I started to meet up with each other almost every week. We even became good friends. Eventually, she and her husband,

Timothy, had become Noah's customers as well. Lucy always wore nice clothes and jewelry. She inspired me to do the same.

I started back wearing my hair long. I took time to lotion my body down and moisturize myself. I watched my weight and started to feel me. I began to feel the love that I had for myself. I had been looking for others to give me that fulfillment. I was looking for other people to give a damn about me. But that wasn't their job.

It was my job to love myself the way that I wanted to be loved. And only I could love me in the way that I craved. Once I fell in love with me, I knew what love was. It's unexplainable compassion that surpasses all understanding. And that compassion addresses all things in every shape, form, fashion, or being.

Once I felt that awesome emotion, I thanked God almighty because only he could create such romantic chaos that embraces the soul. It was He who gave me life, who allowed me to travel to this world through the vehicle called a womb that was driven by Patricia.

He sent me here. He blew breath into me and gave me life and love. And for that and so many more unthinkable things, God, I love you. My prayer to him:

God, I love you, God, I'm in love with you. I love you God. I love you heavenly father. I love you, my creator. I love you, I love, I love you more than I love my own self. If it wasn't for you, almighty God, there would be no me. And I love you more because you gave me to myself.

From that day forward, I acknowledged myself. I esteemed myself. My education of self and life overwhelmed me. After a while, all that was negative started to become uncomfortable. It even burned my ears. I no longer wanted any part in it. I wanted to live! Not just live, I wanted to be alive! The pressure that was brought on by God was to turn us into the diamonds that He knew we were. Then there was the pressure that we brought upon ourselves, like taking in children for the wrong reason. Nevertheless, the enemy can plan for something bad--not saying it was bad that I got the kids--God can use it for our own good. So we had to understand to trust the process that God had laid out before us. Not what we think we should do.

When you trust in God and his timing, he gives you the full package equipped with everything. When we try to skip the process or take the shortcut, we'll continue to set the restart button and repeat the lesson over and over again until we get it, no matter how old we get.

That's what Noah and I came to realize. Every time we argued, God put us right back where we left off.

Later on, Mom would call from time to time. I would always cry whenever she did because I had not addressed my resentment for her. Me being on those pills for so long had me out of touch with life. Everything that was there when I got on those pills was still waiting for me when I got off. But everything was more than what it once was when I checked out. Even our children were older.

One day, Angelica called to me with all of her siblings. Even Noah was there. They all surrounded me as if they were doing an interview on me. "Mom?" Angelica spoke, "we see how hard you're working on getting yourself and us back together again. But every time you come so far, your family starts calling you, and you always end up crying or upset. Especially your mom."

It seems like you want her love so bad that you're willing to compromise your own family for it. And, God forgive me for what I'm about to say but, I hate your family. They have never done anything to help us. All they do is hurt you and make you cry. Then, you start pulling away from us. We're just scared that you're going to go back to those dark days again." Then Manny spoke, "Mama, we are tired of you and Dad fighting each other. We love both of you." Then Que spoke up, "Y'all are our parents. Y'all are our heroes. When ya'll tear each other down, it hurts us because we love both of you." I knew that everything going on with Noah and me had started to wear down on the kids.

I knew it when Angelica and I were watching ex-husbands versus ex-wives on the Family Feud. Angelica asked me, "Mom? How do the people from each side know each other?"

I pointed to the screen and said, "See right there where it says ex-husbands versus ex-wives?

"Oh," she said, "I wonder who the kids went with."

"Angie, do you think about stuff like this?"

"All the time," she said as tears dripped from her eyes.

I could tell that she was filled with worry and uncertainty. I could tell that they started to realize what the hell was really going on. So that family meeting was no surprise to me at all. After everyone had spoken, Manny said, "When you and Dad were fussing one time, Que put a knife to his throat and said he was going to kill himself."

Lord have mercy, Jesus! What had we done? We were trying so hard not to become our parents, but we had become a product of their misfortunes and failures. We were dead smack in the middle of becoming something damn near worse than what we had as a parent because now, our children were talking about suicide!

I looked at our four smart, beautiful, brave, God-loving, God-fearing babies and said, "Babies. Mommy is so very sorry. I take full responsibility for everything. And y'all are absolutely right, and I'm going to fix it, okay?"

We all hugged each other. I came to grips that they were young men and women, and I didn't want to lose my children's respect for me. When we prayed after that, I started allowing them to pray as well.

Whenever one finished his or her prayer, I called on the next one until everyone had said their prayer. Noah had never been a part of the circle. But he started to notice that everything I said, I would always say 'me and the kids'. Usually, before we prayed, we would all bathe and brush our teeth before circling around my bed. One night when we were circling up, we heard somebody open the door. It was Noah. "Hey, Daddy!" the kids greeted him, "Do you want to pray with us?" "Sure," he said. He joined in with us. After each one of us said our prayer, I called for Noah to pray as well. He started to pray:

Oh Allah, thank you for blessing my family. I didn't know that this was what my wife was teaching our children to do, which is to pray to you. Thank you so much for my family…

Noah went on to pray as the overwhelming emotions took control. He prayed as tears of joy flowed from his eyes. I was so thankful to God that Noah had joined us and completed our circle as a family in prayer. And he came to prayer every night. He started to pray before he went to work every morning and prayed with us at night. We would even wait until he came home before we started praying. Then, sometimes when he was still working, we called him and prayed with him over the phone.

In due time, his mood changed, and he started being nicer to me. Still, I was deeply scarred from all of the verbal abuse. The arguments turned into spats and bickering. The bickering didn't last long. I had become less argumentative and started to get back to where I left off in my life, which was about twenty years old.

I liked short shorts and skirts, stiletto heels, and dressing exotic. I had been wearing sweats for so damn long I couldn't even fit into anything that I had that was sexy. I had to continue to lose weight.

When the swelling in my feet went down, I bought the first pair of heels that I could find. I did my hair, fixed my makeup, and looked better than when I was younger. A few days before, I planned to have lunch with Lucy. So on the day of our planned outing, I dressed in some short shorts with a pair of my heels. I thought Noah was going to be gone all day that day. But to my surprise, he walked in the house earlier than the time I was expecting him to be home. I saw him watching me, but I was moving about as if I didn't see him.

"Hey Shawnie. How you doing?" he asked.

"Oh. Hey Noah, how's it going?"

He sat on the couch and said nothing else. I could tell he wanted to ask me where I was going, but he just sat there in shock.

When I went to put my earrings on, I dropped my earring on the floor on purpose. I stood in front of him, opened my legs, and bent forward to pick it up. Out of my peripheral vision, I saw him bite his knuckle. Then I heard him whisper, "Thank you God for giving her back to me."

His little nasty ass! As I stated before, somewhere, Noah and I stopped talking and started struggling. So there were deep seeded things about him that I didn't know and vice versa. Although we were married, we still remained a mystery to each other.

When Lucy came by to pick me up, I walked out the door and left without another word. While I was out, Noah called me on my new cell phone and asked, "What are the kids having for dinner?"

I heard Angelica say in the background, "I'm thirteen years old, I know how to cook. I'm making some fried chicken with corn and salad."

Then I said, "Well, there you go. Fried chicken, corn and salad. Sounds great."

But he didn't hang up. He stayed on the phone breathing, saying, "Um. Um. Uh...Um," nothing was coming to mind.

"Okay, Noah, I'll see y'all later tonight." I hung up the phone.

I stayed out for a long time. I didn't get back until later that night.

When I walked through the front door, I saw Noah sitting on the couch. The first thing he said to me was, "You know a married woman isn't supposed to hang out like that."

"You know, a married man isn't supposed to do a lot of things. But for some married men, that rule doesn't apply."

"Shawnie, can I at least get a hug? It's been so long since I've held you in my arms. There was a time when you loved that."

"Since when have my hugs been so important to you? I craved for your hugs night after night. But you chose to push the music and everything else over me! You abandoned me!" I yelled, "You left me! You left me, you left me, you left me!" I screamed and cried.

He walked up to me and held me so tightly. Damn, I missed that! It's been so long since he held me like that. "I'm sorry, Shaw, baby. I'm so very sorry." he started kissing me. When I kissed him back, it was like eating a meal that was so good that once you took the first bite, all you could do was close your eyes and savor the moment. That was how we kissed each other. It was in a way that we never had.

My tongue was in his mouth, and his was in mine. His hands were all over me. As badly and as much as I wanted him, I had to stop. I wasn't going to make it easy for him. My heart was still broken, and he was going to have to put it back together.

Every day I made it my business to look good, smell good, and dress sexy, even in my pajamas. I walked around in heels and nice lingerie. When I was in the kitchen, he walked up behind me, pulled my hair and smelled it.

"Stop Noah!" I would say.

"What more do I need to do Shawnie? I said I was sorry."

I didn't say anything. Next thing I knew, he was starting to buy gifts and giving me large amounts of money. Then he started to go to the store with me every time I went. He even waited until I got in the tub so that he could bathe with me. Noah started to chase me. I knew it and I liked it.

"Stop playing with me Shawnie," he said.

"How am I playing with you, Noah?"

"Because you're walking around me naked and torturing me."

"I'm not torturing you, Noah."

"Come go out with me. Let me take you to dinner."

"Why now? You didn't want to take me when I was overweight and in sweatpants."

He couldn't say anything else but this, "You're my wife. I own you."

I still paid him no attention.

He continued to pursue me. Anything and everything he thought I wanted, he would buy it. At that time, Noah was making well over $275,000 per year, and he was buying me everything with damn near every dime! Then he started putting his arms around me when we went to sleep. He called me every day when he was at work, making jokes. All I could do was blush and laugh. The children knew that we were happier, and they became happy. They smiled when they saw us playing around with each other. Noah rushed home every night. He couldn't wait to get home to me. One night, he came home and found me dressed up because I was about to leave.

"Where you going, Shawnie?" he asked.

"I'm going out to Rays." So he went to the closet and started to take out some clothes. He took a shower and then got dressed. When Lucy arrived, I grabbed my purse and walked out the door. Noah came out behind me. I didn't ask him where he was going. I just got in Lucy's car.

When Noah got in his car, he turned on the radio and all I heard was *Make it last forever...don't let our love end...let me hear you tell me you want me. Let me hear you say you'll never leave me…*

He was playing Make It Last Forever by Keith Sweat. Me and Lucy headed on over to Rays. We sat down and ordered once we got there. Then I looked across a couple's table and saw Noah being seated. 'Oh my God! No, he didn't!' I said to myself. I pretended like I didn't even see him. Then he sat back and watched me. Then different men came over to our table, offering to buy both Lucy and me a drink. We politely declined and ordered our own drinks.

Then I looked over to see Noah holding up two fingers, counting the guys who had come to the table. When another guy cane, he held up three fingers. I tried my damnedest not to notice him, but he made it hard.

The waitress who was waiting at our table brought me my wine. Noah ordered a Heineken. It's been a while since I last drank alcohol. So I got tipsy fast from the first few sips I took. I started feeling good and loose. Noah saw everything, and the moment he got my attention, he stuck his tongue in the hole of the beer bottle and licked the inside. I started to sweat. Then I began to move around in my chair. I knew how his tongue felt, and the thoughts of that had me about to come out of my clothes. Then he bit his bottom lip before he mouthed to me, "I'm gonna fuck the shit out of you tonight." I read his lips as plain as day.

"Alright Lucy girl," I said, "I'm ready to get out of here."

We paid for our food and left. Before we went out the door, I saw Noah paying for his food. On the outside, Lucy asked, "Is everything okay?"

"Yeah, girl, I'm good," I smiled.

Lucy brought me home and I got out of the car. As soon as she pulled off, Noah started backing in. I got the keys from my purse and tried to open the door as fast as I could to run into the house and get a shower before he came in. But as I went to put the key through the hole, I lost my grip, and they fell on the ground. I picked them up and tried for the knob again. Before I could turn the key, he placed his hand over mine and the other in my hair and said, "Quit playing with me Shawnie." I turned the key and opened the door. Noah grabbed me from behind, "Stop, Noah, stop!" I yelled.

"You're my wife," he said. Then I whispered to him because I didn't want to wake the children, "You left me."

"I didn't leave you, Shawnie. You checked out on me. What was I supposed to do? Let our family go down?

"You could have treated me better. Or talked to me better."

"I didn't leave you. I never told you to get out and I never stopped providing for you."

"But you stopped loving me. And you gave up on me."

"I never gave up on you!"

"Yes, you did!"

"No, I didn't."

"Yes, you did! You told me you did!"

"I might have said that in an argument, but deep down, I never gave up on you! You gave up on you. You stopped trying."

Then he got up on me, "Stop playing with me, Shawnie. Stop torturing me." "I'm not playing with you, Noah!"

I was trying to go up the stairs, but he stood in front of me and blocked my way, "Tell me you love me," he said.

"I'm not going to tell you that because you told me to stop telling you that I loved you."

"I told you that because it didn't feel real to me."

"That's because you stopped loving me."

"I never stopped loving you!"

"Don't you know how badly I craved you?!" I asked as I sat down on the bottom step, "Do you know how many times I just wanted your hands on me, touching me, rubbing me, and feeling all over me? Do you, Noah? Do you know how many nights I wanted to make love to you? All I could do was wish and hold myself together. Don't you know how much I've cried? I wanted to smell you and rub my fingers through your beard. I wanted you so bad that I called your name in and out of my sleep. 'Noah? Noah? Noah, please baby, hold me'. I needed you and you weren't there. Time after time, I was on the floor rocking back and forth with my arms wrapped around myself, crying my eyes out."

"I needed you too, Shawnie. But you chose the pills over me. I begged you to get off those pills. I got on my knees and begged you. I even hid the pills, but you found 'em. You outsmarted me. Then I saw the kids suffering and shit really went sideways because you checked out. What was I supposed to do?

What was I supposed to do if you refused to get out of a burning building? 'Cause I'm damn sure not going to leave our kids to die, too. What did they do to deserve that?! They didn't ask for that, Shawnie.

Do you even realize how far gone you were? The shit scared me! The drugs were like a nigga that you chose over the children and me! How in the hell was I to compete with your choice?"

"You could have fought for me," I said.

"Fighting for you was keeping you out of harm's way. I knew your family didn't give a damn about you, so I damn sure wasn't about to put you in their care. Shawnie, I've never had to deal with this kind of situation before.

How the hell do you go from saying that you would die for us when you wouldn't even live for us? For better or for worse, Shawnie. That's what we promised each other."

"I feel like I don't even know you. You look like a stranger. You've lost so much weight. I don't know you at all, Noah, like, I've missed out on a lot."

"Well," Noah said, "We can reintroduce ourselves to each other," he handed me his hand to lift me from the step. When I stood up, he continued to hold my hand.

"It's going to take time, Noah. One day at a time."

"Stop playing with me, Shawnie," he said again, "Stop walking around me, flaunting yourself in front of me because you won't let me have you."

"I'm not trying to play around with you, Noah."

"Tell me you love me, Shawnie," he said as I turned my head from left to right, avoiding his face that was close to mine.

"I can't right now. I'll have to think about it."

"Please, Shawnie," he said while he placed his hand on my butt.

Then he put his hands in the back of my panties. Before I could say anything, he started kissing me long and hard--the long savory kind of kiss. I kissed him back.

"I miss you, baby," he said, "I missed you so much," he said as he kissed my neck and licked me on the face, "Oh, you taste so good."

Then he turned me toward the steps and bit right through the panties before he pulled them down. He licked my thighs and my stomach. Then he stuck his tongue through the gaps of my fingers one by one. I wanted to stop him, but I didn't want him to stop.

He opened my legs and lifted them over his back. It felt as if I was being inhaled by a vacuum. We were all over the step then on the living room floor.

"The kids might come downstairs," I said, "Let's go to the room."

"Wait just a little bit," he unbuckled his belt as fast as he could. I sat back on the steps to give him a BJ. The last time I had given him a BJ, I was a young girl. But now that I was a woman, I had to handle him like one.

While I was lonely before, I had watched so much porno because I was horny. While I was watching them, I picked up tips from the women. I gave that motherfucka a blowjob that made him stand on his toes!

"Shit!" he yelled, "We gotta go to the room."

I was still tipsy so he helped me upstairs to our bedroom. He took off his clothes and helped me out of mine. Noah had gotten finer than a motherfucker after he lost all that weight. He had the same voice and features, but not the same body and damn sure not the same dick size!

The motherfucker grew some more inches since he lost weight! My body felt different with his. Even when I lost weight, my body had become proportionate. A bigger ass and breast, which Noah couldn't seem to keep his hands off of. Even when I lost weight the first time in my teenage years, I still had the body of a teenage girl. I now had the body of a woman.

We were both nervous. We were acting as if we had never slept with each other before. I touched him all over, familiarizing myself with the blueprint of his body. I touched on his chest and rubbed his head; I pulled his leg up over my hip. I rubbed his thigh and calf muscles. I lifted his leg higher and felt all over his feet.

I sniffed his beard, behind his ears, and under his neck. I held his hands, rubbing each finger. I put my hands between his legs and gripped his penis, which was long, thick, and as hard as a rock. I rubbed his scrotum and all between his legs. Everything I was doing to him; he was doing back to me simultaneously. We were both like aliens discovering the human life form for the very first time. I was throbbing on the inside. I was throbbing so badly that I'm sure he could smell the pheromone coming from me because I could smell his.

I knew he needed me badly. I knew that he couldn't wait to put his penis down my throat, and I couldn't wait for him to do it. 'I'm all yours, Noah,' I said to myself. I could not count how many times we made love that night. But I can say I had enough orgasms to last a lifetime, all in one setting in one night. Although we had a very long night of passion, I wondered, how much of myself was back to him? I didn't know. We had become two different people. We were only the same in name. The years had gone by so fast, and the different struggles we endured caused so much pain that it changed who we were. Part of the change was maturity, spiritual and mental growth, and toughness. We had become like two pieces of iron sharpening each other. Most importantly, there was fear. Not the kind of fear one might have had for God or the unknown, but the kind of fear that comes by way of respect.

Chapter Twenty-Two

Prayers For My Husband

The following day, the kids knew that something was different. They woke up excited and jolly. I hadn't seen that out of them in a while. And I knew deep down inside that those babies felt like they had their mommy and daddy back. It was as if a dark cloud had lifted from them.

Our kids could only see the surface of what was going on inside of Noah and me. The truth was, and I didn't tell them this until they were older, Noah and I were very young. We both had needs and wants. To me, my wants were for the children first. The same with Noah. There were young people our age having fun, going to Freaknik, the Olympics when it came to Atlanta, going to college, and living it up. Then we saw our neighbors afford to take their kids to Disney World and have family fun vacations; our friends had cookouts, parties, new cars, and could afford to shop and enjoy the fun in the sun every summer.

Our life consisted of bounced checks, lack, not enough to make ends meet, thrift store shopping, food stamps, and just straight thuggin' it out. So immediately, we were looking for ways to make extra money. One reason was so that the kids wouldn't have to go to daycare when they were still babies. We had such a hard time, so we shut down, blamed each other, grew apart, and were just plain unhappy, miserable, sad, and frustrated. We just wanted a damn break.

During this time, Noah and I started to fall truly, madly, and deeply in love with each other again. Although we had fallen back in love, there was a part of my soul that was still sore and fragile from the hurt that Noah put on me. The reason why what he said hurt me so badly was because I didn't expect for him—of all people—to be so mean at times. I didn't have to live with Edward to know some of his traits because when Noah got angry, I saw it, and I felt it. He didn't have to touch me physically because his words were so powerful and strong that they made their own punches, cuts, and bruises.

I could close my eyes and hear, '*You don't have shit! Stupid ass bitch! You're laying up on me! You're using me! You come from a family of users! Sorry ass! You're just fucking lazy!*'

But on a good day, it's like, '*You're beautiful. You're a great mom. You're good to me. You do a great job in taking care of us.*'

I honestly felt like I was put on a pedestal and pulled back off over and over again! I tried to get it out of my head.

As we continued to move forward in life, Noah and I began to become more knowledgeable about the world in which we were in, like finding out more about money management. We attended a credit seminar class. I was sure that the class on credit would take a while because they were serving Pizza Hut pizza to the attendees.

In one of the speeches, a woman was telling everyone how important it was to keep your bills paid on time. I thought about the checks I wrote that I knew would bounce. I thought about spending the money we didn't have so that our kids wouldn't get picked on in school. I thought about just trying to participate while keeping up with all of the unfortunate decisions I'd made that put us deeper into a hole. However, a lot of decisions that I made were out of sheer ignorance.

When I recalled every decision, I began to wonder if that was why Noah had resented me for so long. I don't think he knew it was resentment, but I didn't have the educational nor mental tools to understand what exactly life meant to Noah, a young, black man who wanted more out of life. I also wanted more out of life, but I didn't understand how to execute nor plan for it. I had no agendas. But I tried the best that I knew how as a wife and mother with an eighth-grade education. A person equipped with the mind to be an achiever or an over-achiever cannot fathom depression, uncertainty, or confusion. To put it simply, they can see their own path to success and not others. I guess they are so equipped that they are always on the go, sometimes leaving others behind. It seems like they have the mentality to say, "You better catch up."

For me, how could I run without knowing how to walk first? The thing is, someone has to teach someone else how to learn to walk. And it's up to the person who is learning to show that they are willing to walk. If they walk fast enough, ultimately, they will pick up the pace with God guiding them. That's what I wanted from Noah. I couldn't understand how he didn't have the heart to do that. Knowing what I know now, as I said earlier, I don't think he knew to do that. Thus, he outgrew me.

Now, as we sat in the class learning about credit do's and don'ts and what we really could afford and what we couldn't. This time around, Noah was making really good money. The little $575 I was getting per month on SSI was taken down to $80 per month. The lady who was speaking told Noah and I to put down what we made. I grabbed a piece of paper and a pen and wrote down what we brought in. I circled the $88 and said to him as I held the paper up so he could see, "That is what I make...well...get per month. This is what you make a year. I cannot afford to live with you."

I could feel the pizza about to come up out of Noah's stomach. Then I saw tears welling up in his eyes, "What do you mean?" he asked.

"I have to be honest with you and myself. I cannot afford a damn near $300,000 home, and you know it." He grabbed me by my hand and said, "Let me talk to you for a minute," he said as he took me to the side and out of everyone's view, "Baby, this is for our family. That's why I'm out here working as hard as I can for all of us."

"I know you mean well," I replied, "but you say that now. Then I move in with you and it's the same old shit! Telling me I ain't got shit and all of what you do for me. I'm tired of hearing that shit!"

"You are bringing up shit in an argument that I don't even mean. We both say stuff we don't mean!"

"Yeah, well, a drunk man speaks a sober mind. You keep saying the same shit over and over again and now, I believe it because you've repeated it for years!"

"So, where you gonna go?" he asked, "You're just gonna break up our family?" he asked again with tears rolling down his face.

I couldn't watch him hurt. That's just not how I'm built. I didn't have the heart to hurt a person. I might not have been born with an over-achiever mentality, but I was born with a soul filled with love and compassion. If a person wanted to run, I would show them how to get up off their knees one leg at a time. I could show them how to take one step at a time. I can show them how to walk. And with the help of the almighty God, they can run! Run like hell from abuse; run like hell from hunger, from pain, drugs, alcohol, depression; run as fast as they can into the loving arms of God. What I learned from God is that he will run slowly enough with you so that you can run because of all that he has created for you to be. That's what I was starting to grow into.

I didn't beg Noah to stop verbally abusing me. I first prayed for my husband because I understood that it was a mental condition his father had placed upon him; however, I had to do what Martha didn't do. I said, "Noah, I will move in with you, but I want my name on the deed. And my love for you provoked me to tell you that I love you, but I love me more. So, therefore, you are going to learn to bite your tongue because I REFUSE to allow our daughters hear you call me a bitch! Calling a woman a bitch is a fighting word. They have to know that if a man calls them a bitch, then he's capable of a whole lot worse. And if they see me allowing you to treat me like that, then they will lose respect for me because I taught them better." I don't want you to fear me. I want you to respect me equally as I have learned to respect you.

We both have a lot of work to do, but I know we can do this together. Deal?" I put my hand out.

He took my hand and responded, "deal."

On November 13th, a day before Que's birthday, we were blessed to close on our home in an upper Cascade community. That same night, Mom called me, and I gave her the address. When she pulled up to our new home, she couldn't believe her eyes. Though we prayed and were blessed with our house, we still pinched ourselves because we couldn't believe it either!

When Mama left and the kids went to sleep, Noah and I broke in the living room, the kitchen, the family room, the sitting room, the study, the steps, the loft, the laundry room, the master bedroom, and the bathroom. We were fucking all over the house. And we fucked on until the end of 2010 and somewhere at the top of 2011.

That's when we got pregnant with our baby girl, Princess. And oh my gosh, what a princess she is! I couldn't believe that Noah and I could still have babies because it had been so long. Our oldest was also almost seventeen years old, almost old enough to be her father. During my pregnancy, Noah stayed under me, rubbing my feet and stomach. He never kept his hand off of me. He told me once before that the thought of him putting a baby inside of me turned him on.

I walked downstairs one night to get myself a glass of water. He rested his chin on his hands while uplifting himself with his elbows on the breakfast bar, watching me.

"You're so sexy, baby," he said.

I nodded my head and thanked him. I turned to go back up the stairs and all I heard was, "Where you going? Come here." I turned and walked back to him, "How are my girls doing?"

"We're doing good," I said as I smiled, "She's just kicking a lot."

He pulled me to the couch and let the recliner back. The next thing I know, I'm naked and then out of the recliner and onto my knees in the middle of the living room floor, getting hit from behind.

The only light in the room was from the fire in the fireplace. He didn't grab my hair as tight as he normally grabbed it. Instead, he was more careful and patient. The way he made love to me now was different from when we first got together. Plus, the longest he could go without sex was a two-day minimum.

I didn't know what was going on in his head, but I noticed that he had become a lot more attached than normal. He didn't want me to do anything without him. Earlier in the year, I went on a girls' night out with my childhood friends. Before I left, I took care of the house and got the kids settled. They came to pick me up. I made sure Noah was okay and kissed him before I left. Well, my friends and I had made dinner, watched movies, and were having a blast. Then, my phone rang. "Hello?" I answered.

"Momma?" Manny said, "I don't know what's going on with Dad."

"What's going on?"

Then Angelica answered, "It's almost 3 in the morning and he's out in the garage."

"Have y'all eaten? Has he bathed?"

"No ma'am. He even told us to go to bed at 10 o'clock. Ma, he's treating us like little children. Dad hadn't made us turn off the TV and go to bed since we were like ten years old," she explained.

One by one, each of our children told me that they were worried about their dad. But I wasn't the only one who heard them. All of my friends could hear what they were saying. Then Laquita said, "I'll take you home."

I got up and put my things in Laquita's truck. I was pissed! Once I was driven back to my community, Laquita said, "I don't think anybody's going to be up at 4 in the morning."

When we got to my house, Chandra said, "Oh, but wait. The garage door is still open. Maybe Noah fell asleep and left it open."

Suddenly, one by one, I could see each of the kids' heads through the huge anteroom window appearing over the staircase banister to see who was in the driveway. Chandra and Laquita burst out laughing. They were laughing so hard it made me laugh.

So I got out of the car and the girls helped me get my bags. As I was coming up the driveway about to ring the doorbell, out walks Noah from the garage. The girls really laughed. They said, "Girl, your family really loves you."

The kids and Noah were so happy to see me. They traded bags with my friends and brought them into the house. I told them that I had some food in the bag I made at my friend's house. They went through the bags and ate the food as if they hadn't eaten in ages.

I went on and walked upstairs. Noah walked behind me, "Babe, have you tried to bathe at all?" I asked.

"No, because you weren't here to run my bathwater."

So, I ran some bath water and got in myself. Noah laid on the bathroom floor looking like he wanted to cry. I just said, "Come on and get in the water with me." He got up and took off his clothes and got in with me. As for the kids, they were so damn happy they started watching TV, talking, laughing, and having a good time. Even Noah was happy. So happy that the sadness on his face disappeared. So when I told my friends that I was pregnant, they weren't shocked at all.

As for the rest of my journey with my fifth pregnancy, Noah was under me all the time, sure enough, but I also noticed that he was acting as if walls were closing in on him. He seemed frustrated at times, and other times, he'd be fine. Before long, the arguments started up again. This time, I was not going to go there with him. I had given birth to four children, pregnant with another, and I had been fussing with him since I was a child. So by this time, I was worn completely out.

Then he went on a bitch spree calling me selfish bitches] and all kinds of bitches. So I started to look for a place to stay. I was done and he knew it! I told him that this time I had no choice but to leave because I had already taught our daughters that if a man called them that they had to get the hell on because the next step was him getting up in their faces close enough that his spit would begin to shower them. Then he'll lay a finger on their noses. Then after that, the beatings would start. I told Noah that I didn't want to look like a hypocrite to our children. As Noah argued, I saw that the boys had quickly come to my defense along with our girls.

I saw that the arguing could cause a divide and possibly repeat a cycle of our children hating their father like Noah and his siblings hated Edward. I was already tired of the repeated cycles in my own extended family. I was not about to sit back and watch that kind of hell break loose in my own family. I had given Noah more than the benefit of the doubt, dodged the truth, given in, and all of the above. But I was truly done.

Over that weekend, I didn't say anything to Noah. He was like a damn ticking time bomb! No matter what I said or asked, it would turn into an argument. He seemed agitated, frustrated, and angry.

Wednesday night, he took off of work for the following day. Then Thursday morning, he woke up and overheard me asking about an apartment complex and how much it would be to move in and so on and so forth.

He got out of bed and went downstairs. I went downstairs maybe an hour or two later. When I got to the kitchen, I saw Noah lying on the couch with his hands behind his head, staring at the wall.

"Hey, Noah. How are you?" I asked.

"Fine," he replied with tears running down his face.

I didn't say anything else. I went to the kitchen and made myself some breakfast. I took my food with me back to our bedroom.

Once I got an idea of what I was going to do, I knew I needed to talk to him because we had a baby on the way. I didn't want to deprive her of the luxury of having a father in her life when our other kids did.

From our room, I could see Noah walking up the stairs, "Noah, can we talk for a second, please?" I continued when he got to the room, "I'm going to give you the bill information, so you'll know how to handle the business of the house." "So, you leaving me?" he asked sadly, "Everything I've worked for to give you a better life, you're leaving? You mean to tell me you would leave this four-thousand square foot home in the upper Cascade area to move into a small apartment?" "To give you and our children peace of mind and to keep our boys from jumping up at you and our daughters from hating men because they hear how you talk to me. Hell, yeah, I'll leave in a heartbeat. You can't see that you're repeating your father?"

"And you're willing to break up our family and give up on me rather than trying to help me find out what's wrong? You're willing to walk away and subject our kids to God knows what, like your mother did your father? I'm not perfect, Shawnie. It's a lot of shit going on at my job and my customers have slowed down. And now I have to raise another baby with this diabetic, beatdown body of mine. I'm just tired," he said. "Why didn't you tell me what was going on? Are you upset that we're about to have another baby?" "No!" he yelled out of excitement rather than anger, "Hell, no! I'm scared of not being around for her! Now you talkin' 'bout leaving. With all the shit you put me through, not one time have I told you that I was packing my shit and leaving you. You won't even give me a chance to get myself together."

All of a sudden, a light came on, and it hit me! What about all of the stupid motherfuckers, niggas, weak ass, no good ass, good for nothing ass, gullible ass niggas that I've called him? What about me talking to other people about our problems? I've never known him to confide in anyone else about me. What about me overspending money that we didn't have? How he only took a little for himself and allowed me the rest. He didn't go out or hang out with friends. He didn't have a life at the gym and never put his looks or health above the kids and me. He went to work and came home, and it all started over again day after day, and he didn't complain. The most enjoyment he had to himself was watching auto shows on cable TV.

He wanted me to have everything that was beautiful. He placed himself last so that I could be first. Out of all the things I could consider, I didn't consider him. Out of all the people I had forgiven, I didn't forgive him. And for all the hurt I've endured, I'd taken it out on him time and time again because he was not like everybody else. He stayed. He didn't leave me. He didn't toss me to somebody else when he got tired of me. He didn't hit me to make himself feel like a man. He didn't bring harm to his children. He loved me and I loved him.

As imperfect as we were, we had to find a way to help each other. That's the easy part. The hardest part was staying together.

"You're right, Noah," I said, "You didn't leave. So, I'm going to ask you something, and I need for you to be totally honest with me. Honey, what's wrong? I'm listening." Just when I said that, the home phone rang, and then my cell phone rang. I got up and turned them both off. When I did that, I also realized that I had made myself available for everyone else but him. Over the years, people would call me with their garbage ready to throw it in the trashcan that I had created for them in my mind. Trash came in many forms. The same bullshit in different clothes. I had to put a stop to all of that. I had to become available for Noah.

When I sat back down, I started listening to him. I didn't say a word. When he started talking, I noticed that he was talking in circles; he wasn't making any sense. While he was doing his best to explain, he started getting fatigued. Then I asked, "Honey, when was the last time you took your insulin?"

"Just a few minutes ago, before I came up stairs," he replied.

So I went downstairs and got his insulin, a needle, and his meter. I checked his blood sugar for myself. His blood sugar was nearly 400, "That can't be," he said, "I've been taking my medication."

I took up the insulin bottle and looked it over. We were in the year 2011, and his insulin expired in 2009. It turned out that the urgent care pharmacy we had gone to days before had given him outdated medication. We immediately changed doctors and arranged for him to see a different one at a different facility called Kaiser. When he was seen, I finally understood why Noah was a ticking time bomb and why he was so frustrated and agitated all the time. It was because of the mood swings that were triggered by his blood sugar elevating.

Noah was my responsibility and I had to understand that my wife had to be his caretaker. Once his blood sugar and AC levels started going down the way it should have been, he became calmer.

And to think that I could have walked away from this amazing man without knowing he needed help--the same way a lot of our black men needed help. After this, I started thinking on a deeper level about our black men. My heart is broken for them because of the challenges they were and are up against.

I would think about my mother and how she treated my father. But to me, it seemed like a master plan. Literally, because the black man was beaten and sold in front of his wife and children. With that being done to those men who were once known as heroes, kings, and warriors, the woman's strength weakened when he was brought to his knees. The moment their knees hit the ground, so did their crowns of their pride and dignity. We as women lost faith in our men when they lost faith in themselves. Just vision a slave master standing with a strong black man in front of his wife and children getting auctioned off, and there was nothing neither of them could do about it. This physically weak overseer has the limbs of a dog standing next to a lion. But the lion's strength had been taken away by the dog. And with the heart of a lion that could roar and bring down the whole charade, he's afraid of what that dog would do to him if he roared. His hands are shackled and bound to his back. He is then brought to his knees.

He looks into his son's eyes because the intent of the dog is for the lion to show his young cub how he'd better bow down to the dog also. His father sets an example of how to stay in his place and not to fight back. His woman turns her head as she had then given up on him. Now, what is he left beside a shell with flesh and bones and a broken spirit? He is a king no longer. From slaves to slums. From slums to the projects.

Apartment complexes known as the projects that look like a replica of a slave ship. Fenced in, one on top of the other. One way in and one way out. Shitting and pissing on top of each other in more ways than one. The women, like my mother and grandmother, were given vouchers and my grandmother before her. And there'd better not be a man in there or else it would ruin the privilege of not being homeless. The only male in there better be your son.

In some cases, they came out to inspect the apartment to see. My grandmother told me that she had to hide grandpa's clothes, shoes, and the little black and white TV she had bought for her family.

They came by to make sure that priority was well in place. The woman ruled the men with this steak that they dangled over their heads. And he'd better not get wrong with her, or he would risk getting kicked out of a place where he wasn't supposed to be in the first place.

For a young man, because there's no father in the house, he has to drop out of school to help his Mama with his siblings. His father and the fathers before him were shackled with their hands behind their backs and brought to his knees. Then he tries to get a job; no opportunities there because his education wasn't up to par.

This time, instead of being sold off, he's in a chain gang--another plantation legalized by the government. So, what is this young man to do when his woman is holding the fact that he lives with her over his head? She could go 5150 and kick his ass out if she wanted to.

Nobody was going to hire this uneducated nigger. So, where does he go? The whore house and the liquor because he has no home of his own. The only other place he could find was under a bridge.

Chapter Twenty-Three
The Breaking Of
A Curse

It was my mother's birthday. I promised her before that I would help her with her birthday decorations at her house for her party. She was acting funny as usual. I just wanted to be alone and leave.

Even my children wanted me to stop dealing with my mom and siblings altogether. They felt like none of them cared about us. So why should we care anything about them? In fact, they didn't even want my family to visit.

Deep down, I was hoping like Hell I wasn't beginning to repeat the cycle of choosing my extended family over my extended family. Because every time they came around, our kids got pissed!

Then the next two days after Mom's birthday was Halloween. I had my annual Halloween party for our kids and whoever else in my family wanted to join. Jazz always came, so she was there. Then Mom came over in her persnickety manner, which was nothing out of the ordinary.

We were all downstairs in the dining area, preparing food for the night. Then one of my kids did something that made me yell at them. I don't remember what it was about, but then Mama said, "My mother and father did real good by us."

Then went on to say we had this and we had that and how wonderful life was. I looked at Mom and said, "If your life at home was so good, why did you run away so much?"

I wanted to know why she left Zay and me. If her family was so great that it was worth destroying her own immediate family just to justify, sacrifice, save, and risk everything for her extended family. For years, I just didn't get it. So on this night, I had to ask.

When she spoke of Grandma and Grandpa, she always talked about how good they were to her. But if they were that good, why was she always in juvenile and a runaway. I barely saw Mama as a child. When I did, she was always unhappy, pissed, and ready to get the hell on as quick as she got there.

I sat and waited as she started to fantasize how everything was peachy to make me feel bad or a type of way as if I should have been ashamed of myself for something. She was always looking for something bad in me to point out.

To make me feel so low would strike the very ego that I'd come to despise for many years. The ego that showed, 'I'm good. I'm better than anything you can think of.' I just knew she was going to smack her lips like she always did whenever she stretched the truth or exaggerated. And she began to do just that.

By this time, both of my daughters were in the kitchen. They had their own opinions about my mother, and they could have cared less about her. They had already tuned her out like they've always done. I didn't want them to be disrespectful or lose their blessings by exhibiting bad behavior.

"So tell me, Mom, what happened when you were a little girl? What was your childhood like?"

Mom sat at the table about to give us the glorious detail of her childhood, "When I was a little girl," she smacked, "my mom and dad always did right by us."

"Yeah, Mom. But, how was your childhood?"

"My childhood," she smacked her lips again, "My...my...my...childhood," before I knew it, Mom had broken down in tears. Then all of a sudden, she said, "I can't do this no more! My Mama and her brothers beat my daddy!"

The girls heard what was going on, and they came to the table to listen to Mama tell her story.

"Uncle Bubba used to beat us so bad! And my daddy was so scared of him because he was an Atlanta police officer and his family had more than what we had! They knew my daddy drank, and they beat him!

Then Uncle Bubba beat Ronald so badly. I thought my brother was dead! And I had a friend that we used to play with. I was in the house, and Richard was outside with him. I don't know what was going on. But I saw Richard come up to my friend with a gun. He put the gun up to his head and pulled the trigger. I just saw him fall back on the ground. Dead!" She cried hard.

"So, I ran away. I ran away with some friends. And when we ran away, we ended up at this big house. It belonged to a man named Allan. He was well-known in Atlanta; very popular.

He was a dancer, and he and his friend were like local celebrities. Everybody who cut school would go to his house and go down in the basement. So I went with my friends Hazel and Minnie. They were used to going to Allan's house, but I wasn't.

When we got there, they were with other dudes. But Allan kept after me. I didn't know him, and I didn't want to know him," Mom stopped for a minute because she was crying so hard now. She couldn't get another word out.

"What happened?" Jazz and I asked.

"He raped me!" she yelled, "He raped me! And that's how I got pregnant with you! He raped me! He wrestled me down until I gave in!"

The girls, Jazz, and I were all at the table in tears, "Mama?" I asked while crying, "He raped you? That's how I came to be?"

"He did, baby. He did."

"But, Mom," I asked emotionally, "There were three different men saying that they were my father. How did that happen?"

"Well, you know how your Grandma loves fancy things. She ordered things, and when they came in, she asked this older guy that used to come to visit as a friend of the family to take me to pick the stuff up. He liked me, but I had a boyfriend named Willie Thomas. All of this was before Allan."

"Willie Thomas? The man that I met said that he was my father. His mother even had a picture of me when I was very little."

"Yes, we were in a relationship. But Rufus was older and on the slow side. He wasn't my type. But Mama wanted me to go down and pick up her things. She could have cared less about who went and got it or how they got it just as long as it was picked up and brought home."

Mom explained as tears began to fall again. I knew she wasn't lying about Grandma and her nice things because Grandma decorated her house like the Good Housekeeping magazines that came in her mail. She fixed up her house more than she paid bills and bought food.

"So when Rufus took me to pick up Mama's stuff, he stopped by his apartment first. He took me in there and started having sex with me. At the time, I didn't know what he was doing because I had never had sex before.

I wasn't even having sex with Willie Thomas at the time. Nobody told me nothing about sex or anything. All I knew was that I didn't want Rufus. So I continued my relationship with Willie. Eventually, we did have sex.

After a while, I knew I was pregnant. So, I said to myself, 'I'm going to have this baby and get me a check and move out!' I said, 'I'm going to save my checks up, buy me a car, sell it, and buy two more.' Either way, I was going to take that opportunity to get me, my brothers, and my sister out of there!

I didn't want to be hungry anymore. My daddy had a third-grade education, and he made fifteen dollars an hour back when black men couldn't make that kind of money as a brick mason. Your grandaddy helped to build those buildings downtown.

Every Friday he got paid, my Mama wanted him to give her what was supposed to take care of us. Daddy took twenty dollars for himself and gave Mama the rest," she explained as tears continued to roll down her face as she relived a painful and damaging childhood.

"Mom," I began, "What about love? Did your mom and dad hug and kiss each other? Did they tell each other that they loved each other? Was there any type of affection shown?"

"That house was like a dark hole. No love at all! Just cold and dark, and I ran every chance I got!"

"If it was like that, how did Grandma end up with ten children?" I asked again.

"I know she hardly slept with Daddy. Maybe once or twice every other year or so. And every time he slept with her, he got her pregnant. I guess that's why we were all two years apart. But every time he tried to kiss her, she slapped him.

Then her brother started to jump him. When my brothers got older, they started to jump him, too. I guess God got tired of my daddy being mistreated, so he took him on," she cried.

"And that's when I saw you," I said, "You came to see what happened when he died. And you looked at me with a frown."

It all started to make sense to me now. I've met Allan once before, and it was clear to me that she knew I was his child because I saw my face when I looked at his. A male version of myself. So, every time she looked at me, it was a constant reminder of a battle she had lost against a stranger taking something she couldn't get back: her soul.

This man took what was left of an already wounded spirit. She ran away to save what was left of her cracked spirit and the love she had for a father who drank his pain and sorrows away.

I later learned that his sorrows went beyond not being loved by the woman he married. He had already lost his mother to a thief who robbed her and took her life along with what he stole. His uncle and aunt were supposed to raise him and his sisters and brothers but gave them away to custody. So they had to muddle through life the best way they could.

He saw a young lady that he may or may not have liked. But if he was to have a shot at seeing where things could go, he's threatened by her mother who tells him if he wants to be with her daughter, he has to marry her.

Her daughter, not knowing who he was or if she liked him or not, had to marry him. But because she had a bastard child, she'd have better done something because her mother would not have her embarrass the family again.

If so, she would get kicked out for good, so she had better do what her mother told her. In her eyes, he was dumb and stupid. But Big Ma wasn't going to have her daughter in the family way, so Grandma had better hurry up and marry this fool while they found somebody dumb enough to get married to an unwed mother.

Unfortunately, two young people got played to marry each other because somebody didn't want to "look bad."

I say, fuck looking bad! That bullshit ruined innocent people's lives! My poor grandfather went to his grave not ever witnessing an ounce of love in his life. Even though he lost his mother, he should have been compensated by his wife and children - the ultimate gift for growing up parentless. Still, he didn't get it.

As for Grandma, she lived an unlived life. She's eighty-eight years old with wings that have never flown. What I mean is that she never stretched, took a chance, been brave, or stepped out on faith. She never 'went for it.' She never crossed that street out of lack of confidence or fear that something bad was going to happen. She never loved freely to the point where she could openly, wholeheartedly, and full-throated tell a man or her husband, 'I love you, baby.' Never, never, never.

To this day, grandmother's legs have no markings or wrinkles. Her face is that of a sixty-five- or seventy-year-old. Her memory is better than mine. Her body, hips, legs, and thighs have never explained the joy of making sweet, passionate love. And sadly, neither did my mother.

My mother has no idea what love really means. She actually thought that if a man told her she was cute that it was love or that she was wanted. Sex was some unfulfilled confirmation of something that she was looking for but never found it. That's why she had a lot of boyfriends because she was looking for something she didn't know she was looking for. But she knew it was something that she needed.

She thought that the attention she was getting was it. That's why getting attention was very important to her. She loved it, and she wanted it but didn't know why. But what she needed couldn't come from a man or from under her covers. That's why she was never satisfied.

She had what she needed all along but was too out of touch with herself to give it to herself. She was in touch with others but not herself. She didn't know that she needed to become important to herself.

Bubba's wife was a schoolteacher, and him being a cop afforded them a very comfortable life. Bubba and his wife gave their son a birthday party, and they invited all of their children and grandchildren.

Grandma had gotten all of her kids dressed and walked them over to Bubba's house for the party. When Grandma and her children got there, Bubba asked them to leave out of not wanting to be embarrassed by them. So Grandma took her kids and left. That made my mother and her siblings feel less important.

When Big Ma had cookouts and family gatherings, Grandma would keep her 'crumb snatchers' at home. That also made my mother and her siblings feel less important.

Big Ma's baby brother left Georgia to build his life in New York. In turn, he was able to send his kids to a Catholic school. They grew up, graduated college, and made something of themselves. Big Ma wrote her brother and told her how proud she was of his kids and not to let them around my grandmother's children because they were all a bunch of dumbheads. This made my mother and her siblings feel less important. Bubba ended up turning into a stone-cold alcoholic. And even as a hero cop, that motherfucker couldn't save himself. Instead, he took his frustrations out on my mother and her siblings and her siblings' children.

Grandma and grandpa were too afraid to make him stop beating their kids. So whenever he showed up at their place, he took total control.

One time, my aunt had come home from the hospital after her appendix burst. Bubba dragged her around the house, trying to force her to walk. He did the same thing to my baby cousin when her appendix burst.

And Uncle Ronald was a skinny little boy. He played the drums and tried to be in a band. He was beaten by Uncle Bubba so bad my grandparents were scared to move.

Mama said one day she was hoping that he would put his gun down because she was going to get the gun and blow his brains out.

Mama sat at our kitchen table and cried everything out. Her cries went from an adult's cry to like that of a child, like that hard grieving kind of cry a child would do when they are telling on someone. Sort of like 'they hit me' to their caring parents. Her head was down, and her hands were on each side of her head as if she was protecting herself.

Mama was telling on everybody who hurt her. The way she was supposed to have told after what Allan and Rufus had done to her. She was telling on them to me as if she knew that I was going to do something about it. She wanted somebody that cared enough to do something about it.

"Momma?" I said, "Why didn't you tell me this stuff? Why? I swear to God I'm going to kill somebody!" I yelled.

She lifted her head, and, oh my God, there she was. "Hey you," I cried, "I haven't seen you in years!" It was her! I had seen her once before on the day of my seventh-grade prom and then on my wedding day.

She came back! No frowns, no angry face, and no hateful look. Just honest and pleasant. It was my mother! "Hey, Mama!" I cried. I hugged her so tight, "I missed you so much, Mama."

All of us women and young women surrounded her in a circle. She looked up at her strong daughters and granddaughters with a look as if she was happy that we had all made it out of a burning building. But, Lord have mercy, the amount of hell that had passed on from one generation to the next.

My mother was such a fragile soul. I believe the day she witnessed her friend get killed was the day her mind broke. Patricia, Trish, Pat, Patty, and Pal were all a part of her childhood. Each one of them had a personality of their own.

It may sound crazy, but I remember looking at a soap opera and seeing a character with different personalities. I thought it was fiction. But, as it turned out, it was a very real condition known as dissociative identity disorder, abbreviated as DID.

Each of them tried to protect Patricia. Mama was even seeing a doctor and explaining to them that she heard voices in her head, and sometimes, they argued with each other. For some reason, when I was still a child, I knew that something wasn't right.

She could show signs of wanting to love and care for me. Then out of the blue, for no reason at all, she treated me like an adversary.

She was diagnosed with Schizophrenia, Bipolar disorder, and other things. When I saw Mama come out that night, it was as if she was a little girl in a corner, covering up her ears and her head to protect herself.

"I'm here, Mama," I said, "And nobody is ever gonna hurt you again. I promise."

She hugged me back and said, "I love you, baby. You're my firstborn, and I don't give a damn where you came from. I love you." It was so much to take in at one time. Then she said, "I'm sorry. I'm so sorry. Please forgive me for everything I put you through.

When everybody else used me and threw me away, you took me in and never gave up on me. Mama is so very sorry. I didn't protect you. I failed to protect my baby girl," she cried.

"Mama," I said, "You couldn't protect yourself. How could you protect me?"

That night turned into one of healing. All because I asked one question. I had no idea what was about to open. But God guided my words that night. This lady that I thought I hated so much became one of the biggest loves of my life. She and I are inseparable.

We even live near each other. And she has become so protective of me that she doesn't want me going anywhere without her. It's been years now, and we spend mother-daughter time together. And the thing with Ron, I'm not sure which personality it was that wanted him. All I know is that my mother hates him. She said if she ever sees him again, she might kill him.

It wasn't only me that started a relationship with my mother. My children are now crazy about her. And she's gotten herself together as well.

She went from making money off of addicts to taking care of

recovering addicts. She also helps those who are homeless. She had given herself to God. I would like to elaborate more on her story; however, she deserves to write her own story.

We, as mothers and daughters, need to heal. As daughters, sometimes we don't know the side of hell our mothers have gone through. And trust me, they are not 'just that way.' There is a reason why they are the way they are.

Years after Mom told me her story, I got a call from Allan. That was my chance to pick him. I wanted the truth about everything. So I started asking, "So, how did you meet my mother?"

"Well," he said, "We lived not far from each other."

"How long were you two together? Did y'all make plans to have me?"

"Well, no, we didn't plan you. We were at my house. That's where everyone hung out when they cut school. Your Mama was there, and she was with her friends. Then she and I started wrestling around."

"Well, did y'all know each other?"

"Naw, we didn't know each other."

"So why would you wrestle a girl you didn't know? And by the way, how the hell does wrestling with somebody you don't know turn into sex?"

"Well, you know, back then…"

"Hold on," I stopped him, "See, back then, y'all called it 'taking it.' But today, we call that shit what it is. Rape. You have no idea the price I had to pay because you decided you were going to wrestle a beautiful young girl who had to 'take it.'"

Mama and I have moved on with our lives. What I had to make peace with was knowing first and foremost that I am a child of the highest God. With Allan being my biological father, I inherited his talents with a touch of my own.

He was a vehicle for me getting here. But it was God who sent me here. He knew what he was doing and why. That is what made me pro-life.

I am taking my platform and using it to bridge the gaps that the grandmothers should have stood in, or whoever is responsible enough, to pick up the dropped ball called life. But, again, it all goes back to slavery. All the way back to Big Ma and Bubba, who were told to stay in their places, who were told that they were niggers and whatever shred of man or womanhood they had, they had better damn well hold their tongue.

Who better to take their frustrations out on than their loved ones? They feel that it's safe and they aren't going anywhere. Uncle Bubba was not that much of a big shot to his white counterparts. But to his people, he had a lot more than what they had, especially to be 'a colored man'.

Instead of helping his family, he beat them. He made them so afraid of him. He made Mama afraid of him. And that fear passed right on down to me. Leaving me open to where somebody could come into my life and beat me, molest me, and sexually assault me, too.

Although we live in the millennium, from the time of slavery, black people have been a part of the American heritage. Yet, up until this very day, the screams, the yells, the blood, the hurt, fear, uncertainty, and loss still roars within us, only showing more in medical diagnosis in things like depression, ADHD, Autism, DID, Bipolar disorder, PTSD, Schizophrenia, and other mental abnormalities. And they think a mental health appointment and a prescription is going to cure it?

The justice system better leave black people alone about smoking weed because they'd rather self-medicate so that they can deal with the hand that this country has dealt to us!

Mama had finally come out from being trapped in her head. It took days upon days for her to get it all out. All I wanted her to do was keep talking. Then she got to Uncle Richard. Uncle Richard was also a police officer and acted differently from the rest of his mother's children.

I guess it was because he was raised by Big Ma and had a different father. Uncle Rich got into it with grandaddy so much. Every time they started fussing, Mama ran and hid in a room and ducked down in that fetal position because she was scared that Richard was going to kill her father the same way he killed her friend.

Mama hated when Richard visited because he, like Uncle Bubba, went for bad. And they tested their egotistical-ass, testosterone-driven strength out on a fragile family that was also dealing with their alcoholism and God knows whatever else.

Mama lived in fear all the time. She thought that when she got home, someone would tell her that her mother was dead. So she stayed in her head all the time. When she saw Richard pull the trigger and kill her friend, she started saying to herself, "Richard killed my daddy."

As her daughter, I truly believe that, at that moment, Pat came out to protect Patricia after witnessing things that were so traumatic that a child simply couldn't mentally handle them. Out of all of her other personalities, Pat was the strongest.

In my day and time, children had to raise their parents, spouses, and significant others. And the damage goes so damn deep that one or both just can't do it and call it quits. So you have two people, both are some kind of fucked up, but nobody else is going to put up with them.

Noah and I both realized that both of our extended families needed us when we needed God and each other the most. So we didn't wave the white flag to each other. I needed to rescue him, and he needed to be rescued by me.

Given our history, who would have known that we would grow up together to become so flooded with each other?

Some people need threesomes, toys, and other shit. Noah is too selfish to share me with anybody or anything. I'm saying this because many people have asked me if I ever got tired of sleeping with the same man for so many years.

That answer is HELL NO! Our marriage bed, floor, sink, washing machine, car, and whatever is ours. God carved that space and time out of this world for him and me. So whatever hubby wants, hubby gets.

Over time, Noah and I would receive old pictures that our families kept. I saw his picture, and he saw mine. When we did, we laughed and cried. He realized that I was that little girl at the store who kept asking him so many questions. And he was the boy that I looked back at and wondered if anyone was taking care of him. Well, now I know who's taking care of him.

I am in love, and he is as sexually addicted to me as I am to him. I'd call him and pine for him over the phone, "Mmm, Nooooaahh, baby. Come home to me, please." And he'd rush home to me. Sometimes he'll take days off so that we could lay up with each other for days, all the time not knowing we were healing each other and licking the wounds of our childhood and adulthood. Just simply trying to live life.

The world is hard enough, and I'd be damned if Hell will reside in the very place where God and peace should be. Our daughters would smile as they saw me dressing up to look beautiful when their father came home. They smile when they see how he embraces me. Whenever I needed somebody to talk to, Noah would stop what he was doing to listen to me. We would even relax in the tub together to finish the conversations of the day. And no, nothing is perfect. We still have our ups and downs and uncomfortable moments, but that's all they are, uncomfortable moments, and it shouldn't last long enough to undo our emotional well-being. But more than anything, we pray.

As a wife - a trophy wife - I wear many hats. I am his friend, his confidant, and his queen. I am his showpiece, girlfriend, best friend, companion, homie, ride-or-die, lover, nurse, and comforter. I am his toy, stripper, and arm candy. I am his submissive, his lover, his sex slave, his sex kitten, and everything he wants me to be. And I will forever be a well-kept trophy wife.

The both of us will keep seeking permission and the go-ahead from God almighty, and in all things we give thanks. Even for the darkest days, we thank God even more because every great thing is created in darkness, such as a seed planted in the ground. It has to fight through the hot summer and the frigid cold. Still, it struggles to come through the ground and the soil, and when it does, it stands up strong, beautiful, and bold, ready to become all of what it was created to be.

In Jesus' name. Amen.

About K. Phoxx

K Phoxx is a native Atlantan. She rips through the walls and lines that are purposed and intentionally set to keep us in denial of who we really are and what we have done. She's transparent with her recorded diary of how one thing can lead to the next, and how we can overcome the repeat of dishonesty within the family structure and those in our social circle. She sets us free to be open and honest with ourselves, and to create a culture of "being your best self." K. says for too long we've been pretending and keeping conversations about real things that happen in life, such as seduction, deception, and sexuality complexities as a hush. K. puts those conversations on the kitchen table, on the altar, and within reach of the social settings. K. exemplifies how liberation can be reached when we freely discuss these issues, myths and challenges that continue to imprison us and those we encounter. She gives us a real taste of the seduction and deception, and she goes all-in to give us a taste of real-life experiences. Buckle up for whatever K. brings your way! K. Phoxx truth~~